Rachel was born and raised in San Francisco, California. That is where her writing career started with poetry, having had three books published and eventually winning an award for Outstanding Achievement in Poetry.

Rachel's hobbies include horseback riding, swimming, taking long walks, anything to do with cars, and especially working out, where she says, "Work out for no one else but yourself, and to stay healthy."

Laughing Out of Context is Mrs. Zangrillo-Galicinao's debut novel, written from her life experiences in motherhood and from volunteering and speaking at numerous elementary schools.

Her love for children, animals, and traveling have all inspired her in life, along with watching food shows, which brings out her creative side in cooking. Mrs. Zangrillo-Galicinao currently resides in Las Vegas, Nevada, with her husband, son, and parents.

This book is dedicated to my parents, Gary and Lynn. Thank you for everything you have always given me, especially your endless love and support!

Rachel Zangrillo-Galicinao

LAUGHING OUT OF CONTEXT

A Parenting Humor Novel

AUSTIN MACAULEY PUBLISHERS™

LONDON • CAMBRIDGE • NEW YORK • SHARJAH

Ordering Information
Quantity sales: Special discounts are available on quantity purchases by corporations, associations, and others. For details, contact the publisher at the address below.

Publisher's Cataloging-in-Publication data
Zangrillo-Galicinao, Rachel
Laughing Out of Context

ISBN 9798891554160 (Paperback)
ISBN 9798891554177 (Hardback)
ISBN 9798891554184 (ePub e-book)

Library of Congress Control Number: 2024909866

www.austinmacauley.com/us

First Published 2024
Austin Macauley Publishers LLC
40 Wall Street, 33rd Floor, Suite 3302
New York, NY 10005
USA

mail-usa@austinmacauley.com
+1 (646) 5125767

To my son: You are the heart to my soul. You make my life exciting, feeling blessed and inspired in every way possible.

To my husband: Our son is so lucky to have you as his father, looking out for his best interest with love, and standing by to (try to) balance me out when I assume the role of Grizzly Momma.

Mom and Dad: This book is dedicated to you, and any heartache I caused during your roller coaster of parenthood with me. My respect and love for your parenting is endless, and my heart will be forever full with the most beautiful family memories.

My in-laws, Max and Jane: I don't know how you did it with raising three boys, and still managed to maintain your composure through love and support.

Auntie Beverly: I cherish the memories of the fun and adventurous weekends we spent throughout my childhood. Always something I looked forward to, and never wanted to end, hence the crying tantrums when it was time to leave.

In loving memory of my grandparents; Fred, Connie, Nate, and Adelle: You helped my parents raise me, and instilled good morals and life lessons. Parenthood may have changed here and there along the way, but you all made sure as I grew up, family remained the same.

Bree, Alee, and Sarah: True friends make being a mom feel that much more supportive, relatable, and laughable. Couldn't get through days without you ladies, our connections, and our children's friendship.

Aurora: Thank you for always being there for my family, especially my son and me. The love and support that flows between us is family by choice.

Jonathan and Christie: What started out as us being neighbors here for each other, transitioned into a close friendship that I treasure, and parents who I admire.

In loving memory of Enrique: A friend who was a great husband, father, and grandfather, with a heart and smile that drove others to greatness.

Joanna and Steve: Neighbors always bonded by being friends and great parents.

Anna: Where one conversation sprouted into friendship, then bloomed by our families connecting in closeness.

Mrs. Kramar, Ms. Kettl, and Mrs. Barber-Knueve: You all are an inspiration to the "plethora" of teachers around the world.

Mr. West: A principal who is above the rest, whom all principals should aspire to be.

To my publisher, Austin Macauley Publishers: Without you my author's novel journey would not be possible. Thank you for your support, guidance, and most of all, thank you for believing in me.

In loving memory of Jonelle: I am proud to have called you my long-time friend. You had always found strength in the character that made up who you were – amazing, strong, and a determined woman, wife, mother, and grandmother.

Table of Contents

Note from the Author

Laughing Out of Context is based on the same premise as my self-help books—no matter what your situation is, you are not alone. Sometimes, people forget they are not alone, and this feeling is exacerbated by stressful times.

Yes, there are many people that experience the same scenarios—inner personal struggles and parenting struggles. It helps to know that others go through what you go through. Even if the circumstances are not the same, the emotions can be.

One night while watching the movie *Goosebumps 2* with my son, a certain line stood out to me from the movie. The character R.L. Stine gave a one-line piece of advice to the character Sarah, an aspiring writer—*write what you know*, which was originally said by the great Mark Twain.

How true that line is. When you write about what you know, fiction or non-fiction, your words will pour out onto the pages from your heart, and from your knowledge. I am doing just that in this book—writing what I know and experienced, pertaining to the many scenarios in bringing up children.

Laughing Out of Context is chock-full of funny experiences about parenting. It is always important to remember that even though there are a lot of times lightness can be made from raising a child, times can also get extremely overwhelming.

Take a step back when needed to take a deep breath. Or finish up whatever you are doing at the moment, then take a step back. Try and find whatever light and funniness you can in your current state of being overwhelmed, then go ahead and calmly breathe. In that moment, laugh a little, because in the grand scheme of things, this challenging time too shall pass.

If you can't find anything humorous at the moment, just think that someday you *will* laugh about it. For extra needed therapy, repeat soothing breathing exercises of slowly inhaling through your nose, count to five, and then exhale through your mouth, counting to five again.

This definitely comes in handy on my daily basis. Comparatively speaking, think of the breathing instruction during a cool down stretch after a nice workout, or with meditation, or just how breathing is when lying down for a restful sleep.

This is especially a necessity for those days when I come home to find my house like a tornado. Everything spewed all over the place, the dishes are piled up in the sink, and those markers that I knew someday would be a problem for the walls finally came to be that problem.

Breathe

Breathing exercises are my daily go-to, along with eating superfoods, such as leafy vegetables, tomatoes, blueberries, pomegranates, nuts, etc. My personal favorite is avocados. I can eat them daily. My budget doesn't always allow for an avocado a day, so, I will then stick with an apple a day keeps the doctor away.

My pediatrician used to recite that to me every time I had a doctor's visit. These types of foods help give me the mental and physical energy I need every day to keep up with motherhood.

Although, I will have an occasional small glass of wine to help me unwind at the end of the day. This is very rare for me, because I have never enjoyed drinking, but some days call for it.

A nice walk followed by a hot shower also does the trick for my stressful days. Fresh air is definitely my personal remedy for regrouping. Also, try the breathing exercises outside. What a difference that makes.

I have also been known to hide out for a few moments in different rooms of the house to de-stress when my days achieve overwhelming status. This actually works out to be a win-win situation for my son, and for me. In the past, he simply thinks I'm playing hide and seek with him, while I'm really taking a mental moment for me.

The honest to goodness truth in a nutshell about motherhood is that it is one wild roller coaster of emotions. Even though there are so many laughable and joyous times—I know I laughed quite a bit writing this book—there are also tears of frustration and sadness.

I laugh about some of the quirkiest actions my son makes. I cried when he lost his first tooth. I'll get mad when he rummages through my purse, throwing everything everywhere. I have giggled when he's mispronounced certain words, because I know what he means, but it is so darn cute.

I cried when he graduated kindergarten. I'll get mad when he will not listen to me for anything. The list goes on and on, over and over, emotions bringing me up and down, this way and that, then up and down again.

Actually, when I became a parent myself, I ended up apologizing to my mom and dad for everything I had put them through when I was young. Mothers from the mom groups I'm part of have all done the exact same thing, as well as so many of my other friends. For only now we understand exactly what a roller coaster ride raising children is.

One saying in particular encompasses a parent's being: Raising children is the biggest challenge you will ever have, and the biggest blessing you will ever receive. There is no truer statement than that.

Basically, anytime will be a good time to just sit back, take a deep breath, and let this book be a humorous break in your day.

Chapter 1
Shopping is a Dream

Darn my internal alarm clock, I think, wincing. *Mia, can't you just sleep in for once? It's the weekend, for heaven's sake.*

Lying in bed, I wait for the alarm clock to sound, while going over all chores in my head that I need to accomplish for the day. The possible challenges of a quick shopping trip are right at the top of my thought process. I can only hope my son will be good, at least good enough to get out of the store, unscathed.

My mind is constantly on overdrive, even in the wee hours of the morning. Staring at the dark ceiling, I see the slow stream of light peeking through the blinds, letting me know that six am is not too far off. My thoughts start to wander off to motherhood, filling in the little amount of time I have till the buzzer sounds.

***

Being a mom really turns me into a questionable woman. I talk to myself way too much. I want to be invisible most of the time. And basically, I assume multiple careers, undertaking each of their personality traits throughout any given day. I also rely on my many different imaginary hats to help me achieve good mom status.

Even though I'm thirty years young, I'm exhausted by the end of each day with my six-year-old son. Cody is a handful, to say the least, always keeping me on my toes. I truly live up to our city's motto in Las Vegas: The city that never sleeps.

Except, instead of the bright lights of the casinos and hotels keeping me awake, I never sleep for a different reason—motherhood.

Family thinks I must be in clubs all the time with living here. When in reality, I haven't been to a club in years. I am a mom, doing Mom things in the normal everyday world that makes up Vegas. My exhaustion comes purely from Mommy status.

My four-foot tall, hazel eyes, brown hair munchkin is the epitome of a healthy, playful, and a normal combative child. Being Cody is almost as tall as me, Mrs. Short Stuff over here, his larger-than-life personality railroads me most of the time.

Let's just say, I'm lucky enough to have a quiet room in my house where I can go. It's designated for me, and only me. I call it my escape room. The door has a deadbolt on it, so I can relax peacefully without my son, or demanding husband and dog for that matter, barging in.

Momma needs a break.

Whenever I need time for recharging or self-reflecting, or fleeing the scene of a temper tantrum, I head straight to this spot.

My escape room is set up to feel a bit posh, spa-like, which is welcomed from the hectic, and often dirty job of motherhood. A couple other moms who've seen this room have said, "Mia, you're bougie."

My response to them, "Yeah, bougie. With throw-up, or food, stuck in my hair. Or boogers on my arms. I feel totally bougie." Then I purse my lips.

Those ladies will let out a nervous laugh, so I'm not sure whether they mean it for real, or as a joke, or a dig. Some of them aren't exactly good friends of mine as they are just fellow moms from my mom's group, so my intuition telling me comments are a dig might be more accurate. I will strive to be fancier with myself when Cody gets older, but for now, it is what it is.

Two plush couches sit in the middle of the room facing each other, accented with big fluffy square pillows. A modern glass coffee table is in between them, having a large picture book with photographs of over one hundred of the most beautiful places on Earth.

Recessed lighting overhead dims to put me in a tranquil state. And a small glass of wine is always on standby for those extra challenging motherhood days. I inserted a mini kitchen in the far corner of the room, and make sure a nice bottle of wine is chilled for me (okay, maybe this is a little bougie, but I assure you the buck stops here). Snacks are stocked off to the side on the shiny marble counter.

All this so I don't have to leave the room from having my alone time. And possibly risk getting pulled in eight different directions.

Being a mother, I like to say, is very much related to riding a roller coaster. There are ups and downs. Twists and turns around every bend. I am laughing with Cody one minute, upset with him the next. Sometimes, crying will take place from being overwhelmed by it all.

What a ride!

And how in the world did I succumb to the pressures of getting a puppy?

"Cody and I are going to get a dog," my husband Will says to me a few years ago. "Don't worry, we will take care of it."

The mother usually ends up taking care of the pets, and I should have seen that one coming from a mile away.

Our dog Caesar is a Dalmatian, and he is the best, but lots of work, and as I now can predict these types of duties, the responsibility mostly falls on me. As if taking care of a three-year-old—Cody's age at the time we got Caesar—hadn't been enough.

To top everything off, all of Caesar's spots have given me a few spots of my own, of gray hair. I'm sure it is a part of his plan to have me resemble him. I've always heard the saying that people end up looking like their dogs. Must be a collective effort from dogs across the world.

***

My days start off with wonder of how I will need to strategize to avoid bumps and hurdles right from the beginning.

This morning, as on many days, we walk into Walmart, and every other store for that matter, like nobody's business. My shiny brown hair is pulled back in a ponytail. My usual attire of shorts, a tank top, tennis shoes, and shoulder bag, is worn. I just put on a jacket if it's cold outside, but in Las Vegas, cold days are not in abundance.

Basically, I'm prepared for take-off. Cody runs, I run after him. If I'm not in a state of shock, that is. Keeping up with the energy from my son and dog, I stay in pretty good physical shape, which I'm thankful for, but my mental status is another story entirely. A constant work in progress at Casa di Mia.

Stores are where so many of my outlandish Mom phenomena's take place. I envision putting on a hat that makes me invisible to everyone around. Actually, my plethora of imaginary hats is what saves my mental status to take on motherhood, and find a better daily routine. I never leave home without them.

When I pretend to put on a different hat for each task during the day, I find myself breaking into character and doing a better job. I don't see that as weird. I see using imaginary hats as, honestly, imaginative.

Of course, closing my eyes is what I actually do to give me the feeling of vanishing, but people can still see me. My hats, after all, are only visible to me. Only now, my status is questionable, standing with eyes shut while Cody creates havoc.

Thankfully, parents have this universal sympathetic expression we give to each other when seeing young children acting up. As if saying, *I understand. Been there, done that.* This is somewhat of a consolation when I think of attempting our shopping ventures.

I typically walk into a store confident, but finish up in retraction. Naturally, being ready to shop is virtually not going to happen. I am never one hundred percent prepared when Cody is with me.

Now is as good as any time. I mentally give myself a push, and exhale a long slow breath. *Mia, just get a few things, then we're out of here,* I confidently think. Knowing that if Cody does pick out something small today at Walmart, there won't be too much harm in buying it for him.

As soon as we step foot inside, the first thing we see is a table with small cakes and cupcakes. They look mouth-watering to me, let alone my wide-eyed boy. I suck in the spot of drool forming at the corner of my mouth, needing to resist the temptation, and hold my focus on only getting the couple of things we came for.

Set an example, Mia, I tell myself in my most assertive tone.

A round table right next to it has big toy trucks, Nerf guns, and dolls stacked precisely in tower formation. This setup is just so that people have to walk around these tables to get to the aisles ahead. And, of course, many of those adults have kids in tow.

Marketing planning? Yep. Employees are paid to stay up at night, thinking of how they can strategically place every single item perfect for selling. Convenient? Nope, not for mothers or fathers in my eyes. But yes, convenient for the store, and a sure-fire way of making money.

Walking forward, I try to create some kind of conversation with Cody as a possible deterrent. *Maybe he won't notice all the luscious cakes, or the large shiny enticing toys right in front of him, if I just keep talking.*

Do I actually think that will work? No, but a good thought to try. I believe, as parents we have to be creative. Whether my idea works or not is a chance worth taking. Distracting with conversation might save my sanity for today's unscheduled shopping trip.

Not really a surprise, Cody zeros right in on each display. "Mom, can I—?" He starts to shout.

"No, you can pick from the dollar bin, and that's it." Trying my best to cut him off at the pass. My conversation plan has not worked. But somehow, suggesting another purchase does, with at least giving the positive notion that he'll get something anyway.

We proceed toward the aisles straight ahead, when a young boy, about Cody's age, runs by us, screaming and crying. Like the Road Runner from the show Looney Tunes, zipping by, trailing a gust of wind in his wake.

Here is a case of another child breaking away from their parent to make a mad dash to the goody tables.

Time seemingly is in slow motion. I turn, watching the boy make a run for it. My eyes move to Cody standing next to me, who is in full observation of this fiasco. My breath hitches, looking from him to the frantic child, then over to the child's shocked mother.

At first, we exchange the universal sympathetic parenting look. But, our eyes widen, realizing what is really about to happen. An oh-no expression hits us. A laugh escapes me. Nothing is funny in this very moment, but these instances are so off the wall, I tend to laugh out of context.

Regaining my bearings, I slowly turn back to the round tables, and then over to Cody again.

No. No. No. Nooooo! Sounds loudly in my head. *Please not again.*

I try to pretend as if I did not just witness this mad dash. No sooner than I look ahead in desperation to move forward, Cody now takes off, heading straight to the same table as the crazed boy.

Mind you, this pandemonium lasts all of only a few minutes. To me, it feels like an hour. I have come to realize during these shopping moments that if others rush to buy things, those items all of a sudden become the hottest commodities since sliced bread and cell phones.

Go figure.

Yes, now I have an I-want-it-now, I-need-it-now situation. There is crying. There is grabbing. There is taking things and sprinting. One would think these two children were gifted a shopping spree by some game show. The episodes that have people pile as much as they can in their carts in ten minutes or less.

I shut my eyes in hopes that suddenly no one can see me. I've mentally shoved on my invisibility hat. Trying anything, something. But, people see me. What's worse is they gape. Their mouths open wide in disbelief, at the crazy close-eyed lady talking to herself and not attempting to control her son.

When all else fails, I flat out wish I can just crawl under that infamous rock I hear so much about. Rocks that can magically appear when someone needs to hide and crawl underneath them; hypothetically they are quintessential to life.

Although, those are an illusion too, along with my magical disappearing hats. If there are actual rocks we can all of a sudden make appear for hiding purposes, they will be seen everywhere. No one would be able to move past them. Embarrassing moments happen all the time, and face it, people like to hide.

This can't be happening. This can't be happening, I mentally chant.

Through all of this turmoil, I start to wish I didn't come to Walmart today. I wonder why I needed anything in the first place. If a person can just take Cody off my hands for a minute, a couple minutes, an hour, heck even a day, I can possibly regroup from this. But even through all the chaos, if anyone dares to take my son, I will single-handily rip his or her arm off.

Cody might be a tornado at times, but he is my tornado, and no one better mess with him.

Go Grizzly Momma.

A shopping trip shows just how wild parenthood can get.

Basically, just when I think I have this Mom thing under control—today happens, setting me back one mothering step. Even though there are plenty of great times with kids, there are still frustrating moments. No way around those.

We finally make it out to the car, but not before picking up Cody screaming in one arm, two toys in the other, and rushing to the nearest checkout line as fast as possible.

I feel I should be a running back in football by now with all this training. I didn't even get everything I came for. Buckling Cody in the car seat, his hands firmly grasp the extra things he fought so hard for.

I sigh, mumbling under my breath, "Well we can't go back to *that* Walmart again. *So embarrassing.*" I press my hand to my forehead in disbelief.

I will undoubtedly laugh about this one day, but not today. However, there is some comfort in knowing when I return home, I can have that glass of wine I rarely have, but reserve for days such as these.

I breathe out a slow stream of air driving off, and can't help but wonder something. Possibly wondering the obvious. There are cameras placed everywhere in stores, this is common knowledge. With all the commotion between Cody and the other boy, not one employee came to see what was going on?

Glancing up into the rear view mirror, I see a pleased look on my son's face. I nod, thinking, *yep, the marketing employees were probably sitting in the back, watching the security camera screen.* Holding their hands out to stop the security guards from intervening in the mad house display of pandemonium. Then applauding how their strategies are working.

Darn the money-thirsty employees.

Absolutely, shopping with Cody is like a dream. Dreaming is a very fluid concept in the shopping world of my life.

Sometimes, shopping can be a nightmare, where I leave saying, "I will never bring him here again." Or shopping can be a sweet dream, where I leave saying, "That really wasn't so bad. Today, he understood he can't always get something when we go out. I can do this."

Just brainstorming on the days where Cody proves he understands he can't get everything he wants, it could be that we are in a place where he didn't want anything to begin with. And that may be one big illusion, some sort of brilliant child logic when it comes to him appearing to understand.

When what he is really thinking: *I'm holding out for that Target shopping trip, where I know I'll go, because I'm being good right now.*

I'm realizing that I need to give my son a lot more credit with his strategies. After all, company-marketing employees can't be the only ones sitting up at night, contemplating new ways to get people to purchase merchandise. My young genius is staying up thinking, too.

Finger tap to the forehead in this discovery. I will remember this significant breakthrough when planning my next shopping trip, and wish myself good luck. May the force be with me, now and always.

Chapter 2
Picking Noses, Especially Boys

Cody isn't only holding onto his Walmart packages riding home. His most prized treasures—boogers—is stuck to the tips of his fingers. Those light-green things are riding home with us too. I look up in the rearview mirror, and sigh. My mind drifts to all sorts of thoughts.

Picking noses is a gross subject I endeavor to escape, it's really inescapable. On a daily basis, he sneaks one of his fingers up in that tiny space. Around every corner, I bear witness to this action.

My deduction is that a child picking their nose is a pre-requisite in growing up, especially with little boys. I usually don't see little girls walking around with a finger in her nose. But there is the occasional one.

Actually, I've been told that girls run to the bathroom when they have to do this deed. They aren't seen then. Very incognito in my opinion. Goes to show you the natural instinct of wanting a lady-like persona starts from young.

In car seats, in class, or just plain walking around, boys search their nose for the infamous treasure of boogers. There must be a secret quota that needs to be met that is unknown to adults—rolling X amount of mucus into small balls each month.

I can see it now, Cody reporting to a secret headquarters for kids with how many boogers he's picked that month. Another four-foot tall child in a suit or dress sits at their desk. On the other end of the receiver, he or she documents nose-picking quotas.

A *Boss Baby* movie-type scenario. Except for toddlers.

"So, Cody, you only have two hundred boogers to report for last month?" The secret dressed-up child asks.

"Yes, I'm sorry. I will pick more next month, no matter what my mom says," Cody replies confidently.

"Better. You're not picking enough. Quotas are not being met," secret child retorts before hanging up.

Stranger things have been found out. And life has a tendency to be strange sometimes.

Telling Cody to stop putting his finger in his nose is just like telling him to do it—wanting to do exactly what I tell him not to. Instead of being less germ-spreading free, there is more picking action after I tell him to stop. *Ew,* goes my life.

I'm convinced it doesn't matter how wealthy of an upbringing is involved with fancy cars, clothes, private schools, etc. kids are kids. I will still see a child picking his or her nose in the back of a Bentley just like the one sitting in the back of that Honda we passed going home today. This is a universal practice noticeably out there.

In the short time driving home, I must have seen more than five children picking their nose. A Porsche, Mercedes, and Ferrari SUV were also among the Honda. I'm a car enthusiast, cars I notice. And man, are there plenty of expensive cars here in Las Vegas to have as eye candy.

If I had a nickel for every time I need to check my hair and clothes before leaving the house, all because I will find a little green nugget on me, I'd be in the billionaire's club by now.

My husband Will and I can buy an island in the middle of nowhere and have everything chartered in. No worrying about tantrums, or needing to vanish a scene there. No panicking over who will see a booger on me. Cody can walk around, picking away.

Oh that would be nice, if only I can get someone to pay me for doing those self-booger-checks.

Will is seen with a finger up his nose too, making me think he plays more of a role model in this action than I know. He is the tall, dark, and handsome type. Light-green eyes. A well-known graphic designer that I like to say he's a hot IT-type guy.

Suave-looking, demure Italian facial features, light sun-kissed skin, and a handsome white-teeth smile. And his five o'clock shadow of a beard drives my libido absolutely crazy. Very GQ, Roman God in a way, most of the time, but not when I see him doing exactly what Cody does.

The hours spent fixing his dark hair to be spiked just right with gel, mousse, and whatever else he uses to achieve a perfect hairstyle, just doesn't match him turning around and picking his nose. I find this unattractive and gross. And frankly, my mind wanders with disbelief at how many boogers I see in a day.

I used to get queasy, but now I'm just immune.

Caesar sneezed, spraying a multitude of wet stuff from his nose. I thought I would get sick. When I looked down and saw splatters of green on my new blue jeans, I felt I was almost done for. Nausea rose up to my throat from my stomach for a minute. I swallowed hard, and quickly got over it, feeling sorry for my dog.

Caesar has allergies, and I know his mucus bothers him more than me. For his sake, the allergy medicine his vet prescribes works fairly well.

A pivotal moment thus far in my motherhood career occurred years ago during a grocery store trip. Naturally taking place in a store, because most of my preposterous experiences happen in these environments. This is my parenting theme—*apparently.*

Stopping my cart in the produce section, I looked over my detailed shopping list, when I felt a small itch on my arm. I went to scratch it, and touched a little bump. I looked down at what it was and lo and behold, a nice-sized green lump sat right there on my skin. I was mortified, knowing I had been walking around a multitude of people, with remnants of mucus on my arm.

From then on, I make it a point to do a self-check before leaving the house. A small, but necessary adjustment to my daily routine. I now commend myself with becoming highly astute to Cody picking his nose, and usually can tell when he has some well thought out plan of where his boogers will go.

He thinks it's beyond hilarious, placing one of his green nuggets on me. A cute giggle escapes at first, ending up in an all-out belly laugh when I finally discover his treasure.

I most likely would have found this gross pre-motherhood, and I still have my reservations, but the love I have for Cody supersedes all random mucus sightings. But I have to say, I'm never thrilled about finding random boogers in Will's and my bed in the morning.

Cody still is not sleeping in his own bed, making our bed the family rest spot. Can't totally point fingers at my sleeping four-foot tall boy though, because the six-foot-five-inch boy lying next to him might have something to do with the in-bed boogers just the same.

I basically live in a sketchy germ world, but then again, I presume all parents do. I don't feel too bad. I'm still astounded as to how Cody gets his nuggets on my body without me knowing it. Maybe that's why there are extra hugs given. That has to be his way of sneaking in the booger.

The little bugger.

Cody and I were sitting on the couch, watching T.V. I had just told him, for nothing short of the gazillionth time, to stop picking his nose. When I noticed his thumb and forefinger was rolling something in between them. Obviously, he had a booger—a small green yellowish sphere.

I jumped up at lightning speed to get a wet wipe. Who wouldn't feel the need to catch those in something other than your hand? When I got back with the wipe, he had already gone back to drawing.

"Where is the booger?" I questioned. My eyebrow raised.

"There is no booger," Cody replied, nonchalant.

"I saw you were rolling it in between your fingers," I said, skeptical.

"Well, there is no booger now," he calmly responded.

I questioned dubiously, "What do you mean, now?"

"I tried to hold onto it as long as I could." His face was serious and concerning, like he really tried to save it. "You took too long." He shrugged.

"I was gone for only a quick second to get the wet wipe. You couldn't hold onto it for a split second?" I was annoyed, but my annoyance quickly turned to bursts of laughter. The sound of those words coming out of my mouth seemed absurd, knowing what this conversation had been all about.

That moment still makes me laugh to this day. Picturing some heroic scene out of a Jason Statham movie *and* all surrounding balls of mucus.

Mothers and fathers are not the only ones who address the picking nose situation. Teachers face this issue in school as well.

I volunteer in Cody's kindergarten classroom, and other classrooms to help, deciding to make it my sole duty since becoming a mother—to aid teachers, and sometimes, the school's office staff. I don't just call myself a stay-at-home mom. I'm also a Teacher Savior. At least that is what the school's faculty calls me. It doesn't go to my head or anything.

Yeah right, Mia. But it sure makes me feel good. *I'm here. I'm there. I'm everywhere. I am the Teacher Savior!* Envisioning my Superwoman stance in these moments. My imaginary superhero mask straps on, snug.

Then at night when I'm off duty, I have an actual costume to act out my womanly powers with Will. Hey, things need to be kept sexy to also keep my sanity intact. He doesn't mind my superhero role-play in the slightest. Tight blue halter top. Short red skirt. Gold thigh-high heeled boots. I set my vision to after-hours sexy stun rays, and run with it.

When in class, I'm astonished at how many times a teacher will stand and wait for their student until they stop digging their nose. In fact, I hear them repeatedly saying throughout the day, "Stop picking your nose," or, "Get your finger out of your nose," or, "We are not leaving for lunch until you take your finger out of your nose."

The child is taken right to the classroom sink or bathroom sink to wash his or her hands, but mostly *his*. Again, this habit seems to be more prone to little boys. What is visually seen, that is.

Teachers do a world more than teach knowledge from school curriculum. They parent during school, and teach life-long lessons as well.

Truth be told, a teacher's importance intimidates me. Each one educates our future generations. The leaders of our countries started in a classroom. The doctors and nurses who save lives sat in front of teachers. Technology gurus were students once.

The list goes on and on. Everyone's future depends on an educator. If this is not the most powerful job in the world, I don't know what is. God bless our teachers. Furthermore, I find through volunteering, and going to friend's houses, children will lend their ear to some adults more than his or her parents.

For instance, Cody will be more attentive with his kindergarten teacher, Ms. Dorsey. Possibly ceasing to put his finger in his nose from when she tells him, instead of me. Listening to Will and myself is a task in itself. Listening to his grandparents is almost that same challenge. I do not know why this is the case, but these same issues float around my mom's group all the time.

We ladies console each other, concluding this is all part of children growing up. Thank goodness our group meets once a week. Sometimes more, to have Mom consolation sessions. All depends on the severity of a mothering problem, we need to meet randomly, or one of us might tip to the other side of the sanity line.

My hands fly up in frustration.

Parents, guardians, and grandparents are mostly who kids spend time with, so I would think they'd listen to them for sure. But no, it's not that easy. Well, not much is easy when it comes to raising children.

Perhaps it's because Cody is so comfortable with my husband and I, and his grandparents, that he feels he can openly be resilient. Yes, that has to be the reason, so I'm sticking to it. Listening is another hot topic that goes around my mom's group often as we contemplate the thoughts behind how our little ones operate.

We've all grasped the fact that little fingers constantly in tiny noses are all part of growing up. Maybe even part of one's mere existence.

Come to think of it, there was that man getting out of his shiny white Hummer the other day, looking for some kind of national treasure up there. Out in plain sight. Out in the middle of the parking lot. The grocery store parking lot to boot. The idea of him going in to test the produce after his nose invasion leaves me at a loss for words. I'm honestly not sure what to think at times.

By Will adding to the nose-picking event, clearly shows me that adults are just as guilty as children.

Boogers have to be part of nature's way of building strong immune systems. An inevitable action to make the world go round. If there are no germs spread, then there will be nothing to make a child's immune system grow stronger. What comes out of little noses does not do the entire germ-spreading. Coughing, sneezing, sharing food and drinks also have a hand in it.

Needless to say, I want to put Cody in a plastic bubble to protect him, but I know it can't be done.

Digging noses has been big for a long time, passed down from generation to generation. My dad tells me of how my grandfather would constantly tell him when he was a little boy, "Pick me a winner," because evidently, my dad would be picking and rolling the same way Cody does.

I laugh, finding the humility in vain.

While boogers are a gross topic to deal with overall, I oddly find many humorous moments pertaining to them, in a demented sort of way. With only minutes left till we get home, I decide I haven't the energy to tackle the familiar horrific sight of what I see Cody doing in the back seat.

Chapter 3
Eating Vegetables

We arrive home from Walmart just in time for me to freshen up and make it to my weekly mom's group get-together. This week, it's at the recreation clubhouse in my community, so I only have a one-minute drive to get there. And luckily, Will, for the most part, works from home, designing company websites, so he's able to watch Cody a lot of times.

"How was Walmart, honey?" he asks me bending down to hug Cody. I close the door behind us.

"Don't ask." I huff, then give him a kiss. "I have five minutes to get ready for our mom's meeting. You okay?"

"Yep, Cody and I will play some games this afternoon, or maybe watch a movie while you're gone." Will takes Cody's hand, and leads him and his new packages into the living room. "Don't worry about us, have fun." He smiles over his shoulder.

"You might want to have him wash his hands." I rub my hands together in an air-washing act, and tap my index finger to my nose. I add, "And you too."

Will looks down at Cody and says, "You've been looking for gold, haven't you?" Cody nods up at Will as he adds, "That's my boy!"

They both laugh at each other. I shake my head. Blowing them both a kiss, I dash upstairs to make any attempt to quickly fix my makeup and hair from the chaos I was just put through at Walmart.

I don't wear a lot of makeup; in fact, Will says I don't need any with my classic Italian features and soft tan skin (I take any compliment I can get), but I usually apply eyeliner, mascara, and eye shadow. My light-brown eyes will look brighter this way, and less tired. I want to at least appear presentable. Then I walk out the door before you can say chaos.

"How do you get your son to eat vegetables?" One Mom asks at our meeting.

"Hide them in something," another Mom responds.

"You mean like push broccoli down beneath the mashed potatoes?" she asks with confusion.

"No! They will see it for sure. I'm talking about maybe mixing squash in something of the same color. Or bake something that you can put vegetables in, like zucchini bread. Pumpkin bread is great too. Color match, you know," I chime in.

"You're kidding!"

"No, I'm not. Try it, it works."

The subject of eating habits goes around our group. Some argue, others agree. Delving deeper into being picky, conversations center on the vegetable group.

I wish Ella was here tonight. My mind wanders to my best friend who has her in-laws visiting, and is doing touristy things with them. Ella keeps our mom meetings on track.

I decide to interject when no one seems to be agreeing on any veggie ideas. "Tuna fish with cut up celery is a good thought you might want to try. Good flavor combination. Cody enjoys it, and so have—"

Tamara cuts me right off. "Cody likes his vegetables, so of course he likes that, *Mia*," Tamara says to me in annoyance. Making sure to say my name in a singsong kind of way. She motions to the others moms who have trouble in this department for support, but they don't make any moves.

"No, *Tamara*," I throw the singsong voice right back, and mimic her. "Giselle likes tuna fish. I know, because I gave her a tuna sandwich when she was over for a play date a few weeks ago. *Remember?*"

She sits frustrated and nods, making her short curly hair bounce up and down. Tamara's hair is the only short thing about her. She is five foot eight, slender, with shiny dark-brown skin that glistens when she walks. I've always thought she would've been a model, but is an accountant by trade. And pushy. Tamara tends to push people to their limits.

"It didn't have celery in it that time," I move my gaze from Tamara to the rest of the moms, "but, what I was saying is that the celery-tuna thing has been tried on kids who don't like vegetables on cooking shows, with it being a success, so it might be worth a try."

"Hey, Mia, didn't your dog jump on the table to eat the tuna fish with celery one time?" Kristin laughs.

"Oh, yeah." A chuckle escapes. "I had forgotten all about that." I wave my hand in front of my face, then covering it. My head shakes side to side. "I had the table set for dinner. We were having gourmet tuna sandwiches, as I like to call them."

"What makes them gourmet?" Kristin asks, and slants her head.

"I have all the fixings; mayo, avocado, tomato, cheese, mild pepper slices, lettuce, and anything else I can scrounge up from the fridge. All on a toasted bagel, usually."

"Okay, you're making us all hungry, Mia. Stop explaining already." Kristin laughs again. She waves her hands out in front of her to make a point. Other moms nod in agreement.

I chuckle, and say, "When I came back from the kitchen, bringing the drinks for dinner, Caesar had jumped up on top of the table, eating the tuna fish right out of the bowl." A laugh escapes me. "He got scared when he saw me, and leaped down fast and took off, leaving droppings of tuna fish behind him. I didn't even have time to scold him, I was so stunned, and also, it all happened at lightning speed."

"Well, ladies, it sounds like a hit, so maybe our kiddos will like it!" Kristin exclaims, clapping her hands together, showing her excitement.

Tamara shrugs her shoulders up in annoyance, again. She likes to be the one directing others, and most likely can't stand Kristin and me directing the conversation. I've just learned to ignore some of her quarrelsome ways, because she has a lot of good qualities, just doesn't show them very much.

Vegetables are a hot topic actually everywhere. Magazine articles, social media, T.V. shows. I've read so much about kids and how getting them to eat their vegetables is a challenge. This issue is so hot that food shows revolve many episodes solely around children and eating leafy greens.

I witness firsthand at friend's houses the lengths a child will go to avoid the wonders of veggies. Push them to the side and under other food on the plate. Feed them to the dog under the table. Stuffing broccoli in sweater and jacket pockets.

These brilliant plans are all done when my friend leaves the table to get something. Usually for more milk, or another sandwich, etc. which is asked for by their young one. Now, a parent can be absent for a minute. Because a minute is all the kid needs to get rid of the goods.

Sure, I pretend not to notice vegetables disappearing, but I see everything. I get the occasional *please don't say anything* expression if they clearly have seen me watching.

However, this challenge is one thing I haven't had to worry about. Thank goodness, I have that solace, kind of like Cody's good-vegetable-eating is an eye in the storm for me.

For example, he will be a hurricane four running around the house. I won't say five because things can always be worse, *sometimes*. Then he will stop for dinnertime, which includes vegetables. Cody will eat his asparagus and broccoli with ranch, or whatever is out. Veggies seem to taste better with ranch, so that's a sure-fire hit. Then in a flash, he's off again.

I see friends daily having eye's in the storm with their little ones. Good in school, polite, no picking of a nose, good general health, neat, a good eater, a hugger, just to name a few. To me, this calm time provides a nice temporary relief on any day. I enjoy several of these examples, and I am so thankful for them.

With Cody being a good vegetable eater comes an interesting acquired knowledge, one that I would have never thought of. At two years old, he ate so many Gerber packaged carrots that his skin developed an orange tinge. Until asking the doctor, I had no clue eating too many carrots can even do that to a child's skin. It's the beta-carotene. Not until they get older, their digestive system filters carrots better.

Who knew—well, I learn something new every day. And learning new things helps develop better motherhood routines. I'm all for that! Even though Cody loves his vegetables, I still am glued to cooking shows that highlight substituting certain food with them.

I'm stuck on cooking shows in general. Baking shows too. The Great British Baking Show is my favorite. Paul, Mary, and Prue have provided me with helpful tips, resulting in better bakes. Including not being afraid with incorporating veggies to make any bake great.

Such an eye opener.

Cody's and my favorite is when I put artichoke hearts in a mini pie. Artichokes are a winner in our household. The pies are a hit, except for the times I completely burn the crust. Hence, why I need advice from experts in cooking shows.

Incidentally, baking tips is not what draws me into The Great British Baking Show. Here, the contestants support one another, helping his or her fellow competitors if they are struggling. These actions make me happy. I watch this show with Cody to teach him a lesson that a competition doesn't mean kindness should not be involved.

Thoughtfulness with humanity over anything else, in my mind.

I do find it fascinating when I find out how to incorporate vegetables into meals without knowing they're there. This way, I can pass on this valuable information to other parents who may not have this knowledge, and do need help.

"Okay, ladies." I decide to interject the many side conversations going on. "I do have a tip I'd like to share. From Food Network Star." This gets all their attention. Most of us love the show.

I go on to explain, "Substituting rice with cauliflower." Chatter starts to break out among each other. Some moms shake their heads. "I know. It sounds sketchy, but I tried it with Cody, and he was none the wiser."

"Tell us, Mia. Sounds interesting," Juliette says. This mom rarely comes to our gatherings, due to her busy flight attendant schedule, but loves to get involved as much as she can.

I smile, and tell them about the show's episode as memory serves me right. "Instead of using rice in some meals, use cauliflower. If you blend up cooked cauliflower, it will have a somewhat grainy texture, mimicking rice. Put the finely chopped cauliflower in a bowl or plate, and then put some Bolognese sauce, meat sauce, over the top."

"Or a good helping of mac n' cheese instead of Bolognese, it will work the very same. These two examples will mask the look of the cauliflower. The kids will see the white, appearing as rice. And cauliflower does not have a strong taste, so the Bolognese sauce or mac n' cheese will overpower it. Essentially making vegetables kid-friendly with the flavors they love." I wave my arms above my head with this discovery.

"Oh, great tip!" Juliette has a wide smile.

Other moms nod in agreement.

I remember the day I put on my chef's hat and went to work. Deciding to try the cauliflower tip out for myself. Bolognese sauce was the choice to cover. Let's see if Cody detects my substitute. *I grinned.*

Since the chef demonstrating on Food Network Star was a dreamy, tall, dark, and handsome Italian man with a charming accent, I thought the audience might say they liked the dish only because of him. Maybe they were in some sort of trance, and would like anything this Italian God made.

Boy was I surprised how accurate he was.

Cody didn't know it wasn't rice on the bottom, even though he would have eaten it anyway knowing about the cauliflower. He ate the whole bowl without noticing I made the vegetable switch, then wanted seconds.

This tip is a winner to pass on. That episode sure makes me think of all the tricks that mothers and fathers perform at times for their children—phenomenal!

Right before us moms went our separate ways from our gathering, I pulled Claudia to the side. She's a shorter Latina woman, light-brown skin, wavy black longer hair, and the cutest accent, being Spanish is her first language. Claudia is mostly confident, always up for conversation and smiling.

For some reason, she is so nervous with trying new things for her son. Maybe for the possible temper tantrums. She does not like arguing, or fighting, and is an excellent mom, wanting her son happy. If only she can be more confident in herself and more stern. Meltdowns are all part of childhood. She has the most problem with veggies out of anyone in our group.

"I'm serious, Claudia. You have to try the cauliflower thing. Jared will eat it," I urge her.

"Don't be so sure, Mia. Whenever I try something new, he's onto me like sauce on ribs." She sighs.

Sauce on ribs. What a very clever Texas thing to say, I muse every time Claudia says these cute sayings she's picked up from their family trip to Texas.

"He's onto you because of your nervous laugh thing. If you didn't look like you just stole a pile of loot every time you give him new stuff, he wouldn't suspect a thing. Your habit tips Jared off." I slant my head. My expression imploring, *you know I'm right.*

We both giggle. Claudia nervously. She just can't help it.

Chapter 4
Food, Just the Way They Like it

That night, after our meeting, I put on my imaginary detective hat, to get me motivated in figuring out why I hear the eating stories I do from my fellow moms in our group. I fire up my laptop in bed and get comfortable. Thinking of all the eating scenarios we tell.

I question one very important thing in contrast to picky eating—*eating boogers*. I compare this odd behavior to why children turn specific foods away, but will turn around and eat what comes out of their nose. Two very different topics, but controversial together.

Some kids say various foods are gross, mainly vegetables, and that occasional dinner looks disgusting. This all to me is baffling, when a lot of youngsters will eat what comes out of their nose. I at least hope it's out of *their own* nose. I've seen this one too many times, and gasped in horror watching the spectacle.

What a mind boggle.

However, my hand will be the first to go up if asked who has issues with your child and picky eating. Another one of my adventures in motherhood. I don't know how many times I hear Cody say that he doesn't like something before he even tries it. It's not like I'm an adventurous cook, making exotic things. I never think there will be a problem.

Salmon to me is reasonable. Chicken dishes are reasonable. Butternut squash and zucchini are reasonable. Oops, getting into the squash zone. Even though the squash family is fruit, they are still considered vegetables by most. Squash tastes savory, and are mostly used as vegetable side dishes. I can see the mistaken identity.

Since Cody loves his 'vegetables', squash in my eyes is acceptable. For some reason, he has never taken a liking to it, so that is a borderline 'vegetable' he doesn't like. I think him not eating squash has something to do with how I prepare it.

I mash it up once cooked. But I need to remember what looks good to me may not necessarily look good to him. A lesson somehow I keep forgetting. Deserves a quick slap to my forehead. *Bad Mia.*

Situating my invisible detective hat on, that somewhat looks like the hat worn by Sherlock Holmes, I finally had the idea a few months ago of telling my tenacious son that he's having fruit with dinner. This was an exciting plan for me to try and attempt to fool him with giving squash another chance. I would make it different too, where it would look like pieces of fruit on the plate.

No such luck.

The squash didn't even make it to the table before he was onto me like white on rice. We rarely have fruit at dinnertime, and he knew something was up right away. I really should have thought this one through.

Routines among children create stability and something they thrive on.

By me giving Cody fruit at dinner was not part of the normal. Basically, my plan turned out to be serving him a red flag at dinnertime.

"Great idea, Mia. You might as well have come right out and told Cody you were giving him squash." I remembered scolding myself out loud.

I then put on my daily imaginary Chef Mia hat, professional kitchen style, and got to work, since the detective hat led me down the wrong path in this instance.

I had one more idea up my sleeve before throwing my hands up. A few days later, I decided to switch the usual fruit given with Cody's lunch to squash. Cody has fruit during lunch most of the time.

I had bought a package of precut butternut squash at the grocery store, as it can be hard and time consuming to cut. Face it, moms never seem to have the extra time. Then proceeded to make it.

Well, it turned out Cody ate half of what I gave him and appeared to enjoy it. This had to be partially because of the butter that I had put on top of the cubed squash after it was cooked.

My boy sure loves his butter.

Added bonus when Cody didn't question why butter was put on fruit. A momentary worry while giving him the plate, but skirted by a miracle.

We've recently started making our own butter. A fraction of the store-bought price and it tastes great. It's a fun activity for Cody while learning the science of food.

One pint of heavy whipping cream, half teaspoon of salt, one Mason jar, and shake till a ball of butter forms. Our arms get a small workout. We have quality mother-son time, learn, and have delicious butter for the next couple of weeks as icing on the cake.

That one day, I put a mental check mark next to overcoming this small hurdle of working with Cody's logic, and squash.

As once said by Neil Armstrong when setting foot on the moon, "One small step for man, one giant step for mankind." This definitely applies to parents just the same.

Cody does fuss at times over not eating certain foods. While my friend's children want the crust cut off the bread. Tamara, complains to the rest of us moms constantly about the bread issue during our group gatherings. Fueling our child complaint sessions.

Thus, picky eating always fascinates me. From seeing it firsthand through Cody, I have to investigate into why children pick and choose so much when it comes to food.

Let's not have another bad solution like the squash thing. Okay? I think to the nonexistent Sherlock Holmes hat on my head.

I shuffle my legs out in front of me sitting on the bed, and type away into the Google search engine. Turns out the answer might just date back to many centuries ago.

A study done by the Monell Chemical Senses Center explains in an article that one strong possibility for picky eating is it's in our genes going back to our caveman ancestors. And it might just be a natural defense mechanism to not eat something that will make you sick.

"If you're a caveman and you're two or three years old, it's not a great thing to be running around and eating berries off all the different trees," says Marcia Pelchat of the Monell Center.

The center's research shows that over fifty percent of children are picky eaters, but most grow out of their habits simply by repeated exposure to the undesired foods. Positive experiences make these foods more palatable and proof of not receiving harm from them.

Wow, such powerful food for thought, literally. This valuable information certainly helps me tap into understanding Cody's actions.

Not useful for Tamara so much, her daughter is not so picky in what food she eats, only the problematic bread crust. But Tamara will still complain about my findings, no matter what. She's our group's local complainer.

The article simultaneously gives me reassurance that I did do the right thing with how I pursued the obstacle of getting Cody to eat squash.

On another side of being picky, I also hear many stories from my fellow moms that food is being pushed away, because it's not in a fun design on the plate. Or even, everything needs to be in alphabetical order in how food is arranged. Myself, I do not experience this side of picky eating. But I do enjoy all the different stories I hear.

Being a mother is so colorful.

I see these moments as kids exploring his or her natural fun and creative sides. It's possible kids may also get a kick out of seeing their moms and dads doing extra work for them. Giggling on the side. Can be a ploy to create more time together too. In any case, the logic is brilliant.

Challenges in picky eating honestly can add up pretty quickly, and can drive me a bit crazy on some days. I take comfort in knowing I'm not the only one tackling this challenge just by reading article facts alone, like the one from the Monell Center. This helps me to shrug off what I can, and try to keep an occasional unwanted eye twitch under control.

Darn that eye twitch.

Little do I know my eye twitch will return a couple days from now.

Chapter 5
Learning to Pay with Money

After the temper tantrum I end up experiencing once Cody realizes his forgotten purchase from a couple days ago, my only choice is to return to Walmart. Feeling my sanity is worth way more than arguing the trip back to the store.

I plum forgot a couple days ago to get that toy Cody had saved up for. And it slipped his mind after racing the other boy to the theoretical grab-all-you-can goody tables. My thoughts driving to Walmart this morning are, *what could go wrong?*

A lot goes wrong. I let out a long exasperating sigh. Here I am driving back home from Walmart, yet again.

"Mom, you won't get rich that way!" Cody exclaims, upset at me from the backseat of the car.

I've been in the beginning stages of teaching Cody how to pay for things with his own allowance, and think this trip will be a breeze. Wrong. It ends with him so upset at me, and for reasons that are completely outlandish, well to an adult anyway. Plus, he got the toy he saved up for.

I really have to keep in mind how he thinks for these shopping days. There is a reoccurring theme here, and I thought by now I would have learned to be better prepared for stores, or for parenting, or for life in general.

Right. Like that can ever happen. "Tough noogies," Cody will say.

Motherhood throws me curveballs left and right. Plans unravel right before my very eyes.

***

Thirty minutes earlier.

"Okay, your item is $10.81. And my item is only $1.57. You only have two five dollar bills, which is a total of ten dollars." I took out the money for a visual explanation. *"You are short .81 cents. I have a twenty-dollar bill. If you*

give me your two fives, I will pay the tax for your toy," I explained to Cody at the self-checkout register.

Cody didn't question my explanation and gave me his two five-dollar bills. I put the bills in my wallet. Then took out my twenty and put it in the bill slot. The register gave me my change, and I put the change in my wallet before leaving.

"You stole my money!" Cody yelled at me, walking back to the car.

"Honey, what are you talking about?" I asked, very confused.

Not to mention embarrassment set in with thinking what would some people think hearing him. I picked up the pace, wanting to get to the car faster. Who knew what unpredictable thing he would say next?

"People like you are put in jail, Mom!" He practically screamed at me.

My eyes sprung open. Oh, I hate it when I'm always right.

I can't get him to the car quick enough now. He already blurted out the jail comment. What's next? *Insert awkward-guilty-face moment. I spontaneously gave a weird laugh to the lady walking by. She tried not to stare, but couldn't help it.*

I piled Cody and the bags in the car. Jumped in the driver's seat and locked the doors. Safe! I blew out a puff of air and attempted to regroup in a calm manner.

The details appear simple enough with how things went down at the register. Okay, maybe not so much in hindsight. I used too many numbers, switching them around and going back and forth.

"You gave me the ten dollars to pay for your toy. I told you that you were paying today," I say while looking up in the rearview mirror.

"Yes, but you put my money in your wallet, not in the machine. You stole my money, Mom. That is not how you're going to get rich." Now his eyes begin to well up with tears.

And I'm left in even more confusion about how he thinks I stole his money. I mean, I put a twenty-dollar bill from my wallet into the machine, and even paid for his tax of .81 cents.

The whole way home, I keep explaining the same thing of how the money exchange went down. He clearly isn't buying a word I'm saying. All he knows is that I put his two fives in my wallet and not in the register's money slot.

It took a while, but just before we pull into our driveway, he finally comes to understand that he didn't have enough money to pay for his purchase, and also the fact that I had to make up the tax difference. Plus, I had to pay for the item I got with my larger twenty-dollar bill.

Phew! What a long drive home.

Not to mention having to deal with the crazy drivers on the road. Every single time I go someplace, I see the worst road behaviors. Las Vegas has to be the watering hole for bad drivers, honestly. Red light runners, cutting people off, speeding, tailgating, and everything else you can think of. It's like those people are the only ones who have somewhere to be.

While I'm in the car being called a thief and trying to reason with my child, erratic driving around me only adds to my frustrations.

I always remember my dad's saying, "You have to drive for everyone else on the road." A lesson held close since learning to drive.

The store trip does end on a good note, with a positive outcome. But the self-checkout experience and drive home from Walmart is a brutal one. Cody considers me a thief the whole time. However, he takes away a lesson about money.

I learn something as well in that I need to let him pay separately for his purchases. Cody can then see his money going into the machine. That is, at least until he gets older and understands more. Another mental checkmark for a better motherhood routine. Teaching in paying, noted.

I wish I can foresee what logic will be used when learning about life, as do the many parents I talk to. This way, we can better comprehend certain situations, and be more prepared. Possibly even walking more on the sanity side of the fine line of parenthood.

Then again, I think, *what fun would that be?*

I won't have nearly as many stories to tell.

The only consolation making me feel better about this particular shopping trip is I hadn't had any smaller bills than my twenty. Surprisingly, not have enough change either to give Cody the exact .81 cents for tax.

I always have a lot of coins. Why not this time, Mia? I remember mulling over on the drive home, while words of thief and jail time were thrown all over. *So, I had to pay with my larger bill, and the situation couldn't have been avoided.* At least that's what I tell myself now.

Later that evening, I relax in my escape room, staring at a favorite painting of mine. A Wyland masterpiece of a whale mother and her baby swimming in the ocean hangs over one of my couches. A picturesque sunset—a mixture of orange, pink, and blue, is painted over the ocean—gorgeous! I revel in it.

In that moment, I sit back and find some humor in what had transpired today. Being a mother requires wearing many different hats for the multitude of jobs we're faced with daily. For a brief moment, Cody had thought I wore a thief's hat at Walmart. And probably, some other people did too, hearing him yell at me.

I chuckle, knowing how speed walking back to the car with a panicked look on my face didn't help the I'm-not-a-thief-stealing-my-son's-money situation.

"What encounters will come up next?" I say in a whisper to myself, and close my eyes to try and de-stress.

Chapter 6
Privacy, or Lack of

I have always known the meaning of privacy, but I'm not entirely sure the word even exists anymore. I believe *it is still* a term. I'm going to go look it up right now.

Yep, privacy is still a known word. In fact, it is in the dictionary to this day. To my parents out there who don't think it actually exists, me included, I just confirmed that it does.

Privacy: The state or condition of being free from being observed or disturbed by other people.

I clearly see Cody didn't get the memo about this. While retreating to my escape room happens quite often, this is reserved for longer recuperating sessions. The master bathroom toilet on the other hand is frequented for a quick go-to recovery.

I have one of those small nooks with a toilet in the master bath, a toilet closet is the correct term, where the door locks; added bonus. Let's just say I use the restroom even when I don't have to, to find some quick solidarity. Even a few minutes helps to regroup from a Cody challenge.

Somehow, he finds me there anyway. By me making the toilet a retreat habit, no doubt. I don't necessarily hear him coming, but will see his hand spontaneously slide in that small gap underneath the door. It's quite scary if you think about it. Everything is quiet, and then all of a sudden fingers appear in that narrow margin. Tapping, wiggling, and moving side to side.

There is no secret to everyone I know, I enjoy my horror movies, but that doesn't mean I want to live in one. To be honest, real-life is considered a horror movie, given all the things that go on these days. Real-life is stranger than fiction, as my favorite saying goes.

The lack of privacy doesn't stop at Cody following me around all day, it continues into bedtime. Sure, he starts out in his own bed, but does he stay there? *Nooooo.*

I get up and walk out of my escape room to tuck Cody in. He starts to panic. As if the store confusion today wasn't enough, I now have to deal with bedtime shenanigans.

"I'm afraid of the dark," he says, grabbing my arm.

"There's nothing to be afraid of, honey." I smile at him, holding my breath a little. Feeling anxious that tonight's talk won't help in keeping him in his bed. After the stresses of today, I need some adult extracurricular activities release with Will.

His eyes grew to the size of small UFO's. "But a monster is under my bed."

For theatrics, I bend down below the bed frame. "No monster under here. Only a big dust ball."

"You cleaned yesterday. Not a dust ball. A monster!" Cody sits straight up with a stern expression.

"Yes, I did clean. But I didn't get under your bed." I try to think fast on my feet. "Now go to sleep."

"No, I'll start sleeping in my bed tomorrow. I promise. I'm sleeping in your room." He jumps right out of bed before I can say another word, and runs down the hall to Will's and my room.

And he's off! Glancing at my watch, I notice he's set a new record. This is the longest Cody's gone before getting out of his bed to run to ours. *Must be the dust ball diversion technique. Play off that more next time, Mia.* I think.

If I had a dime for every time Cody said he will sleep in his bed tomorrow, I'd be a billionaire by now. That combined with the money I would make for booger checks would buy me a yacht to go with our personal island.

Overall, Will and I need to get creative with having personal private time, if you know what I mean. *And* I think you do.

A lot of fear spawns from monsters and the dark. This is universal from young. I remember being the same as a kid. I didn't have to watch scary movies to be afraid; this type of fear was just ingrained in me. I wasn't alone either; my friends had the same fears. We talked about them a lot. I'm positive I got most of my ideas from my cohorts. Just as I'm sure that Cody gets a lot of his ideas from his friends. They talk about the dark and monsters too.

Times may change, but the game of growing up remains the same.

Lack of privacy is just one of those things I learn to accept as part of motherhood, and part of going through the stages of raising Cody. I'm getting my share of the effect with having my little monster attached at the hip, so to speak.

Life wouldn't be the same without my constant five o'clock shadow following me around.

"Cody, go to sleep right now, and stop squirming around," I tell him sternly. My side received a second leg kick during another summersault.

Good, Mia, that can go along with the bruised ribs. Which I'm sure never fully healed from Cody kicking me during pregnancy.

I'm convinced monsters aren't the issue here, wanting to practice for the circus in Mom and Dad's bed is the main goal.

"Ouch! Cody, stop it!"

Chapter 7
Distorted Actions...Borderline Horror Movie

Pouring another cup of coffee in the morning is a must after dealing with the nightly tossing and turning of a six-year-old. Two cups is my max. However, I know more will be ideal, but I really don't want to bounce off the walls all day. Adding an America Ninja Warrior hat to my collection isn't really in the plans. That might be going a smidgen too far.

As I watch Caesar from the kitchen window, he's running this way and that, entertaining himself in the backyard. I'm thankful he can do this, especially in these early hours. Cody sleeping in on the weekends gives me some time to prepare for the day. This is Mommy time to hopefully get energized.

Taking another sip of coffee, a chuckle escapes me at the memory of last night's Cody show. He likes to amuse us doing some sort of routine—comedian style, usually, horror style every time in between. Many of his actions, I have to say, are more on the creepy side than funny.

I can't believe how many of his moves and facial expressions can frighten me, and even Will sometimes. Caesar is rarely frightened. He might just be immune to Cody's actions from a dog's point of view. I wish I had a good resistance to being scared, but when it comes to my son, I don't.

The difference between feeling terrified from a scary movie and Cody's chilling scenes must be because now the hair-raising fears are right in my own home. As opposed to in a movie, sinister is seen through a screen, done in Hollywood, and far away from inside the walls from which I live.

Figures in the dark. Shadows lurking around corners. Horror movies fuel the deepest of my fears. Cody only reinforces those terrors instilled in me by the movies. Kid's behavior can be considered outright horrifying in appearance.

When Cody first found out how flexible he is with bending in these mysterious ways, I watched and wondered in amazement at how the heck he can perform these actions. Honestly thinking, *this is really a creepy sort of thing when you stop and think about it.*

If I see a figure walking toward me backward on all fours along the floor, head tilting back, looking upside down with a sly smile, I'll be frightened beyond belief. Sprinting right out of the house screaming will be my first inclination. Thus confirming any odd thoughts to the neighbors.

I'm not the only one who'll get scared and run in this case. I tell my fellow mothers and fathers of scenarios like this. Having them picture an entire scene happening in the pitch black.

Nothing but quietness. The only sound you hear is the scoffing of small hands and feet against the hardwood floor. Nails occasionally scratching. Your child gets closer, nearer *and then*, silence. You stand still, pupils fully dilated, trying to make out something. A sound. A movement. But nothing.

And then your child leaps up out of nowhere. Making your hair stand straight up like you just stuck a finger in the light socket. *"Ah!"* You scream, a bone-chilling shriek pierces the air. I couldn't sleep for a week after experiencing this very same thing.

The mothers from my mom's group also confirm that running and screaming is exactly what they will do. Some have done it. Specifically, Kristin has done this, who is a kind-hearted, petite mom. Mostly quiet.

One rainy night, Kristin had the cops called on her, of all people. Her daughter spooked her, waking Kristin up from a deep sleep. She had just seen the movie The Grudge with her husband. Kristin said she could've sworn the ghost from the movie was creeping alongside the bed, then she sprung up, screeching.

"I ran out of the house, screaming at the top of my lungs. I was so startled. My neighbor, who's always posted at her window watching everyone, called the cops," Kristin explained, shaking her head in disbelief. "Ceila had her hair hanging over her eyes, grunting the whole time. She looked like the ghost." Kristen looked down, wary, and said in a soft voice, "Exactly like her from The Grudge."

I felt better after hearing her story. At least I have never had the cops called on me. *Hopefully, I'm not speaking too soon.*

Scary actions aren't the only things to be afraid of. Cody tests out certain noises that are just as frightening. Whether he hears these sounds in school from other kids, or from being out in general, he replicates them. I'll never get a more goosebumps feeling than when I'm engrossed in my favorite nighttime show and out of the blue, he makes a horrifying sound. Grunting or clicking sounds come from behind. I leap up in an instant.

We're being invaded by aliens! I think in a moment of hysteria. The movie *Signs* comes to mind. My high ponytail swings as though I'm in a Kung-Fu fight. I quickly notice it's only Cody, and huff out a breath of relief.

All those noises certainly make my heart skip a beat. Being I don't get much quiet or alone time, the spine-tingling sounds seem to follow me wherever I go. They're a constant reminder that I'm truly living in a haunted show. Giving my lack of privacy a terrifying twist.

It doesn't take much imagination to get scared when my little one is first trying out new things. He is innocent in the matter, simply because he has no clue what terrifying ideas are dreamed up in movies and books. Young kids are natural at creating spooky phenomena, and comedy; sometimes, they go hand in hand.

To think that horror authors, movie writers, and directors spend countless hours trying to conjure up themes to terrorize the general population. When all they need to do is sit and watch a toddler in action. As he or she tests their flexibility while exploring new sounds, ideas will start to flow.

Maybe these professionals already do that. Which explains some of the scariest movies I've ever seen right there.

Ninety percent of the time, I'm elated to see Cody succeed at figuring out how to accomplish new ways of getting his balance and trying new sounds in finding his creative voice. Seeing him proud of himself because he's trying something new and succeeding is heartwarming.

The other ten percent of the time I spend wondering if I'm in the wrong house. *This cannot be my child twisted in the way he is. Run, Mia, run!* I honestly feel a James Wan film to be exact, explains a portion of my life. *I should be the one afraid of the dark. Not Cody.*

One thing I've acquired, as part of my daily routine, is to keep at least one light constantly on, and sleep with one eye open. This hopefully will get me through this stage without being completely scared out of my wits.

Still, I haven't figured out a way around Cody's hand sliding underneath the toilet room's door. That gets me every time.

Chapter 8
Going to Bed, and on Time

Just like in previous days, we approach our nightly bedtime routine, in hopes that this time, Cody will sleep in his bed.

"It's time for bed," I announce, standing at Cody's door.

"No, just five minutes," he retorts to stall the inevitable I'm-sleeping-in-your-bed-tonight scenario.

"Okay, five minutes, *but* that's it." I walk away to make my usual nightly preparations.

Five minutes later.

"It's been five minutes. You need to go to sleep." My second attempt.

Meanwhile, I have the strangest feeling of déjà vu. Like I've been here before, same words always being spoken. *Wonder why, Mia?* Face it, my life is based off the premise of a broken record, and being a mother spins me around on that same tired phonograph day after day.

"Not yet. I'm finishing up this one thing really quick. Hold on." Cody's second attempt to put off bedtime.

"How long will that one thing take?" I ask, my frustration escalating.

"Only five minutes."

"Okay, finish up quickly. Then it's straight to bed in *five* minutes. You have school tomorrow."

Five more minutes later.

"Now it's seriously off to bed. It's been another five minutes." My third, and going to be my final attempt at putting Cody to bed.

"It has not been five minutes, Mom. I have not finished my thing yet. Just hold on, will you." His third attempt at stalling.

Cody loves to use the phrase *hold on*. Everything is hold on. This is one more repetitive phrase that will pass, eventually. Before hold on was *obviously*. Before obviously was *so, anyways*. The list goes on and on.

"That's it. I have given you the extra time you wanted. You are just going to have to finish up your thing tomorrow," I demand.

"You never let me do anything!" Cody shouts back.

"I just let you have fifteen more minutes," I say, standing back in his doorframe.

He huffs.

I have been through this exact same situation a hundred times, never witnessing him actually wanting to hit the sack. If he's tired, he drops wherever and falls asleep. Not voluntarily either. *At least he's getting rest*, I will assure myself, feeling I lose another battle.

Naptime has the exact same dilemmas as bedtime. Cody stopped taking naps at four years old, but the arguments that occurred up until then had been almost daily. All surrounding a nap.

Cody got so tired, while combating me every step of the way, his eyes started to droop. They closed in mid-comeback.

Finally, when Cody laid down in our bed; yes, even during naps he took possession of our bed, I remembered Will came in one time and said, "Try to use nap time for yourself to lay down and get your rest, just like the old saying."

I looked at him and let out a big sigh, rolled my eyes, then walked out of the room. I ranted under my breath. "Whoever invented the saying to rest when the kid's rest must have been invented by a man. Because what mother can rest during the day? We have a million and one things to do, and can't get a lot done when the kids are awake."

Will, on the other hand, has no problem putting household chores off to lie down and rest. Me, a whole different story. Moms in general are on a completely opposite wavelength than their other half's when it comes to this napping subject.

I would wait until my parents left the room after putting me to bed. I'd climb up and break out of my crib as a toddler, and leaped out of my bed when I got older. Then go stomping out of my room like a soldier would march in the military.

"I am staying up!" I shouted, entering the living room. I marched over to sit by my dad on the couch, if it was nighttime. He was mostly the soft touch with letting me stay up later.

When teenage years hit, I went to bed on my own, only because I knew I'd be staying up talking on the phone. Whispering of course, because yes, I was supposed to be asleep.

What a difference between younger children and teenagers.

I don't always have a hard time with this issue. There are those moments where Cody simply runs himself so ragged, he drops in mid-step and falls asleep.

His younger cousins do the same thing. Play till they drop, we joke. It's almost as if the kids feel they will miss out on something big if they go to bed.

I will say one of the biggest arguments we have is in regards to bedtime.

My cousin, Sybil, and I sat around my fire pit, sharing naptime stories. She told me about a time when her youngest girl was playing with all her friends in the backyard, relentlessly playing without wanting to take a break. She saw her daughter start to wobble in mid-run. Her eyes drooped, nodding off.

"Basically, she looked drunk. Mia, you wouldn't have believed it." Sybil laughed.

She jumped up and got to her daughter just in time, right before she fell fast asleep. And literally while playing.

"I say that is pretty hardcore, if you ask me," I told her.

We adults should have the stamina children do. A lot more work will get done. But hey, in all fairness, after work, house chores, cooking, and running after our high-energy kids, we are beat. I barely crawl my way into bed at night.

Endurance is clearly the key to mothering. And coffee, let's not forget the coffee. I hear tea works in a pinch also. I'm not a tea drinker, but my mom is. She says when raising me, she depended on this liquid gold (as she likes to call it) to help her get through her mothering days.

Basically, a little caffeine goes a long way to endure for us moms.

Chapter 9
Toys Overrunning My House

The sun is shining brightly through my kitchen window. Not a cloud in the sky. A perfect Las Vegas Sunday morning until Cody yells from his playroom upstairs, "My toy broke! Fix it! Fix it! *Mommy*!" The waterworks start flowing full blast.

I know it must be one of his new toys from Walmart. I trudge up stair by stair. The crying gets louder and louder. *Why is it whenever I buy something new, it breaks?* I question myself, shaking my head. *I didn't even want to buy that in the first place.*

Thirty minutes later, the well-made toy, or so it appeared to be well-made, is fixed. But not before the tantrums I had to withstand. First, the Walmart mad dash fiasco. Second, the store outburst of me stealing his money. Third, the broken-toy blowout. All in the span of one week, and all over toys.

It all seems such a blur. Who knew buying something would be so traumatic? No, not always traumatic, but yes, sometimes. And pre-motherhood, I didn't know that part of a parent's job description would be a handywoman.

I know I didn't go to school for that profession. But I learn fast, and have to integrate a handywoman's duties into my daily routine. Yet another motherhood hat I wear. Many days, I think about going into the hat business. Imaginary brought to life.

My ad will go something like this. "Parent's Unlimited—Job Hats For Less. Make parenthood more fun and wear a hat for each duty we do. We have nearly all careers covered, so come in and buy your new hat today, and make parenting more fun."

Arriving home from any shopping trip with brand-new toys, books, games, or anything extra Cody has his eyes set on, is exciting for him. Only now he has to figure out how to play properly with his new belongings before it's too late and one of them breaks.

Even pre-existing toys often don't stand a chance depending on what kind of day he's having, and what imaginary hat he is wearing. One day, he's a construction worker with his hard hat on, trying to hammer the coffee table.

"No, not the coffee table, Cody!" I panic. "Mommy's place to put her much-needed coffee." I really do get defensive over coffee the more I think about it.

Then he tries to fix his play set that doesn't need fixing. Another day, he is an artist, coloring more than just his paper.

"Cody, the walls are not meant for crayons. Your coloring books are."

Next trip is Home Depot for paint. He moves onto creating a new picture on the pages of his hardbound, non-coloring book. Things are made pretty well, but even the best can only take so much before Mia Handywoman Extraordinaire springs into action.

That night, following an exhausting day of repairs, while doing my routine house check of making sure the doors are locked, and Cody's stuff is relatively neatly put away, I stumble. "Ouch!"

My foot starts throbbing. A dinosaur lay on the floor spikes facing upward. Never fails. There is always that one figure I miss seeing.

For items made to not be considered dangerous for a certain age-appropriate group sure seem to be dangerous for adults. Kids can zigzag around their toys in their sleep as eloquently as a cat, but adults are the ones who fall prey to the toy harm.

Whether Cody has had harmless-looking infant sets, or toddler action toys, or small chapter books, it quickly becomes apparent—anything hurts badly enough when stepped on. Or worse, stubbing a toe on.

Those tiny letter, number, and animal board books, made specifically for the safety of infants, proves to not be so safe for me. I have encountered stumbling on those more times than I care to think about. Pain shoots throughout my foot and up my leg. No, those are not harmless *at all*.

Maybe the books are easier for an infant to hold in their hands with tiny fingers. They are safe to not be swallowed. But man, step on a few of the books the wrong way—instant pain.

Same goes for those big plastic links that are shaped like trains, cars, or whatever shapes you buy. Each link is perfect enough to make you hobble for an hour. And let's not even talk about Hot Wheels and action figures. All parents who I know have had a run-in with those.

These small items are so easy to spread throughout the house. And this happens because Cody is interested in something one minute, until he moves on to the next interest. The problem is, he will just not put things away. His belongings land where they may as soon as something else catches his eye.

Finally, when he's asleep, and now I have my prime chance to sit down, relax, and watch my own T.V. show—*aw*! I plop right down on the couch and onto a Spiderman action figure. The arms and legs happen to be sticking straight up.

Cody was never really into action figures, only a couple. He's, however, completely into dinosaurs. So yep, you guess it. I'll plop right down onto, just my luck, a stegosaurus. For my dinosaur buffs out there, you already know what a stegosaurus is famous for—their seventeen broad plates lining the length of their back. It smarts landing down on those.

Being a broken record continues with saying, "I thought I told you to clean up your things." This has to be one of the top ten statements a mother and father say.

Every parent I talk to deals with this cleaning up issue. I want to avoid any injuries, first and foremost for Cody, but for me also. With his stuff lying around, I find myself getting hurt more than I ever thought I would.

Worst injury to date was stubbing my pinky toe on Cody's crib. It didn't break, but my toe had a minor fracture. I wasn't paying attention, rushing around to get chores done, and crack.

I not only felt it, but heard the cringeworthy sound.

Mia, don't rush, remember the crib-toe incident, I mentally chant whenever I find myself in a hurry. This never fails to be a helping aid. Fueling my daily goal of a better motherhood routine and good mental stability.

Moments in particular where I start to become frantic are when I have company coming over. I do my best with last minute cleaning, so the house looks presentable.

Over half my time is spent picking up toys, books, and clothes. I cut corners and shove whatever I can into the hall closet. This is my biggest timesaver for preventing the over-rushing. My only hope is that none of my guests will open a closet door and Cody's things cascade on top of them.

That will be bad. Very bad.

"I really need to get more storage bins," I often say out loud one minute. Placing my hands firmly on my hips, I blow out a slow sigh of exhaustion.

In the next minute, I find myself buying extra storage containers just for the toys and books alone. Following are second and third trips back to the store, buying large bins for the smaller ones.

It's all about the consolidating, is my motto. What I won't give to solve the challenge of the ongoing consolidation war in my household, and in the millions of homes across the world.

I enter my escape room after I figure the couch is not as safe to relax on after sitting on, not one, but two toys. Ending my day in here is per the usual on Sundays anyway. I put on my detective hat. I think for a while on this consolidating business. When nothing comes to me, I move to my trustworthy toilet closet. No ideas here either.

"Come on detective hat, work." I tap my head. "I need a solution. Consolidate. Consolidate. Consolidate." Not only do I talk to myself, but I tend to converse with my imaginary hats too. In private that's not so bad, but in public, it's really not a good look.

By twelve am in the morning, an idea came to me back in the escape room. (I could not seem to sleep until this was all figured out—serious business!) My butt had fallen asleep on the toilet and I had to move back to the comfort of my plush escape room sofas.

Our finances are in order. We can get a small storage unit at the Cube Smart Self-Storage place down the road! The biggest container for my smaller containers. I jump up in mid-thought. "Detective Mia has done it again."

Not too long ago, my fellow moms and I spent the whole afternoon talking about how we love when our kids get gifts that already come in fun storage boxes.

For instance, when it's time to open presents on their birthdays, we pray for things that already come in containers. Fun keepsake collectible casing is the goal.

Mother and Child alike are smiling and excited. Excited for two different reasons, of course. Our children are happy to receive what they have been dreaming of. We are elated the gift came with a box to put it in at the end of the day. Having these types of discussions within our group helps me to know how other moms have the same trials and tribulations as myself.

Now, getting my messy son to put all his things into the actual containers, instead of leaving everything all over the house, is a whole other story in itself.

"Happy consolidating." We moms laugh.

Chapter 10
Getting Ready for School

Monday morning arrives with the promise of a new week, new start to tackle school rituals.

"Wake up now. I've spent ten minutes trying to wake you up. Cody, you're going to be late for school." I nudge him.

Lights are all on. Shutters open. Covers pulled down to the bottom of the bed. My way of making it almost impossible to stay asleep. He grunts.

"Honestly, you don't want to go to sleep at night, but you want to stay asleep in the morning. That's backward, and not going to happen." *Oh no?* "Get. Up." I literally have to pull Cody up to a sitting position in order for him to open his eyes.

We barely make it out the door on time after a quick cereal breakfast.

Having to go anywhere since becoming a mother is very challenging. The process to get ready for school definitely overshadows everything else. I do all but pull my hair out. And I don't want to do that because I will be bald before I know it.

Maybe Cody thinks, *I don't want to go to school today.* Or simply, *I don't want to have to get ready to go anywhere.* It's most likely a combination of both. Whatever the reason is, he cannot pick up the pace when I need him to. Unlike the playing-till-he-drops thing, needing to get ready to leave has the opposite effect on him.

All of a sudden, Cody becomes a snail when it's on my time. But when it's playing time, boy oh boy is he a lightning rod. He turns into a super-fast snail just like the ones in the movie *Turbo*.

I take into consideration the early hour needed to get up for school. That alone can take time with waking up, and being sluggish. Slow moving is apparent when eating breakfast. I am not a morning person, as well as many adults are not early risers. It's only logical that we have these certain traits dating back from our childhood years.

Cody's pediatrician once told me that the personality a child exhibits from the age of five will be his or her disposition for the rest of their life. Since then, I pay very close attention to everything, being aware of this juicy bit of knowledge. Cody's four-foot tall personality is big already. If this is any indication of his adulthood, watch out.

Articles are written with how to make school mornings easier with putting outfits out the night before. Also suggesting making lunches the previous night as well. These wise words of advice sure do help me. I highly recommend this advice to my fellow mothers and fathers.

As far as the hurry up and eat a nutritious breakfast aspect, I'm still working on daily. But I did find through paying attention to what Cody eats before anything else, and what his favorite breakfast foods are, I'm then able to plan school mornings easier.

When it comes right down to going places in general, specifically having appointments to get to on time, I struggle still in this department. I might be ready to leave with all the necessary items in hand, even Cody has a specific toy he wants in his hand, but something, somehow, comes up.

After a long Monday at school, we stand at the front door, leaving for our dentist appointments. I push the numbers on the alarm keypad and Cody miraculously forgets he needs something else to bring in the car.

We fix this problem and are back at the door, when he has to go to the bathroom. Even though I'll ask him about a million times before we have to leave if he has to go potty, I'm assuming he goes to the bathroom one of those times. Alas, he finally has to go just as we're walking out.

"You're going to make us late for our appointment, Cody," I say, watching him walk into the bathroom.

"No, I'm not," he retorts, closing the door. I hear him lift the toilet seat.

"You should've gone when I told you to before," I tell him, now more irritated in tone.

"Well, I didn't hear you."

I blow out a sigh. The struggle of leaving the house is real. *How do I make this easier?* I ask myself and cringe. My eyes squint shut. Hand presses tightly to my forehead in disbelief. Unfortunately, I don't believe a clear answer is on the horizon. Kids will be kids. Growing up wouldn't be the same without traditional youth tactics.

Begin the leaving process earlier than possible, is the only solution Detective Mia has come up with in the past. That only works sometimes. I've spent many hours in my escape room trying to solve this mystery. Create early lead-way in timing.

This way, when last-minute things come up, or mind-changing happens, we still might have a chance to be on time. I still keep attempting this small solution in hopes it will work. When it does, I'm surprised, and have a better day.

I can never forget the days we're halfway to our destination and a meltdown booms out of nowhere. Cody forgets one of his belongings at home. In that case, I have a choice to either turn around and go back home for what he wants—this would stop the meltdown, or we can continue driving the rest of the way. I know if I do the latter, I run the risk of an ongoing meltdown.

What a dilemma. Big sigh. And asking him why he doesn't think of bringing what he wants to in the first place makes him cry even harder. *Nope Mia, definitely don't ask that again. Last time was enough,* I end up saying to myself as we pull into the parking lot of the dentist.

I contemplate pleading full insanity when we finally reach our destination. Realizing what a fine line I really do walk with staying sane at times. The choices are endless I'm faced with daily.

"Please be good, and don't pull any stunts." I park the car and look at my grinning son in the back seat.

He just smiles back at me. My expression turns to worry, getting out of the car. I hope that smile is a means of an acknowledgement that nothing out of the ordinary will happen, and he'll be good.

Chapter 11
Wearing Clothes in the Wrong Places

"Appointment with Dr. Ng for Mia and Cody," I tell the lady sitting behind the reception desk.

"Yes, I see you both here. You may have a seat and we'll—" Before she finishes her sentence, her eyes grow wide, looking to the side of me toward the back of the room.

I quickly turn around, only to see Cody is no longer sitting nicely in the chair I told him to stay in. He is jumping from seat to seat, having removed his shoes and socks to put them on his hands, like boxing gloves.

Swinging at the air like he's trying to swat something flying around. Not jabbing as boxers do. Cody looks like a boxer who took one too many hits to the head and is trying to still keep fighting, but is swinging at birdies circling overhead instead.

"Cody, stop it, and sit down. Right now!" I march over, trying to keep my voice as hushed as possible, but to get my point across.

The other patients start to stare, but an older couple smiles at us. I'm thinking they must have grandkids and understand what life is like with little ones. I awkwardly smile back, coughing out a repressed giggle.

Why am I starting to laugh? This is not funny! I can't seem to control my laughter, which is also not a good look, ever.

Finally, I get Cody to calm down enough to sit in the dentist's chair and carry out our appointments. With his shoes and socks properly on his feet. The only thing left to do is for him to go to the toy bin and pick out a treat before we leave. What started out as an iffy visit turned out okay. Cue putting on my relief hat.

"Mom, look what I got!" Cody says with enthusiasm from the back seat of the car, showing me a bouncy ball he picked from the bin. He pulls it out of his side pocket.

"That's cool, honey." I start the car and begin to pull out of the parking lot.

"Wait, Mom, look what else I got!" He reaches in his other pocket, revealing a small notepad.

My eyes spring open, panicking for a second, peering up in the rearview mirror. I stop the car. "Um, Cody you were only supposed to take—" My words trail off. *This is going to be bad, Mia.*

"And this." A third item comes out. A Spiderman eraser packet. "And this!" He now produces a small squishy monster.

I continue from earlier, "You were only supposed to take one. You take only one thing, Cody."

"She didn't say that," he retorts. Of course, referring to the hygienist that showed us to the front desk.

"There's a sign to Please Take One." In all fairness, the sign is way above a small child's height. Almost above my own five-foot mark, but that isn't saying much.

More panic starts to rise. My eyes fixate on the road and I start to drive off. Occasionally, I glance up in the rearview mirror like someone might be following us.

They're small toys from the dentist's complimentary kid's basket, Mia, not jewelry. The employees are not going to hunt you down, or call the cops, for those toys. I try to put myself in check.

"Well, now we have to change dentists," I mumble to myself. Breathing out a slow stream of exasperating motherhood air.

The shoes and socks incident at the dentist is not the first time Cody wore clothing and shoes in the wrong places.

Cody's natural comedian tendencies leads him to the novelty of purposely putting clothes on wrong. Which has become part of his spontaneous comedy hour—a show he puts on for Will and I. There are countless times when he's put his socks on his hands and pants on his arms.

My personal favorite is the underwear worn as a hat. Now, this is pretty gross, and parents see all the possibilities of dirtiness. But, watching him run around the house, laughing out loud with his underwear on top of his head is a showstopper for me.

I suppose this is one of those teaching cleanliness opportunities. With me not being able to control my hilarity totally discredits any firm stance I have. These times do not fuel my finest educating minutes. Also, by volunteering in school, humorous situations work their way in, even through planned lessons. *That* is embarrassing.

A month ago, I was helping Cody's kindergarten teacher, Ms. Dorsey, with grading papers. She paused her lesson plan to answer the classroom's phone. It was the administration office, so she was occupied for a couple of minutes. That was just enough of a break for one of the students to grab a basketball and put it under his shirt.

Damion started walking around, patting his basketball stomach, whispering he was pregnant. Ms. Dorsey's back was to him, looking at her appointment book, engaged in conversation with the person on the other end.

It was up to me to make sure class was in order. I tried so hard to keep a straight face and tell Damion to stop. My voice was as hushed as it could possibly be.

One, he wasn't supposed to be walking around class. Two, it was not appropriate to be playing with a basketball in class either. I guess clothing aren't the only items that can be worn in the wrong places. Basketballs can be too, in a cool pregnant look.

I got him back to his seat just in time. Ms. Dorsey returned to her lesson plan. I kept grading papers. Noticing at a glance, I had forgotten to take the basketball back.

She saw! Oh no, Mia, what to do? *I was about to laugh at pregnant Damion who wasn't supposed to be pregnant.*

Of course, I did the only logical thing; bent down underneath my table in the back of the room. Reaching up and on top of the table, I pushed a few papers on the floor, so I could have something to pick up. In turn to hide my giggles. Plus, how could I have seen Damion take the basketball in the first place, if I was distracted by picking up my mess?

I thought, yes. It worked. She didn't see I was laughing, and I get to keep my Teacher Savior title. *No one got in trouble with the exception of a couple of questions to the pregnant boy.*

Cody took home his friend's basketball idea. For weeks, he was pregnant, walking around the house. At least I didn't have to deal with any drastic hormone changes, so I was okay with my expectant son.

Classic situation of kids liking to imitate their peers.

I'm not as lucky now with going unnoticed as with the Damion moment from before. The teachers have caught on to my making-a-mess-on-purpose thing. No one mentions it, but I can tell with certain expressions. At this point in my mothering career, I'm used to decoding odd looks from others. From talking to myself alone, the open-mouth gapes just keep coming.

By giving it a try with not creating a distraction, I've started having my share of interrupting quite a few academic sessions by giggling.

Don't get me wrong, there is nothing saying we can't laugh in school. The teachers have their moments when they cannot hold back. The students definitely get a kick out of this. But we realize when children shouldn't be doing or saying something because it's not a great example for all the kids.

I guess I should set an example as a volunteer, *since* I am invited to help—I shouldn't start a laughing frenzy by any means. Let's just say I've left school, thinking, *well, I won't be asked back next week, or ever again.* And then laugh out loud about the day, like I haven't learned my lesson.

I shake my head at myself, and my can't-help-it ways. I try to stick with turning around if I feel a snicker coming on, so students won't see me. But that doesn't always work. Kids are smart, and they know when you think they're funny. If a child sees you chuckling at them, instinctively, he or she wants to keep doing their actions even more.

All this opens up a can of worms, and it doesn't stop there. The other kids start imitating what their friend is doing. Their classmate is receiving a laugh, and they want one too. As I can always predict, there is a mass, and possibly uncontrollable, problem. Multiple students doing actions they shouldn't.

And by talking about funny-doing-things-that-they-shouldn't-be-doing, I'm referring to nothing harmful by any means. Making silly expressions, or twisting themselves in weird flexible ways. Incidentally, this takes me right back to the chills of being borderline horror.

When I volunteered in a different kindergarten classroom, little Tommy took off his shoes and put them on his hands, which got his peers into a hilarious fit. Not bad, but disruptive.

I lectured myself. Don't laugh, Mia. Don't do it. *I did it. I couldn't help the escaping chuckles.*

Cody probably sees Tommy doing this type of stuff on the playground, and Tommy might just be the culprit who fueled the dentist's appointment turbulent actions.

Wearing clothes in the wrong places also stalls the getting ready part of going out. It's cute most of the time, but when I have someplace I need to be, this never fails to delay leaving.

Comical moments can test my limits the very same as finding them funny. I'm honestly sending mixed signals to Cody, and what's worse is, I know it. But I can't stop; situation out of my control. I'm only human, or as I like to say, I'm only a mother being a human, who makes mistakes.

Trials and errors.

I am right back to a wheel of emotions—laugh, cry, mad, and not necessarily in that order. I may pass crying altogether, and go straight to mad. Or I may cry a little because of being so frustrated and mad. It really just depends on the day, week, month, or frankly, the minute. Round and round, mothering emotions go. Where they land, no one knows.

But for the most part when Cody wears his pants on his arms, acting like a mummy or Frankenstein, I'm completely amused.

Chapter 12
Wearing Adult's Clothing

When I was about seven years old, I started trying on my mom's heels. I would wear them in the house, pretending I was an adult. Naturally, my feet wobbled. Most likely, you don't see women wobbling in heels, but I thought I looked exactly like an adult woman strutting around. My parents got a kick out of watching me. All the practice I got growing up, I believe actually helped me to feel comfortable in heels today.

My story is not an unusual one. Kids just love putting on their parent's clothing and shoes. My friends and I laugh constantly about this. A lot of memes on social media prove this type of action too. Let me say, wearing oversize clothing is definitely cute.

At night, my husband Will and I watch episodes of *Kids Are So Darn Cute* with Cody. There are only new shows once a week, on Monday, so the rest are reruns. But tonight is a favorite night of mine with a new episode.

After the eventful dentist experience this afternoon, I'm ready to sit down, relax, and enjoy. Cody is excited, and loves seeing his age bracket saying and doing funny things. Tonight is a special new episode showcasing young children's unbelievable knowledge.

"She knows all the bones in the body!" Cody exclaims, pointing at the T.V. in awe as a little girl, about five, recites all the bones in the human body. Mostly naming the major ones, or she'd be on stage all night with humans having over two hundred bones in our bodies.

"Yes, isn't that amazing, honey?" I sit, shaking my head at how this young child is so smart.

Step up your game, Mia. I order myself. *Teach more at home.*

"I want a bone book." Cody turns to me. "I want to learn the bones, too."

"Okay, I'll look for one online tomorrow after bringing you to school." I hug him tight.

Almost like he read my mind. I smile.

Every time he gets into something new, or sees something someone else does that interests him, he wants to learn about it right away. Then put his own spin on whatever it is he's trying to perfect.

"No, look now, please. I want to learn now, and tomorrow the bone books might be gone," my ambitious four-foot tall son says, looking at me with general concern.

"It's bedtime, Cody, right after the show. There will be books tomorrow, don't worry," I try to explain.

"Mom, I need to learn bones." He now starts to get upset. Clearly believing all books on bones will be sold out by tomorrow.

"Yeah, Mia, he needs to learn bones," Will chimes in as he stretches. He runs his fingers through his thick dark hair. "Just look now, and order a book. How long could it possibly take?"

I glare over at him. *I can't stand when he doesn't back me up when I'm trying to make a point, and that I don't do something right away when Cody asks.* I envision my foot stomping down, hard. My lips purse in a thin line.

Will's shoulders go up seeing my frustration, and he makes a funny face. He does that when he knows he's going against what I'm saying. That annoys me the most, even more than any nose-picking.

He's trying to make me laugh. Well, I'm not laughing. I stare him down. The hazel in my eyes pierce the green in his.

"Alright." I look over to Cody, then back to Will. My eyes narrow, giving him a look of, *we'll talk about this later.*

"Come on, shows over. Bedtime." Taking Cody's hand I lead him upstairs to wash up and go to bed. This time, no arguing, I'll just put him in our bed. He can definitely stay between Will and me tonight. No hanky-panky will be going on anyway when my giant over six-foot tall kid goes against my mothering.

Even though I enjoyed watching the kids and their amazing minds tonight, seeing skits of toddlers pretending they're grown-ups always takes the show for me.

Boys and girls wear fancy clothing, acting very mature, or sometimes have oversize clothing on to appear as an adult. Altering his or her voice to be deeper or higher in tone to be mature.

Boys wear hats that practically cover their eyes. He'll tilt his head upward to see. Then the suspenders holding up large pants and having an adult tie thing always gets me. Add in girls wearing oversized heels, teetering side to side, finding her balance, and you have a first rate comedy show.

That was me when I was young; adorable in heels that were way too big for me.

Cody, in his comedic ways, enjoys putting on his father's shoes to clomp all over the place. Surely ideas from *Kids Are So Darn Cute*. I've laughed till I cried, and nearly peed once, then laughed at that. It's like watching one of those clowns in their larger-than-life red shoes, except the clown is miniature in size.

Although, I don't like clowns, but watching my son, I love.

I'm positive watching the movie *IT*, and reading the book by Stephen King, terrorized me years ago. That man is a genius. The movie scares me so much that I won't look at clowns in the same way again. Thank goodness I can put that aside to enjoy watching Cody. Or else, I'll have to put wearing oversize shoes as a borderline horror story.

I always remember that kids will do anything over and over again if they know they'll get a laugh. Hence, why I need to turn around at times if I see Cody doing something he shouldn't. Yeah, that really does not work. He knows I'm cracking up.

Once, he found lingerie tucked away in my dresser drawer. It was a novel idea to try the newfound apparel on with having absolutely no clue what these garments actually were. Not to mention, Cody's gone into my bra drawer, too.

Cody marched about the house with several of my bras underneath his shirt. He looked quite odd in appearance for a child, especially being a boy. My satin teddy once went over his clothes, stretching it out in the process. A pile of mismatched clothing has glided along the floor. He strode back and forth.

Poor lingerie will never be the same again.

To him, the pieces of unmentionable items are just more adult-size clothes to fuel being a comedian. Anything to appear more grown-up, as with wearing his father's pants. But no, lingerie is to be worn in private, not for the thought of regular attire. Unbeknownst to him, of course. He does not know what lingerie really is.

I'm sure there are exceptions seen—lingerie being worn in public comes to mind, but that's definitely a red flag. The cops will be called at that point. A downside to wearing oversize clothes is the largeness can be a safety hazard for smaller bodies.

Cody was four at the time, he used to love wearing his dad's shirts in the house. They looked huge on him, but adorable.

One afternoon at naptime, he had Will's shirt on and wanted to sleep in it. My husband and I were turning our bed down. Cody began bouncing, hopping, and making quirky expressions before lying down. Acting as silly as he could.

The minute he did a 360, his foot caught on the hem of the white undershirt, making him fall. He fell headfirst, hitting his forehead on the corner of our bed frame. Everything happened so fast.

Will was closest. He reached Cody at lightning speed.

All I saw was blood coming out quite a lot, squirting up the way some fountains do. Okay, maybe that was a little graphic, but I'm creating the visual for that split second.

Will is medically trained, so he took charge. How lucky I was to have him there, even though my maternal instincts would have worked in a jiffy. We rushed him to the hospital, applying a good amount of pressure to the cut on the way.

After careful examination, the doctor advised to use surgical glue to close the wound, instead of stitches. Being it was only a surface cut; it wasn't as bad as we first thought.

I asked the doctor about why the blood came out so much for only a shallow wound. He told me that small lacerations on your head or face will look worse than they actually are. There is a good blood supply in this area.

Learned something new that day, and there is no scar whatsoever now. After that incident, I don't let Cody wear those large shirts anymore. I don't like to put a wrench in his joy of comedy, but a mother has to step in and do what she has to do.

Needless to say, I feel I could have absolutely prevented the whole situation by foreseeing him tripping on the dragging shirt. I know I'm not the only mother who thinks of how injuries can be prevented. Stories told among my mom's group are similar.

"I should have seen that coming," we say often.

Fact is, we strive for optimal safety prevention with our children, but unforeseen things still occur. That's all part of growing up *and* simply being a kid.

When Cody hit his head, it wasn't the first time he wore the oversize shirts. It was the millionth. The fall had been an accident, but I did learn from it.

Most accidents at home happen from things we do daily, even to a point we can do a chore with our eyes closed. The problem is we get too comfortable, and mistakes occur. I need to keep this in mind.

I remember the time my dad twisted his ankle coming down the stairs. Going up and down the stairs is something he does daily, and mostly not thinking about it. He missed a step, and was laid up for a month.

Caesar's breeder told me when she cut her finger badly while slicing an apple. Preparing apples is an everyday routine for her, feeling she can do it with her eyes closed. One day, the knife slipped, not paying as much attention as she should've been, and stitches were needed.

I keep everything in my memory bank. Will's shirts continue to be off limits. Well, what do I see next? Cody finds new adult-size clothing to wear, and puts on a new comedy routine. He is resilient, and just can't help himself.

Chapter 13
Donation Time

Since a few weeks ago, where those new toys were purchased from the momentous trips to Walmart, I decide the time has come to visit the infamous subject of donating some of Cody's unused things. Room needs to be made.

"Don't take my toys! I want that. I want that too. I'm still playing with that. You're stealing my stuff, Mom!" Cody wails with tears streaming down his cheeks.

I begin to tear up as well, because I don't want to see him cry. Telling me I'm stealing his stuff is my personal favorite though. Along the same lines as the chapter *Learning to Pay with Money*. Only now, I want to donate to help other children.

When I see various items from my little one lying around for years collecting dust, a natural reaction would be to think he's no longer interested in them.

Big mistake, Mia. Big, big, mistake. Cody takes a mental inventory of all his things and where he's put every single item. I, of course, didn't know this at first, but learn fast throughout the years.

I'll leave everything for the time being, but mentally tag them for when I make my next donation. Logical, since so many children go without, and Cody has outgrown a lot. He has more than enough to entertain him as it is.

Add in the things he recently obtained from our chaotic Walmart ventures, the house is being stuffed to the gills.

Words of caution—donating is dangerous territory.

From the minute I start gathering unused toys, books that are too young for him, clothes, etc. I immediately have one hundred percent of Cody's attention.

Very strange, he will purposely not listen to me when I'm asking him to do his chores, or to clean up. But now, my messy child is all ears and eyes, running over to see what I'm doing.

Panic begins to set in with witnessing items being moved around and some placed in bags. Pleading commences with how he will clean up, and then begins to do it.

I end up with my hands firmly placed on my thighs, kneeling down on the floor, and pursing my lips. Thinking, *isn't this ironic? The place gets organized right when donation time rolls around.* Interest suddenly restores for everything.

Shortly after Cody turned four, I attempted to collect for my first donation round. His hands couldn't fly fast enough to grab items out of my collection bags, and out of my grip.

I stood stunned, frozen in place, as if I watched a hurricane ensue around me. He hasn't played with any of this for years. My mind set into a whirlwind, sparking another motherhood first, and lesson. When new mom instances happen, shock and confusion hits me like a ton of bricks.

Ah. There's a first for everything, *I thought.*

It's not like I would donate anything that is his favorite from any of his stages. I tried the best I could to reason with him at the time, knowing my son was beyond smart. At times, I've actually forgotten Cody's age with how mature he could act.

"But don't you want to help other children have toys, games, and books? There are so many that aren't able to have these things," I said.

"Yes, I want to help," he softly answered, contemplating what he could do, because he has such a big heart.

I watched him rummage through a drawer. "Here!" He ran back with a small round plastic container holding a bouncy rubber ball in it.

He'd gotten it out of a toy machine, the slender stand-alone ones that require a quarter in the coin slot.

His smile said it all—elated to be giving something to another. Granted, giving something that he really didn't want in the first place, but he was happy to be donating nonetheless.

All I could do was sigh and thought, Mia, you can't donate this.

But I smiled, because the temper tantrum from a moment ago was gone, and he beamed from ear to ear, showing he wanted to give and help.

Not what I was looking for, but giving is giving, and from a toddler, that's a big deal.

Rearranging Cody's things after donations is also a perfect solution to keep his normal room appearance. Sometimes, he's none the wiser. Donating, then cleaning—accomplish two birds with one stone.

I came up with this small solution once I finally got wise to carrying out certain tasks when Cody was out of the house. If there's one thing I've learned since becoming a mother, it is the need to get creative with avoiding breakdowns. At least for now.

Only by me solely putting myself into his shoes lets me realize what's important to him at his age. Also, he doesn't want to part with anything. Thus, the tantrums at donation time.

A quick reminder of the saying; walk a mile in someone else's shoes—this often does the trick to keep my mothering on the understanding side. I actually like the original wording; walk a mile in his moccasins—deriving from a Native American aphorism.

Moccasins just sound so comfy. I should get us a pair.

The only decision I'm left with is to accept his now generous offering of a Green Lantern action figure. He got it in a goody bag from his friend's birthday party, and knows he will never play with it. Next month, I'll just wait until he's either in school, or with his grandparents. Making sure he will be out of the house, I then can collect unused things for donation.

I stand up and turn to walk out of his room, thinking, *waited till he was out of the house. Why didn't I think of that in the first place?* I shake my head back into the present. Staring in the reality of now at my upset six-year-old in front of me.

You never learn your lesson, Mia. A long sigh escapes.

Cody then makes a comment that stops me in my tracks. "Remember Mom, all children get toys. Santa goes to every house and delivers toys."

I have to think about a response to this, because he's right with how the Christmas tradition of Santa goes.

I respond, "Yes, Santa goes to all homes who celebrate Christmas, but this is only once a year. Imagine if you only got one thing, maybe two, one time throughout the entire year. How would you feel? Plus, don't forget there are cultures who celebrate different holidays, where Santa is not part of their tradition. We want to help all." This appeared to be an answer he could work out, since he gets quite a lot during the course of a year.

I'm not entirely sure I gave the best response, but that's all that came to mind. He seems satisfied, and moreover, he appears empathetic by nodding his head. I smile back at him, seeming to have gotten an important point across in this very moment.

Cody then surprises me. He goes to pick out a few of his belongings to donate. On his own, placing the items in bags.

Proud mommy moment.

I never truly know of all the questions that I will be faced with as a mother. I devote much of my time to figuring out good answers to my son's many questions. I do have to say, I'm not really looking forward to the, 'Where do babies come from?' question. Whenever that may be.

However, there is a certain line from a show called *Full House* that sticks with me. One of the daughters in the sitcom asks her father, "How come you always have an answer for everything?"

He replies nonchalantly, "What I don't know, I make up." He shrugs and then grins at her.

This makes me laugh, because it is true. I don't always have the answer to everything, and I have to think fast on my feet often. I've ended up embellishing a little along the way.

Donating items and the arguments that come along with it is not my struggle alone, fellow moms face this same issue. We have plenty of spirited discussions about the challenge of donating. There are mixed feelings about the subject. And don't anyone get Tamara started.

She is against giving anything away. But she's always been a pack rat, so we moms can't truly go by her. For such a chic woman in appearance, Tamara will gladly throw down verbally with any Mom about the injustice of getting rid of our kid's stuff.

Even though there are many toys collecting dust in the corner, and books Cody has already mastered reading, to him these are his personal entertainment things. To me, another child less fortunate can be happily enjoying them. He is slowly coming around.

I believe that finding a content middle ground will occur as Cody matures. For now, I donate small items when I can, and work with his way of thinking.

Donation time is a segment of my life that is somewhat stressful for me, and I don't mean just because of a possible tantrum as a result. Making room for new stages in Cody's life means he's getting older. No matter how many times I'm driven to the brink of insanity; I also don't want him growing up too fast.

It's almost like deep down, I want to keep going through the younger years of a roller coaster—wild!

Chapter 14
Negotiating—I Said I'd Never Do it

In the past, I remember hearing two things from others, even saying myself pre-motherhood, "I will not negotiate with my child to get something done, or threaten them to get something done."

Day to day, my routine changes; always on the search for a good solution to not use these tactics. I didn't bribe Cody to give toys for donating, or tell him there will be a consequence if he doesn't donate. And that is a nice consolation in my mind.

As a teenager, my parents took me on a Mexican Rivera cruise. I quickly learned that people negotiated in stores. The cruise staff told us that it's simply their way of life, and the residents expect tourists to haggle prices. I never liked the feeling though, like I was trying to get something for nothing.

Cheating the store vendors. When in actuality, a couple of friends that I had met on the ship told me that in Mexico, the merchandise is priced higher. The storeowners expect tourists would talk the price down.

I didn't like negotiating then, and I don't like it now. The Mexican cruise motivated me to be one of those people that said I would never wheel and deal with my child.

Supposedly, Mexicans do enjoy the haggle interaction. I'm not sure how accurate this information is, but going back and forth with amounts to pay isn't my thing.

But alas, no one can ever plan how parenting will go to a tee. Just like there is no book that can give parents infallible solutions to all things in raising children. I end up doing things solely to prevent making a scene.

I say I won't do it. *Stay strong, Mia. Find another way, you creative mommy you.*

But then barter occurs out of my mouth before I know it. Realizing going back and forth does become essential. Especially if I see a meltdown coming, or a temper tantrum rising. Panic sets in with what to do to avoid humiliation. Being a mother is so off the cuff. Through situations experienced, I have to learn to find hilarity. If I don't, I will drive myself crazy, and partially have.

Working out an agreement is mostly done in purchasing big-ticket items such as houses and cars. Realtors and car salespeople. Oh, how quickly I found out negotiations is very commonly seen in my line of work too—motherhood.

When it comes to negotiating, I think about a scene of going back and forth till finally there is an agreement reached. The same as how they haggle in Mexico. Very adult-like in action, however in reality, not so much. Cody is a natural-born negotiator at his young age, whether he knows it or not.

More common than not tantrums are over something small like a lollipop, a tiny stuffed animal, or even a sticker. Which later had been passed off to me as perfect donation goods. *A lollipop, Cody, really?*

Cody can't get something every time we shop. I endeavor to stick to this plan. All my work put into strong attempts not to negotiate or threaten flies out the window one disastrous day with a trip to the pet store. Cody was three at the time, and right in the middle of the grabbing-whatever-he-can-reach stage.

I'll never forget it.

Caesar needed new chew toys. It had been during his teething time, and face it, us dog parents need all the appropriate toys we can get. They are way better to chew on than our hands and feet. Although, Caesar always wants what we tell him no to. Sounds a lot like children, if you ask me.

We got what we went in for, and made our way to the cashier in front. In a flash, Cody started to panic. "Wait! Wait! I need toy for me!"

I knew what would be coming next. "Not again. Please not again," I pleaded to myself.

Before I could respond, or run and hide, I wasn't sure which one to pick, my turbo son ran back down one of the toy aisles. I watched him in a foggy daze. He moved side to side like a cagey panther. Becoming frantic. His hands grasped anything they could reach, which were only from the bins on the bottom shelf. But that was enough, believe me.

I stood there, about to cry watching the chaos, but I laughed instead. Not because anything was funny, but because I started feeling a sense of insanity. Laughing out of context arises at the most awkward times.

Only my son. Only a toddler.

I finally snapped out of it and came to my senses. "We are here for Caesar. We are not getting anything for you. It's Caesar's day. This is a pet store anyway, for animals, not humans, Cody," I sternly reminded him.

Nothing I said would have mattered at this point. Cody was already in tornado fashion, sucking up toys left and right. Dog's toys, mind you. A temper tantrum on the rise with no looking back.

We ended up exiting the pet store that day with what we wanted for Caesar. And also with Cody holding tightly to a squeaky giraffe stuffed animal in one hand, and a Nylabone (chicken flavor) in the other. Two Chuckit fetch toys nestled snuggly, one under each arm.

Why he fought so hard for the Nylabone, I'll never know.

I felt in utter shock. My hair had been in a neat ponytail walking in, and a disheveled half-pulled down mess going out. My purse slid down my arm hanging in the crook of my elbow. My shirt stretched to one side. My pants marked up from Cody's shoes and dog drool.

Caesar kept his nose stuck to my leg like glue, unsure of the child whirlwind he had just witnessed. I had a kind of staggered limp walking to the car, trying to juggle my two boys, one with two legs, one with four. I looked like I came straight out of a battlefield.

Needless to say, I did not want to return to that pet store for a while or ever. My disruptive son. His crazy laughing Mother. A blur of events.

There are other stores, Mia, *I assured myself.*

But in my state of shock, a notion hit me. Will I run out of stores to go to? What if this happens again in the next store, then the next?

Not one thing worked for that particular day, mostly because I mentally had checked out.

I'll try a small negotiation first, even the once in a blue moon tiny threat, when saying *no* a million times does not work. Giving in will be my last result, if all else fails, before complete mind exhaustion. I resorted to my last option at the pet store that one day—giving in.

At any store, I frequently find myself saying, "I *will* get you something later, but not now."

Cody replies by me needing to get him *three* things later. Then I respond by letting him know I will get him *two* things, and that's my final offer. And boom, we've just negotiated a deal. Now, he will be getting two things, which was never part of the plan in the first place.

At least I don't always give in. Thank goodness for small favors.

The ice cream store is a popular tactic too. I keep that one in my back pocket, because Cody can't resist ice cream. This will eventually save me from buying items that cost more.

One scoop in a cone instead of buying toys or games should work.

Of course, depending on the situation and the level of severity I'm faced with at the time, a trip to the ice cream parlor might not do it.

I notice not just from Cody, but other children also learn fast when it comes to what is more expensive. Getting the best value in return for their haggle is of utmost importance.

Darn technology and the internet sometimes. Valuable tactics readily available. YouTube specifically can be extremely handy, but this site can also be my downfall with Cody finding pertinent information so easily. He's just too smart, as kids are nowadays, with all these resources at their fingertips. My little neurosurgeon genius.

Uncle Ted was a neurosurgeon, so possibly, his brain mechanisms have passed down to Cody.

Another thing I said I'd never do as a parent is threaten. When I need to use a threat, it goes kind of like this: "If you don't clean up your room, you will not go to the birthday party on Saturday." Nothing harmful, but I'm aiming to get a point across that there is a consequence for not doing responsibilities.

If you think about it, this is true in life. If I don't pay my house bills, I will have consequences of not having a place to live. Or not have a car to drive if I don't pay the car bill. This is a learned lesson as kids mature.

Honestly, I'm teaching now what he needs to know later on—consequences. I tell myself this so I feel better if I've used a small threat. But in actuality, I'm trying to convince myself. A zebra will always have stripes. A giraffe will always have a long neck. A threat will always not be the best parenting.

I know threatening is not a great way in mothering, especially in the younger years. But, I'm only human and I do try my best. Most of the time, I scramble around with what to do. I'm not thrilled I use a small threat, but on some occasions, desperate times call for desperate measures.

And before I know it, I have said, "No dessert if you do not clean up your dinosaurs. One of us will trip and get hurt," or, "No allowance if you don't stop burping out loud in public." This in itself screams *desperate times call for desperate measures*.

Using negotiation tactics and tiny threats is not at all my finest hours. Motherhood is a whirlwind of constant decisions spinning around me, with the occasional side of laughing out of context.

I do what I need to in survival. Okay, that is a bit over dramatic, but not too far off from the honest to goodness truth.

Chapter 15
Attention Span, or Lack Thereof

Hitches in my day do not stop at spinning out of control in stores. Being pulled in one direction then the other with Cody's attention span, gives me a run for the money.

He is wholly concentrated on a single task, and will attempt to turn any conversation to it, no matter what I'm talking about in any specific moment. Brings new meaning to losing my train of thought.

When I'm talking about subjects different than Cody would like, he mostly replies, "Okay." Then goes on about his hobby, toy, or whatever he wants.

I breathe out an exasperated sigh, knowing full well what I just said went in one ear and out the other. I choose to let my question or conversation go, for the time being anyway.

Why keep repeating myself? When things are important, I hope to finally get an answer in relation to what I'm asking. Not be derailed by Cody's lack of regard to what I have to say. This has to be how the saying, I feel like I'm talking to a brick wall came about. In regards to kids.

I've recently started answering myself. Even conversations take place, just me, myself, and I. No reason to be concerned, I don't think. Hey, I have to make my own fun around here. Still, if anyone looks in my windows, they might think something's wrong with me. Again, confirming any odd thoughts for the neighbors.

On another side of Cody having a lack of attention with questions and answers, is I lose *my* focus. Children like to talk, that is no secret. They always seem to have so much to say, even though it might be only one topic at the time. Cody repeats things over and over again. Giving details like I've never heard before.

My task list for the day all of a sudden gets wiped out when he chatters for a solid two hours. Then I plain forget what I'm supposed to do. I'm always busy, as the other parents I know are the same, and failing to remember my agenda for the day is very disturbing. There goes *my* attention span.

En route to one of the rooms in my house, I'll stop in mid-step, and my mind goes blank. My mom attention span issue—forgetting the task at hand by a constant overload of information from my child. This is referred to more commonly as mommy-brain, or parent-brain as I like to say. Hey, I'll always include fathers. Dads are more involved now than they've ever been. Parent-brain is completely appropriate.

As a result of my mommy-brain, I have to find other avenues to be sure to remember tasks. Detective Mia hard at work investigates and finds diamonds in the rough—post-it notes and sticky tablets. These are a gold mine, and now are my number-one solutions to staying on my daily track.

I proudly say out loud, "Post-it notes are my best friends." Without those notes, I will be lost.

Our long talks can go on for hours, repeatedly giving me mommy-brain. Therefore, the post it notes are in use all day, every day.

My talkative boy varies from whatever he's stuck on at the moment—his current hobby and/or obsession. I'm astounded I don't have habitual whiplash from him going back and forth with his likes. One minute, it's all about trains. The next, it's all about planes. Then it's all about cars. And then repeat.

Another mom once explained this exact scenario, except she has a daughter. One minute, it's all about the movie *Frozen*. The next minute, it's all about LOL products, then Doorables come into play. Where she knows her daughter will have to collect them all.

If our children's obsessions become combined all at once, it will literally be mind-overload. Thank goodness things come in stages.

I only have one trip to a chiropractor on my book to-date. A visit for a sore neck. I constantly convince myself that the soreness is from whiplash with Cody's changing of interests. It can be stress from trying to keep up with him in general. Also, I can't forget Caesar and his on-the-go ways. In reality, it's probably a little bit of everything.

My neck starts to hurt just thinking about it.

Often, I wonder how marketing teams come up with their specific plans for children's interests. All I know is you have to know your target audience and speak to them. That is the only way to be successful. Marketing personal knows exactly how to project ideas to feed a kid's fascination.

If there's one thing I know, when it comes to birthdays and other holidays, buying presents for my ever-changing son cannot be done too far in advance.

For example, the *Thomas the Train* appeal lasts all of about two months until he makes the switch to the show *Chuggington*. That lasts all of a few weeks. Then when I go to buy presents for him, Cody already moves onto another attraction.

I'm glad a good Boxcar Children mystery book, board games, dinosaurs, and sea creatures always stick with him. I at least have those safe alternatives when I'm not sure what else to get.

Given I'm a planner, I take solace in doing my errands in advance. I have had to literally train myself to wait on buying gifts. Motherhood of a toddler pushes me to do my best to adapt to changes and overcome them.

As the U.S. Marine's slogan goes, 'Improvise, Adapt, and Overcome'. This works for the Marine Corps, and it applies to mom-life just the same.

Chapter 16
Brutal Honesty—TMI

TMI-Too much information.

TMI is behind the most humiliating scenarios I experience.

I am sitting at the kitchen table, taking one slow sip of coffee after the other. It's nine o'clock at night. I choose my Keep Calm, You're Strong, because You're a Mom, mug to drink out of. To give me the reinforcement I now need for tonight. I'm also wearing my Positive Vibes Only short's pajama set. This is to back up the mug's attempt at positivity.

My freshly washed brown-wavy hair is twisted up in a hair clip. I shake my head in disbelief, thinking about my night. Not a good one. I had my two-cup coffee limit this morning, but the dinner from this evening calls for another cup.

The direct, right in front of you, TMI reveal happened tonight. While out at a big family dinner, Cody announced to everyone that I had my period and was bleeding all over the place.

Wow, and right when the food came to the table.

He must have heard me talking to myself earlier, complaining about my period. *My eyes shut tight.* Why? Why do I do that? *I scolded myself.*

Little pitchers have big ears, as Lucy's mom once said in I Love Lucy. And how true that was. When you think kids weren't listening, they were.

I nodded.

Thinking back to the many shades of red my cheeks turned, crawling under that table had been all I could imagine doing. No, I didn't do it. But the thought of closing my eyes and pretending no one could see me crossed my mind at the time as worth a try.

Sure, I sat at the restaurant's table and laughed off what Cody just said. Out of pure embarrassment, I pretended to act out and smile. Then shook my head as if thinking, man can he make up stories.

But I instantly remembered that most the family at the table had children of their own, and knew how kids candidly spoke the truth. Maybe crawling under the table didn't seem too far off.

I get up to grab a Snickers from the pantry. The memory of tonight, and having my special time of the month, calls for one. I take a big bite, and sit back down.

Cody will pick the most inappropriate, awkward moments to spill out TMI, like at tonight's family dinner. I shake my head. Closing my eyes, I scan my memories of TMI.

I would not want to consider bringing Cody to work, if I had an office job, after hearing what my fellow mom Kristin confided in our group this afternoon. I wouldn't even think about giving my company's daycare program a try. I think I'd reconsider. Kristin apparently had no choice in bringing her five-year-old daughter Ceila to work about a few weeks ago.

"We weren't in the building even ten minutes before Ceila told every one of my co-workers, including my boss, that our neighbor called the cops on me for running in the street, screaming." Kristin threw her arms in the air.

"She conveniently left out the part of her scaring me half to death before I ran. The next day, I had to do some serious damage control at work." She lowered her head in shame. "I'm thinking of a career switch."

Ella consoled her, "Don't worry what they think, honey. No one knows what others go through if they don't live with them. Besides, doesn't almost your whole office have children?"

Kristin nodded yes.

"Well then, they should understand," Ella swayed her head side to side in her spunky signature way. Shiny black hair flowed, "and if they don't, who cares. All of them should be as good of a parent as you." She winked.

The rest of us moms were all in agreeance. Poor Kristin. I had looked at her with the parent universal sympathy expression. Although, that and Ella's talk, didn't seem enough consolation for what had happened to her.

Kristin is proof of how information can be spread all over the office building in just one day. Knowing my son, he is without fail at the ready to divulge everything to make conversation. He loves to talk. Obviously, Ceila does too.

The indirect not in front of you TMI reveal is just as bad, as it happened yesterday when I volunteered in a first grade class.

It was time for the kid's art special. The children lined up in an orderly fashion at the front of the room. The teacher stepped out to talk to the principal while I stood with the class. One of the girls turned to me, telling how her grandma farted all last night, and boy did it stink. Then following suit, another child jumped on the bandwagon, and told of how his dad pooped in the car because he has the flu.

"He just couldn't make it to the bathroom. And the car really smelled after that." The boy held his nose for special emphasis.

As I would've guessed, a couple more students had stories to share as well.

Before I knew it, I got such an earful of personal details. One right after the other. I knew very well how kids like to do what their peers do. The poor parents and grandparents didn't even know what indirectly was being shared.

I felt mortified for them. They probably would never find out, but you never know. The child might go right home and say, "Guess what I told a volunteer at school today!"

At such a young age, kids don't realize how humiliating this can be for their loved ones. In fact, they are generally excited and proud to be sharing this valuable information.

Everyone knows they are only small and don't grasp the concept of privacy yet. But that doesn't take away from the fact that personal true moments are being divulged so easily.

A major side to brutal honesty is no holding back on what is being thought of at any given second. We adults call it 'brain to mouth filter', or lack of 'brain to mouth filter' when it comes to grown-ups. I've seen countless adults lack this filter, to say the least. But the difference between small children and a grown-up is that we know better.

Children are just learning, and thinks he or she is doing a great deed by telling exactly what his or her thoughts are. The younger the child, the more he or she is unaware of private information causing embarrassment.

"Wow that guy has a BIG booger in his nose!" Cody, at almost three, discovers one day in the grocery store. Here again provides me with another hand-slap-to-my-forehead instant. The guy stands right next to us in the checkout line, as my little one innocently gazes up in awe at the stranger's nose.

I remember turning every shade imaginable. Uncomfortable laughter taking place.

"Look at that lady's hair. She looks like a lady Frankenstein!" He so eloquently points out another day, around the same age.

Talk about wanting to close my eyes and disappear with the wave of a wand. *Harry Potter, where are you? I need magical help!* I often think, imploring him.

Remembering those instances as just a couple of perfect opportunities to teach about what is, and what is not, appropriate to say out loud. I'm happy to announce that Cody had learned from those situations until I realized he hadn't.

Nothing, and I mean nothing, could have prepared my husband and me for a future incident. The worst experience to-date. I take another slow sip of coffee, reading my mug's saying again, and then take a big chunk out of my Snickers bar, before thinking back.

It was a warm summer night. My parents, Will, Cody, and myself were having dinner out at a barbecue restaurant. Cody just turned three. Three is evidently the age to really be aware of.

Will saw a couple of men who had been past clients of his, so he decided to go over and say hi. He also brought Cody to meet them. Innocent enough, I would have imagined.

Our table sat within ear range of hearing the men and my husband talk. They had the usual small conversation of how is everything going, and this is my son, and the men asking Cody questions such as, how old are you. When all of a sudden, I heard Cody say, "You look like pigs."

Whoa! What? *My eyes flew open, staring directly at my mother and father sitting across from me.*

Of course I did the only logical thing to do. I pretended as if we were involved in deep conversation. Like I didn't hear a word said. Our table was only two tables down, so I had to act well. Make it look convincing.

Problem is, I am not an actor. And in hindsight, I'm sure I seemed way too animated. Drawing attention to myself from other patrons, when I wanted the exact opposite.

A few minutes later, Will returned with Cody. He told us what happened. Naturally, I acted astonished, because I didn't hear a thing. If only I hadn't.

He said that the men just laughed.

Obviously they'd laugh. They both seemed like nice guys. What else were they going to do? *I thought.*

Each of the two in shock, and did what I have done at family dinners, time again—use laughter to mask the embarrassment.

Will and I both had a talk with Cody about things that could hurt another's feelings. As we finished our dinner, we told him what he said should not be said out loud. It could hurt a person, even though he didn't want to be unkind.

The subject had been brought up before that night, but he was only three, and things went in one ear and out the other daily.

Apparently, a rather large picture of a pig hung on the wall behind the two guy's table. Cody couldn't help but stare at the picture. And being both men had a little bit more meat on their bodies, he wanted to say something about this great comparison between the pig and both of them.

Not that it's an excuse, because it's not, but for a three-year-olds logic, discovering things are the best. And what better way to celebrate this newfound triumph than to blurt it out. Young minds learn so much every day. I've seen it at home, when out and about, and in school. For Cody, this scenario was only a comparing-cool-thing he came across. That's why he let the words fly.

No safety net of a filter with a three-year-old, obviously. He loved when he unearthed anything new, and he needed to immediately let others know. We parents get caught in the crossfire, so to speak.

Ride it out, Mia. The brutal honesty gene will eventually be controlled. *I had pondered in some sort of shocked trance after dinner that night. I envisioned me wavering on a surfboard. Hands held out to balance, surfing the wave of no filter.*

But wait, there's more from that night. As we were leaving, we waved goodbye to the two men, me pretending like I had no clue what had just happened. As Cody waved goodbye, he shouted, smiling, "Bye pigs! Bye pigs!"

The restaurant patrons I'm sure could tell he was genuinely excited that he knew them. The people had to be confused though at what he was saying. At this point, I was mortified, turning those obscenely odd shades that no one ever hears about.

Evidently, the talk from ten minutes ago about what to say and what not to say didn't stick. Neither had the earlier talks about the Booger Man and Lady Frankenstein blurt outs.

Batting a thousand over here.

The men half raised their hand at us goodbye, as to not alert everyone that the boy was talking to them. All of a sudden, I felt a chuckle coming on in thinking this had to be the worst experience ever, but at the same time, so absurd. I also turned a bit insane in the moment. Basically, about to belly laugh out of context.

Before that could happen, I did the only rational thing to do, run back to our table, skirting past any possibility of hearing Cody say, "Bye pigs." I pretended to check if we had left anything behind. I looked around the table, under it, and scanned each chair. Stalling my best until my escaping chuckles subsided.

I flashed an awkward smile in the men's direction and stumbled out of the restaurant.

When it comes right down to it, I'm really not good under humiliation pressure. I rub my thumb and index finger against my forehead in the pained thought, and take another bite of the Snickers as positive reinforcement for the time being.

I never will forget that night, feeling terrible for those men. It all could have been handled completely different, but I panicked. No one is blessed with flawlessness, and I am the prime example of that. Thankfully, I have that once in a blue moon glass of wine at home. Perfect for nights such as the barbecue one.

Cody never fully explained why he said what he did when leaving the restaurant, especially after Will and I spent time telling him what can hurt people's feelings. Probably because he knew it was bad after the fact.

I'm convinced children have this brutal honesty gene they are born with that cannot be controlled until older. At least that's my theory, and makes me feel better with any motherhood blunders. Making me relax for a tiny bit less stress in my daily routine.

Tonight's family dinner hadn't been as bad as the one from the barbecue restaurant, but still embarrassing nonetheless. Periods are hard enough to deal with. The mood swings, emotional outbursts, bloating, headaches, cramps, having anxiety about everything, you name it, women get it at this time of the month.

Throw letting the world know (exaggerating here, it was only the family, but felt like the world had been told) that I have my period, sends me into retraction. Children don't understand periods and that it is a huge privacy issue, let alone men don't either.

Will walks into the kitchen and looks at me. He sighs. "I don't see the big deal, Mia. You're overreacting. Periods are perfectly natural, and my aunts, your mom, and my mom were all there. They know all about that stuff anyway," he says to me with no empathy. He pours himself a cup of coffee.

"Please don't bring your mom up at a time like this," I say, and add, "I saw her criticizing look, thinking of what I must be doing wrong in my parenting."

"Oh, stop it, Mia. She was not."

"Come on, Will, she doesn't think I do anything right. And, cooking—"

He cuts me off. "Mia, you know that's not true. My mom just tries to help, that's all. She's sweet with how she talks to you."

You're seeing the train passing by, but you're not hearing the sound of the choo-choo. I think back to a comment Ray made from the show *Everybody Loves Raymond. Will just doesn't hear the obvious.*

"She's critical, masked by acting overly nice." I flash him a sideways glance. *He knows I'm right.*

Will inclines his head, shaking it side to side, and breathes out a long sigh. I scrunch my face, glaring at the top of his head. "On that note," I say with sarcasm. I get up and this time, pour a quarter glass of wine, ready to head to my escape room.

Then add, "Well, you wouldn't understand with what happened tonight. It's a woman thing, and there were the men of the family there, too."

As I walk out of the kitchen, I hear Will mumble to himself, "I hate this time of the month."

My feet practically make stomps all the way down the hall and into my private oasis, closing the door hard behind me. Mumbling to *myself*, "You hate this time of the month? Try being a woman going through it." My hand waves around in the air, having never been more annoyed. "You whine over a stupid hangnail."

I stagger over to one of my couches, defeated from the dinner's humiliation outburst, and Will's insensitivity, and plop right down. Reminiscing over all the crazy times I want to crawl under a table, and where I want to run and hide. Wondering why the heck those are the only solutions I can think of when in panic mode.

Taking a sip of wine, I let out a long slow stream of air.

How could I handle this better next time? I think in one moment. Then; *oh, please let there not be a next time like this?* I think next.

Chapter 17
Taking a Test

Finally, Friday arrives. I feel like I've been put through the wringer this week, not only because of the plethora of tasks given to me at school, but also needing to deal with the uncomfortableness of my monthly friend.

And the abundance of TMI thrown from every angle hasn't helped throughout the week either. My mind set on being ready for the weekend and to mentally get back to a sense of normalcy. Well, what's become normal for me anyway.

Cody and I get home from school, and I ask my weekly Friday question of, "Did you complete your AR tests at school for the week?"

AR—Accelerated Reader is a computerized program that provides names of books to read affiliated with it. Tests are taken after reading the book. This program allows teachers to know how well their students comprehend what they read through a series of questions.

I'd been reminding him since Monday that he needs to get two tests done, and better to do it sooner than later. This is a weekly routine of mine. I'm not a procrastinator, and I encourage Cody to not wait till the last minute to finish anything either.

Never too early to start teaching this to kids, even in kindergarten.

I'm also the type of person that believes extra time should be allotted in the week for things that come up unexpectedly. If no surprises arise, then I will use my spare time to relax or even get a chore done in advance. Oh, the hopes of this happening more often than not.

Cody tells me that he got only one of the tests done, and did it today. I ask him what the percentage on the test was. He tells me only forty percent.

The only AR test he took during the week, and at the very last minute, he didn't even pass, runs through my mind in aggravation.

Only five to ten questions are on the test. Eighty percent or higher needs to be scored for it to count as a pass. We read this particular book a few times, and it seemed he had a good grasp on it. I go on to question him about why he thinks his score is so low. Get ready for this, his response, "I took the test in Spanish."

Okay, this would be fine *if* Cody is bilingual *and* can read Spanish. But he isn't bilingual and he cannot read Spanish.

"Wait. What?" I say.

"I didn't see any other option. Only to click on Spanish." He shrugs.

Ay dios mio. Something doesn't make sense here.

"Why didn't you raise your hand and simply ask Ms. Dorsey for help?" I then ask.

He responds, "I thought the test only was in Spanish. There was not an English button to click on. It was my only choice."

Ugh. My face scrunches together in pure frustration.

He has no problem participating in class. On top of that, he readily volunteers to bring up when he sees an issue, especially with pointing out a rare occasion when his teacher makes a mistake. He only wants to help, and be sure Ms. Dorsey knows when something is wrong.

She has enjoyed telling me of these moments. Teachers can't help but find their times of cuteness within students. I've been in a classroom and have observed these once in a blue moon occurrences where a teacher has not known one thing or another. I must admit, I revel in it.

Teachers are only human, like me. I will then daydream.

Still superhuman, but not without imperfections. Maybe even reachable. To this day, a teacher makes me nervous, knowing their auspicious power.

Reminds me of an interview I watched on T.V. with Judge Judy. When the interviewer asks her if she's a feminist, Judge Judy replies, "What is feminism?" She laughs. "I don't really even know what that means."

I feel good knowing Judge Judy doesn't know about this. Proving she is only human too. A brilliant woman, nothing gets past her, but maybe semi-reachable.

Seeing Cody's reaction to this entire AR scenario clearly makes perfect sense to him, not seeing why he needed to alert Ms. Dorsey. To me, it makes no sense at all. And his teacher is the most willing to answer questions and help.

I then emailed her to see if Cody can retake the test, and see if she can find out why only the Spanish option appeared. Generally, once you finish an AR test, the computer won't allow the student to do a retake. I'm hoping, since

Cody took the test in Spanish, maybe the computer will accept it now in English.

Honestly, I start off upset, but mid-way writing Ms. Dorsey, I end up not being able to stop a fit of giggles. At this point, I find everything totally outlandish, and am convinced Cody must have clicked on a wrong button in a rush. If he hadn't procrastinated, there would've been no rushing.

I stand at my kitchen window, watching Caesar play in the backyard with Cody, and take a moment to stop giggling. I check my phone. Ms. Dorsey responds within a few minutes admitting *she* can't help herself laughing out loud.

She had never come across this situation before, but pointed out there's a first time for everything. She went on to say that his AR program appears fine in English, so he must have clicked the Spanish only test when logging in, probably in a rush.

Ha! My maternal instinct was right. Go momma. I cheer inwardly and perform a couple dance moves. Attempting the moonwalk, but that doesn't go as I plan. Then I laugh at that.

And that is exactly my point in case, to not procrastinate. Straightening up, I think to make this somehow into a new chant. Envisioning myself holding a picket sign with neatly printed letters, reading something like this: Always my point in case, to not procrastinate.

Ms. Dorsey confirms that unfortunately, the system will not let him do a retake. But Cody does learn a valuable lesson from today and what not to click. And always ask for help if something seems wrong.

He also learns for the most part not to leave things till the last minute. Or so I hope.

Chapter 18
First Day of School

I'm constantly thanking my lucky stars that Cody likes school, and he loves his teacher, Ms. Dorsey. She loves him too. I think it's so important for children to have a good relationship with their teachers. Since Cody and Ms. Dorsey have a strong bond, and Cody is excellent in school, I know she won't be too hard on him for what happened with AR.

If anyone would've told me, my sometimes-combative son will love school that first morning of kindergarten, I would've told them they are nuts.

The memory is so clear now.

"I don't want to go to school," Cody announced from the backseat.

"Honey, you will make so many friends and do tons of fun activities. It will be great, you'll see." I smiled, glancing back.

Nothing more was said. I pulled into the school's parking lot. Got his Jurassic World backpack on, one strap at a time, and handed him his matching lunch pail. I kissed his forehead before we started walking to the class dot, where I could see other kids already lined up. Their parents stood next to them. Tears started to prick at my eyes. My baby was about to begin kindergarten.

"Take my backpack. Heavy." Cody started shrugging the straps off his shoulders.

I quickly blinked back the tears.

"Sure." I slung one strap over my shoulder, and took his lunch pail while I was at it.

It's not heavy, I thought, but decided not to question it.

From a distance, I saw other parents in line carrying backpacks, and arms full of jackets and other things, standing next to their children.

I figured it was normal at the age of five to help your kids carry school stuff.

Right as I stopped to adjust his backpack from sliding off my shoulder, he took off like a cheetah. I froze for a split second, stupefied.

Wait, what's happening? *I thought, stunned.*

Cody started running in the opposite direction of the blacktop with all the kids, back toward the parking lot. My legs sprang into action before my brain could process what was going on. I ran after him, watching his body swerve this way and that. Side to side. He was clearly looking for our car.

"CODY, STOP!" I screamed.

He pulled on a couple of door handles as he moved. Of course, none of them worked, because neither were our car.

"NO!" He shouted back.

At that very moment, life seemed such a blur. As I ran, my eyes scanned the parking lot and drive-through lane for cars coming in. Making sure they saw a child was on the loose, all while staying laser-focused on Cody running like a wild man.

He started running in large circles when he didn't find our car. When all else fails, make it hard for the 'enemy' to catch you. Me being the 'enemy' at that point, trying to make him go to school. It's never easy to catch a moving target.

Cody must have picked this trait up from Caesar. He did the exact same thing to avoid me catching him in the backyard. Caesar never wants to go inside, except for the times our neighbor's dog was out in their backyard barking.

He's then been scared out of his wits, scratching at the door to go in. If I really thought about it, Caesar's a big baby, just like my childhood lovable Doberman.

Moms and Dads turned to stare at us. Some had to put their hand above their eyes to block the sun, so they could get a better visual of the fiasco. Although, none came to help, which I duly noted. Thanks for that.

I had to make Cody stop somehow. Get him onto the blacktop area, and out of the danger of school traffic. Maybe a teacher could help me, which by now would have been nice if one of the on-lookers got a staff member to help.

"CODY, STOP NOW!" I attempted to swerve in the opposite direction to throw him off his neat circles. And it worked! He changed direction, running straight.

"NEVER!" He yelled back, sprinting toward the school. In his state of panic, he didn't even realize he was heading for the place he had been rebelling against.

By this time, I had started huffing and puffing, out of breath. Not even realizing the backpack and lunch pail were still in tow, adding a small amount of unneeded weight to the chase.

What a clever boy. He unloaded the unnecessary baggage as to not weigh him down, to make a quicker getaway.

Should've seen that one coming, Mia, *I scolded myself.*

I threw on my imaginary Olympian track and field hat, invented for take-off and dash moments such as this, and really put pedal to the metal. Just as I almost caught up to him in the school's front courtyard, an older short slender lady, short-black hair, scooped him up.

"Who do we have here?" She tightened her grip, so he couldn't get loose.

Cody kicked and wailed with tears.

Hunched over and breathing hard, both my hands grasped my knees. "Cody." I barely could speak. "Ms. Dorsey. Is. His. Teacher." I looked up, breathing frantically.

"Calm down, Cody. I'm Ms. Dorsey." She smiled at him with the warmth of Santa Claus, and oddly enough, he stopped crying. "We will have a lot of fun this year. I have all kinds of activities planned for us. Okay?"

He wiped his eyes. She put him down and grasped his hand, giving me a wink. "Why don't we head inside with all your friends?"

He nodded slowly, stifling back a sob.

I put his backpack straps over his shoulders, and handed him his lunch pail. I gave him another kiss on his forehead, then he walked off with his teacher. Hand in hand, Ms. Dorsey led him to their classroom dot and walked him and the rest of the class inside.

I stood in the same spot for what seemed like hours; in reality, it had only been a few minutes, until I mustered up enough energy to head back to my car. That is where the waterworks came pouring out. The unforeseen fiasco, my son's first day of school, the embarrassing odd looks from other parents, all caught up to me at once.

I felt sad, scared, worried, and a bit humiliated. You know, all the feelings of the daily motherhood roller coaster.

"I can't even start school out normal," I cried to myself, grabbing a tissue out of my purse.

I ran after my child like a mad woman.

Look at that mom. She can't even control her son. *Parents must have been thinking.*

Not like I should care what they think, they are parents of small children and should understand. But I found myself feeling embarrassed nonetheless. Slowly, I wiped a few tears away with my fingers. A couple of knocks on my driver's side window made me jump.

"Are you okay? Can I help you?" A woman with beautiful tanned-skin asked through the window. She had large brown eyes that appeared concerned, and straight silky-black hair. A bit of an Egyptian Goddess, in my opinion.

I rolled my window down. "Thank you. I'm fine. Just having a first-day-of-school moment." I half-smiled.

"Oh girl, I feel you. My son is in second grade, and I still have those first-day moments." She sighed, gazing up into the bright blue sky. "My name is Ella. What's yours?"

"Mia. Thank you for checking on me by the way. That's so nice of you." All of sudden, I started feeling better.

"Hey, you want to get a cup of coffee, or something? Share some mom stories, the good, the bad, and the ugly." Ella giggled. "I can't truly start my day without coffee. I don't know about you." Her head swayed side to side, matter of fact.

"Ella, you're speaking my language." I nodded sharply. "I'll follow you."

We met at the local Starbucks down the street, as later discussed, just in case the school happened to call with one of our son's going out of control. We would be close by.

"You should have seen me. Weaving, skidding, almost falling a couple of times. It was a mess. I didn't see it coming either," I explained the disastrous morning to her. I took another sip of my coffee. Cup size—Venti. Leaving room for cream.

She laughed. "Sorry, I don't mean to laugh, but being a mom is so eventful. We never know what will come up." I laughed with her, nodding. She added, "Well, I haven't had a first day as eventful as yours, I am sorry." Ella chuckled sweetly.

"But Marcus didn't go without a small scene for his first day of kindergarten." She took a bite of her blueberry scone, and said, "I had to carry him in, kicking and screaming. Switching from holding him on my hip to in front of me, because his legs were flying fast and furious. My hips and ribs were sore for weeks."

We both shook our heads, laughing.

Ella continued, "The most amazing thing was how the teacher reacted. We had Ms. Dorsey too. She had to bob and weave a little bit, but got Marcus to calm down in a matter of like a minute. As I watched her in amazement, I knew instantly she's done this all before."

She waved a hand in the air. "I knew right then and there, I wanted to dedicate my time to volunteering, feeling how much these teachers must have to deal with each day."

I agreed with Ella, and from that moment on, I too made sure to volunteer as much as I could.

After that morning, Ella and I became fast friends and volunteer buddies. She too was a stay-at-home mom, but called a Teacher Savior. I'm not mad, because if I had to share my Teacher Savior title with someone, I'm glad I shared it with Ella.

Shortly after, she joined my mom's group I had become a part of two years back from signing up with a place called Toddler's and Mommies. A group of us became friends through our weekly visits, and decided to start group meetings of our own for only us moms.

Such a brilliant plan. Those get-togethers saved my mental status so many times. The other moms felt the same.

I explained to the moms my escape room concept, and my imaginary hat's dress code. Another mom passed on the toilet closet retreat idea. Ella utilized all ideas, as I did.

"Mom necessities. Can't live without them now." Ella laughed during one mom group therapy session. That's what I called it, being it was a particularly hard week for most of our group. We mainly sat, shared, and consoled each other.

After meeting Ella on the first day of kindergarten, I have a lot more faith in random mom support—then, now, and in all the future adventures to come.

Chapter 19
Repeating Things Over and Over

Saturday is now in full swing, eating breakfast. A.R. test snafu solved from yesterday, onto tackling the weekend.

Toast, eggs, fruit, juice. Bacon is a favorite of ours, but I can't handle the grease going *pop pop pop*, up and out of the pan. Splatter guards do protect from the extra grease going airborne, but then I think, *just what I need, another item to wash, and more mess.* I tell this to myself when Cody asks for bacon. My house rule is order bacon out.

"Mom, what are you doing?" Cody looks up from drawing, still at the kitchen table.

"Washing the dishes," I say, holding up the sponge.

"Mom, when are you going to be done? Mom?"

The repetitious word is starting earlier each day. I sigh. "In a minute, honey. Why?"

"Because Mom, you take too long, Mom. Mom, mom, mom, mom, are you done yet? Mom?"

I look over my shoulder at Cody intent in his masterpiece. Repeating mom like it's nothing, normal for him. Maddening for me.

"Almost. Just stop and be patient. Okay? The dishes don't wash themselves, you know." I smile at the top of his head. He's finishing coloring in the dinosaur he just drew.

"Is that a Pterodactyl?" I ask.

"No, a Quetzalcoatlus," he responds.

A what!

Cody looks up, seeing my confused expression. "It's another Pterosaur."

"Oh." *Totally knew that one.* "Good job, honey. I love your drawing, and love how much you know about dinosaurs."

He looks back up. "And Pterosaurs. I know a lot about them too." Cody pauses, noticing my eyes go blank. "Pterosaurs are not dinosaurs. They were a cousin of dinosaurs."

I make a slow smile and kiss his forehead, then go back to the dishes. *My little genius.*

"Mom, mom, mom. Mom!"

"Yes?" I question. *We're back to this now?*

"Is that your last dish, Mom? Mom? Mom!"

"No, it's not. Please be patient. I'm almost done."

"How many more dishes, Mom?" Cody asks. I peek over my shoulder at him. He's still coloring.

I sigh. "There's enough of them."

"Mom, what are you doing now, Mom? Mom, still not done yet, Mom? I want to play."

Huffing, I can't take the badgering so early. I place the sponge down overly gentle in the sink, making every attempt to control my rising frustration. "I have to go to the bathroom," I state, turning on my heel.

Back to my toilet closet in the master. Not that I have to go, but I need a break from the word mom. *It's too early.* My mind feels exhausted already.

Fingers slide under the gap of the door. Tapping the tile.

He found me. Eyes widen. Terror. Dun dun duuuunnnnn. Cue scary movie sound.

"Mom, are you pooping in there?" Cody whispers underneath the door.

I burst out laughing. Only moms can experience frustration (to the point of anger), turning to horror, then poop comes into the equation, and all in a matter of less than five minutes.

"Mom, why are you laughing? Does it smell, Mom?" He giggles loudly, making me laugh even harder.

My days won't be the same without the overuse of Mom, Dad, or Grandma, Grandpa, etc. Hearing my official title over and over, even when I'm looking right at Cody *and* having acknowledged him twice already.

Okay, let me think back to how many moms were said this morning in the span of a couple minutes. I count at least twenty-five. My mind starts to fog with the realization.

I nod and think it can be interesting to conduct a little experiment. For the rest of Saturday, I'll walk around with my always-handy post it notes, tallying up how many times Cody says mom. I tally a whopping one hundred and six moms by the end of the day.

It's gotten to a point that if someone actually calls me by my first name, I end up saying, "Huh? Who? Me?"

I decide to call my cousin Sybil and tell her about my tiny experiment. She has four children. Sybil times my number by how many kids she has. We instantly flop down on our couches from delirium at this very real equation, and briefly pass out. The line goes silent.

Mental stability also takes a hit when my ambitious munchkin gets on a subject *and* repeats it time again. And then rehashes it for good measure. Harping on the same thing every waking moment.

If I ever chance going to a parenting seminar, and the repeating issue comes up, I'll be the first one waving my hand in the air. Or my giant yellow number-one foam hand. Whichever, I have both ready to wave.

I'll be quick to leap out of my seat, and shout, "I can relate! Me! Over here!" Arms flailing, jumping up and down, number-one foam hand flopping back and forth, my hair bouncing up and down. Maybe the chair knocks back to the ground in my hysteria.

Through all daily conversations with parents, I definitely won't be the only one jumping up with his or her hand waving high in the air.

This is one of the many pastimes of a child, heck also with teenagers, and many adults for that matter. It just boils down to wanting something so badly that Cody believes if he does not constantly repeat himself and remind me and Will, his grandparents, aunts, uncles, etc. they are going to forget what he's saying.

By the way, he gets this trait from his dad. Will talks about plenty of items he wants till he's blue in the face. You can say I have repeating in both ears on most days.

Double whammy.

Obvious proof that Cody is simply a mini version of my husband.

Thank goodness he inherited excellent concentration from Will (he totally looks like me though, except his height is all Will). This allows projects to occupy Cody's attention for a while. A breath of fresh air for me.

Nonetheless, Cody thinks talking about interests no less than a thousand times causes failure to remember—repeat on nauseam.

To be honest with myself, maybe after one or two times, I might forget. With my schedule being so busy, hence the post it notes—I have many mommy-brain instances. But for the most part, I'll remember what he says, or asks me for his birthday or any other occasion.

Give me some credit here. But that may be asking too much, given the facts.

Plus, during a repeating session, whatever I need to say tends to go in one ear and out the other. Well, except for when my response includes vital information about whatever Cody's been laying into me about for the past month. He will be all ears now. Then he knows I've been reminded enough. Or so I think, until two hours later, when he'll remind me again.

Sometimes in the middle of my answer, he'll be right back to repeating. Meanwhile, I believe, interrupting isn't acceptable in school, so why does Cody think it's supposed to be free will at home? He'll just cut me off. Right in mid-sentence.

Each subject can last anywhere from a week to months, depending on how long he's interested in a specific show, movie, toy collection, etc. Then, just when he stops talking about the biggest news from over the last several weeks, I exhale a deep breath. I have a sense of relief. Only to start a brand-new subject a day later. Yes, I'm rewarded a *whole* day's break. Thank goodness for that break, though.

Although, Godzilla has stuck around for a while, at least nine whole months. Reminding me of a safe purchase for his birthday, Christmas following suit.

He talks about making Godzilla movies, or at least monster movies. Every waking moment, in fact. Definitely not the first obsession, but they've been around the longest to-date. I'm actually starting to imagine Godzilla and monsters will stick as part of Cody's career in the movie industry. This appears to be his dream—working in movies.

Go Cody, you can do it!

I bring up the challenge with repeating to my fellow moms during an emergency meeting I call for today. I'm almost pushed to my limit, and my ears feel as though they might fall off. Comfort from our mom's group is in need, and now.

Each woman speaks her piece, going around the circle of us, venting similar frustrations.

"OMG, Mia, I could cry most days, and sometimes do with Marcus repeating himself." Ella covers her face with her hands. "Mom this, Mom that. I want this from Star Wars. I want that from Lego. Over and over, he repeats. I'm glad for school, and the break it gives me."

"Try three kids stuck on repeating things all at the same time. I could go insane for sure," Audrey says while shaking her head. "Mind exhaustion."

"Oh, I bet, I couldn't imagine three children. I only have one, and my ears are on overdrive," Kristin jumps in, sympathizing with Audrey. "My Ceila and her Barbie's are out of control. In the store alone, she'll explain the Barbie Dolls she wants, about twenty times over. The looks I've gotten down the aisles were enough to make me run."

"And you don't need another running incident, Kristin." Ella waves her index finger side to side, trying to mock an overly-serious expression, but fails as she adds, "The cops being called on you for running out of your house was bad enough." A giggle escapes.

Kristin burst out laughing, along with everyone else.

"So true." Claudia chuckles.

Turns out we end up walking away this afternoon with being rejuvenated. We come up with no solution, but by talking it out, we all feel each other's support, and most importantly, not alone.

One confident foot in front of the other, heads holding up high, we strut over to our respective cars. Even Tamara has a look of satisfaction from today's emergency meeting. She makes a slow nod in my direction and winks at me just before getting in her car, one stiletto at a time. Having a sense of self-assurance in mom power, each of us moms are going home to face children of all ages, just waiting to repeat themselves.

Mothers and fathers know we're all in the same crazy and sometimes highly experimental boat. I often envision us all in a yacht instead of only a boat. This makes me feel like parenting is more high-tone and luxurious. Luxury is needed, even if it's only in a hallucination.

Through my awkward mom moments, like using a wet wipe to take off a booger from my arm; *nice*, my yacht trance will save me.

Detective Mia has a two-part theory. First, by harping on the same subject is a ploy to eventually drive adults nuts. We proceed to give into our kids with what they want, in turn saving our mental stability for a brief minute. Or, second, maybe we have already been sent over our breaking point by the repeating, and talked into buying merchandise without any knowledge of doing so. In that case, we have temporarily blacked out.

Another theory can be, going nuts may not just be a coincidence with a grown-up potentially blacking out from our repetitious kids. There might be an undiscovered game plan by the entire population of children. An idea thought up so creatively that only youth knows about how to get what they want from their parents. Tricking them in a way. Thus, we grown-ups have not caught on, or decoded it to this day.

Again, only theories in the making. My detective hat is on frequently and I'm hard at work solving one mystery at a time. I sit here at my computer, logging notes, thinking Area 51 cannot compare to what has not yet been found out from a child's cerebral mind.

Can someone please tell me why parenting hasn't been declared the eighth wonder of the world? Seriously.

Chapter 20
Excessive Talking

My weekends are full just from the countless nonstop hours of information I receive from my son. I'm grateful for school, and the mental break, as my best friend Ella had said at yesterday's emergency mom meeting.

Saturday pours right into Sunday with Cody talking continuously. Harping on subjects, repeating his points, repetitious words—mom overload.

How different small children are from teenagers.

Words need to be pulled out of a pre-teen and teenager's mouth to get them to talk. Extracting teeth is easier.

I see this with my friend's older children and know this from growing up. Myself, I find the lack of talking highly suspicious, because teenagers spend so much time on the phone with their cohorts. Clearly, they can converse. I know they're not on the phone in silence. Although, speaking from experience from my teen years, being on the phone in silence can happen. I used to fall asleep often during late night chats.

My thoughts; teenagers do not speak as freely as their younger years, because adults simply are not cool enough during this stage of them maturing.

Um, excuse me. I can get down with my bad self. I'm cool, I think to myself. Well, maybe this older statement could discredit my coolness completely. *Trying too hard, Mia.* Quick slap to my forehead.

I'll try to refrain from saying it when Cody enters teen years.

But this phase too shall pass. Also, older kids start having the need for more independence. I grew out of my quietness around my parents at about twenty.

I know one thing for sure, at Cody's age, I had no problem sharing my words in abundance. My father tells stories of how he would talk, talk, talk, as a child like me. As the old saying goes, the apple doesn't fall far from the tree. By genetics, Cody's bound to be a talker as well. And boy, can he talk.

I'm consumed by no less than two hours of nonstop chatter at a time. Plus, yes, the same subjects from the last chapter are thrown in the mix.

Sometimes, I think, *how can someone so small have so much to say?* I mean, adults have way more going on, and they aren't as gabby. Come to think of it, some adults are, but that's another story in itself.

Obviously, the world is all new to my son. Once verbalizing comes about, he can now express his thoughts about each fascinating event he sees. I've been around way longer, so a lot of what's out there becomes old hat in a way to me. The world's an exciting place, and when Cody discovers things, he has to tell about it all. And that he does.

For instance, pots make loud noises when hit. Sponges hold water until they're squeezed, and then the water magically pours out. When the middle of a steering wheel is pushed, the car honks, making a loud noise. And of course, another good example is the lights up high on silver polls. They turn green, yellow, and red to put on a light show for people.

In the beginning, he didn't realize these lights are actually meant for driving purposes. To Cody, a light show is being put on every few minutes.

There are a plethora of discoveries waiting to be told, taking at least one whole hour to describe each. Somehow, it truly does take that long, and that accounts for the excessive talking. Hundreds and thousands of these revelations absorb a lot of time every day.

My mom and dad have repeated a saying to me several times, "Once a child starts talking, you'll wish they held off a little longer."

I don't wish Cody held off longer, but I do wish I had breaks every now and then when Cody's home.

Part of our weekly ritual is taking a Sunday afternoon casual drive. This Sunday is no different than every week. The car is filled with observations and questions. Farting and pooping is at the top of the subject list. Somehow, all conversations revert back to the infamous number two.

Cody will laugh till he farts. Then he cracks up about that. In a couple cases, skid marks have been left in his underwear in the past. It must be more of a boy thing, because my experience with girls, topics don't usually venture into anything butt related.

I presume young children get through explaining and asking what they want by their teenage years. This may partly account for the quietness between teens and parents. I'm thinking. The other part may be puberty, and that opens up a whole other can of worms in itself.

Teenagers and the flashy, yet sometimes embarrassing, world of puberty expand into another level of questions. These are mostly discussed among friends. That right there explains a lot for the shortfall of communication at home.

We pull in our driveway, returning home. My mind certainly needs a few minutes break from the ongoing chatter. I go to sit on the toilet longer than needed in pure silence, beginning to think about my own motto for excessive talking: Enjoy it while it lasts, because the teenage stage arrives sooner than you think, where I'm wishing for more conversation.

I blow out a slow stream of air, knowing that now I need to tackle the excessive laundry before nightfall, because momma will need to relax tonight.

Chapter 21
Excessive Laundry

The weekends are known to me as my excessive days. No break from talking. No break from laundry.

As the sun sets, marking the end of Sunday, I've now finished six loads of laundry, and had my ear talked off for two days straight. I visited my escape room and toilet oasis no less than a combined ten times, aside from me actually having to go to the bathroom that is.

Complete mind exhaustion is an ongoing challenge I endeavor to solve. Impossible to make go away, but I've discovered tricks along the way to ease my routine.

Detective Mia on the hunt for easier motherhood. The promotion will read for an imaginary sitcom I dreamed up.

Spending time in the laundry room will be at the forefront of the episodes. Cody will be behind me, throwing all his clothing in my direction. Good thought, because that's basically what happens.

I haven't experienced laundry like after becoming a mother—one load after the other. Naturally, my near-daily multitasking, because there are mid-week loads too, includes a laundry chant; washing, drying, and folding.

I'm so used to my chant by now; it's second nature to me.

Newborns should be born with a caution label. CAUTION-Newborns cause a high magnitude of messes resulting in excessive laundry. Must keep detergent and cleansing agents in stock at all times, and many bins to make sorting clothes easier.

One thought comforts me, ever since the beginning, a trick up my sleeve: My grandmother, and all my ancestors before her, had to do laundry by hand. Scrubbing every piece in a wash basin. Then drying every single item by putting them through a wringer. Followed by hanging everything up on clotheslines with clothespins. To finish this major ordeal, afterwards, all has to be folded.

We have modern-day conveniences of washers and dryers. I simply can't imagine having to wash bedding by hand, along with clothes and tablecloths, etc. When did these women, being women were the sole homemaker's back in older days, have time to cook, shop, and clean house?

Let alone have enough energy to make more babies after finishing all that laundry, by hand. This astounds me. Especially during the potty training stage, and also if the child goes through a bedwetting period. The loads of bedding by itself are a project.

Anytime I'm feeling overwhelmed by laundry, I go back to thinking, *what if I had to do it all manually?* Then I feel better. I mention this little trick to all parents. It might just make their day.

The laundry decreases as Cody gets older. I semi-think the slow down occurs for all kids, but that is not the case. Fellow moms assure me the excessive cleaning still keeps on going with their kids in sports, or some having a constant need to change clothes.

Apparently wearing multiple outfits a day is big with girls.

"Savannah has to change her outfit no less than four times a day. Four times! My washer and dryer never stop," Zoe complained to us last week when we organized a picnic at the park.

We spread out on a large blanket; us moms discussed while our kids ran around and played.

"One outfit comes off and goes straight into the laundry basket as another one goes on. Then that outfit comes off soon after and goes into the wash, and so on," Zoe explained. She was exhausted just talking about it, since her washer had been only on its third load for that twenty-four hour period.

Poor Audrey too. She had spiked her thermos of fruit punch and lemonade. Fruity Vodka is what Audrey called it. That very morning, her three kids had gotten into the paint drawer, unleashing a colorful house. The clothes took a hit as well.

"I always lock the drawer. How did I forget? How?" Frustrated tears formed in her eyes.

The rest of us stared at her with empathy. We nodded and pouted. The washer and dryer would be on overdrive in her house that day. Audrey took another sip from her thermos, looking beside herself. At least she lived within walking distance from the park for after the Fruity Vodka was finished.

It does seem there is a whole other side to the parenting of girls that I am totally unaware of. Also the sports side I'm not familiar with either, being Cody doesn't show interest in sports. Still the consensus seems to be the abundance of dirty clothes is definitely more with infants and toddlers, boys or girls.

Between the spitting up from the infant stage, and the spitting out of food in the toddler stage, laundry never stops. The onesies, the burp cloths, the bibs, the blankets—all constantly changing throughout the day faster than you can say washroom. Oh, and I can't forget the crib sheet, swaddlers, and those bouncy play gyms, also are laundered frequently.

If someone had told me pre-parenthood that I will be cleaning bouncy play gyms as part of my laundry routine, I wouldn't have believed them. I'd think, *why do those need to be washed? I can see wiped down. But put in the washing machine?* Insert a puzzle look.

Hard to fathom this before becoming a mom.

I do have a bouncy play gym experience that happened to me many times.

I put Cody in his adorable baby-blue ocean-theme bouncy gym. The seat had a comfy material that hugged his butt when he sat. He would get a kick out of the spinning toys fastened to the secure ledge around him. He squeezed the lion, making a squeaky sound. He moved the large plastic beads along the wavy wire. He loved it, and I loved watching him playing.

I thought one really nice thing about these gyms was that while Cody played, he also stayed immobile at the same time. Which came in handy for catching up on cooking, cleaning, or simply taking a much-needed break, especially from constantly running after him.

When he became mobile and always on the move, chasing after Cody was a full-time job. The bouncy gym proved absolutely perfect for my mommy break, while playtime continued for him.

I had an unforeseen challenge. While he bounced up and down plenty of times, he would poop. Yes, poop, and a lot of it. It was almost as if the springing action pushed his number two out, and upwards. Cody's back, all the way up to his neck, was smeared in brown.

The intense smell alerted me every time. Carefully, I took him out of the gym, seeing pudding-like consistency squished all over the seat, too. I had to bathe him, take the gym apart, clean up any excess brown clumps, and then stick it in the washer.

For the grand finale, I would disinfect every single toy fastened to the gym's ledge. You know, just in case little fingers had wandered elsewhere and then back to the toys.

By this time, I had given up on dinner, or whatever else I was doing, and decided that my comforting old school laundry thought wasn't helping me either. My ancestors didn't have these types of fancy gyms to contend with back then. Basically, the easier-not-having-to-do-laundry-by-hand trick didn't do it for me during these all out cleaning sessions.

I knew I had to come up with a solution for future messes.

The time I would make for this playtime would now be made around when he usually went number two. Finally, I figured out about when pooping was most likely to occur. I made sure I didn't put Cody anywhere near this structure, or swings for that matter.

Once I finished my poop detective work, large clean up moments became less. I still had sporadic cleansing, because we know how toddlers have surprise droppings, and messy ones too.

Laundry became a lot less.

Pee also could be an issue with it seeping out of the diaper, soiling the gym's seat. Pee came more often, so there was no way to really gauge that. I did the best I could think of.

I share this bit of knowledge with others in hopes my small remedy will help. Another aspect to exuberant laundry is the potty training stage. This is a whole different ball game. The good and rewarding side to potty training is the heartwarming feeling when Cody shows to be so happy when he succeeds in going to the bathroom all by himself.

Needless to say, I go through an emotional stage watching this all unfold—my baby is growing up. Yet, another part of the mother emotional roller coaster.

When my little well-oiled machine starts controlling his call of nature, all things stay cleaner *slightly* unsoiled that is.

However, leading up to this stage is the challenge of many bathroom accidents. At this point, the laundry is still at an all-time high. A crazy time for me. But starting with Pull Up diapers, training becomes easier. Cleaning becomes a bit less, and laundry, more undemanding.

Although my patience span, not so much easier. Being in the Pull-Up diaper stage, I can see the money pit with diaper buying end in sight, and it can't come soon enough.

Then my need for the washroom escalates when taking away the Pull-Ups. Watch out for those random moments when kids can't make it to the bathroom. When accidents happen, clothing takes a hit along with your carpet, flooring, bedding, car seat, or wherever you might be. There goes the washer again, and out come the paper towels and cleansers.

I should have bought stock in paper towels and cleaning products in hindsight. Not just because of one potty training stage, but two, with Caesar. A good month goes by before my four-legged boy catches on with going to the door every time nature calls.

Throughout potty training him, at least he never went poop in the house, a huge relief, since there's no safety net of a diaper with dogs. Even diapers aren't foolproof, as seen with Cody. Pee will seep out of the seams around his thighs. This baffles me, because every time when changing him, I swore I pulled those darn seams out to prevent seepage.

Back when Cody was three, one night he went to the bathroom in his underwear and it was not an accident. That night had been in the beginning of taking away the Pull-Ups.

Cody said, "Look!"

I happened to be sitting on the floor right next to him. He stood.

"What, honey?" I smiled.

Cody stood there, giggling. A slow stream of pee flowed down his leg, creating a puddle on the floor.

"Cody, no!" I panicked, carrying him right to the bathroom.

When asking him what happened, he said, "Pee's out, no diaper."

I told him to not do that again. I couldn't be too mad, because I knew it's only natural for kids to experiment. But scrubbing pee from carpets wasn't my idea of ongoing fun, if he decided to continue his science testing.

"We don't let the pee out anywhere other than the toilet, sweetheart," I *explained.*

If I stop and think about it, parenting really isn't all that glamorous. Between the pee, poop, scrubbing, and laundry, being a parent really is a messy job. But hey, someone's got to do it. Someone has to raise our future generations.

I show up every day, physically ready to work, but my mental stability is oftentimes on standby, questionable, and waiting to see what the day has in store for me.

More often than not, I'm on my imaginary yacht. Comforted by the company of a bunch of mothers and fathers sailing along the Mediterranean coast. We're holding glasses of Dom Perignon, lounging on deck as we watch the sunset.

I bask in a feeling of glamour. For a quick hallucination moment, other parents and I are living in a lap of luxury. Our own Lifestyles of the Rich and Famous—Parenthood Edition. Robin Leach sometimes narrates in my trance.

Chapter 22
Mom Social Media Envious

"What is it about these darn cones? Isn't it bad enough they're all over Vegas? Now I have to deal with them at school," Ella says in frustration after dropping off Marcus. She takes another sip of her Caramel Macchiato.

Starbucks has become a once a week ritual for Ella and I to meet in the morning after bringing the kids to school. Designating this as our best friend time.

Today is especially needed with the newfound craziness of dropping the kids off. Someone apparently thinks it's a good idea to set up a labyrinth of orange cones at the school to make mornings easier. Not spacing them correctly at that. Well, it isn't easier.

Parents driving on the wrong side of the parking lot, including me, with looks of confusion. Weaving in and out of cones like in Driver's Ed class, not knowing where to go. Horns blasting off at people going the wrong way. Mothers and fathers trying to walk across the parking lot with their children, dodging cars, to get onto campus.

Recent morning times have been a regular sideshow as it is.

"I know, right! A mess. Like all I see when driving is orange. Beyond irritating, with crisscrossing around cone mazes set up for construction sites here. If they were set up to build more middle and high schools, I'd be more understanding, but no, just for more homes."

"Yeah, and nowhere to put all the kids moving into Las Vegas." Ella pounds her fist down on the table.

"Have you heard back from the principal yet about the school chaos?" I ask, sipping my Venti coffee.

"No, have you?" Ella slants her head to the side, making her shiny black hair sway like silk. She purses her full lips.

"Not yet, but she needs to know the new cone system is not working." I shrug and grin, admiring how my best friend makes swagger and beauty work so well hand in hand.

I seem to always have disheveled plastered all over myself. *Make more of an effort, Mia,* I mentally scold. *Moms need to take care of themselves, too.*

"She should be out there watching how the new system works. I find it odd she isn't. Don't you?" Ella asks me, raising an eyebrow.

"It is strange." I pause. "I'm a bit skeptical as to why Principal Shea isn't out observing, especially a new system that's put in place."

"I kind of don't feel like offering to volunteer today," she mumbles into her coffee cup.

"Yeah, me neither."

"You mean not even for Mr. Sherman?" Ella raises both her eyebrows this time.

I know she thinks the fifth grade teacher likes me, because he requests my help every week, but I think he just knows he can count on me, that's all. "No, not for Mr. Sherman, either." I sigh and give her a sideways glance as if to say *really?*

She shrugs and closes her eyes, then smirks.

"Well, I feel with all the Teacher Savior responsibilities we take on, *we* should at least get an answer back from Principal Shea." She glares out the window, huffing.

"Ella, we said we wouldn't let the Teacher Savior title go to our heads. Remember?" I try to keep a straight face, but am unsuccessful, and can't suppress my giggles.

She starts to laugh with me.

"Well, maybe you won't let it go to your head, but I do. Hey, we do a lot for the school, and I don't see many other parents jumping at the chance to help." She raises her eyebrow again as if challenging me to say she's wrong.

I won't dare. I don't want to start an argument with Ella, and besides, she's absolutely right.

"I do have to confess, the title might have gone a *teensy weensy* bit to my head one day," I decide to admit while squinting and making a small size gesture with my index finger and thumb.

"Do tell." She sits straight up now, ready for the story, like a schoolgirl anticipating juicy gossip.

"Last week, I commented on a Facebook post from an acquaintance I know through Kristin. You know Kristin in our mom's group."

Ella does a slow nod.

"Her mom friend, Ruby, has become a mutual friend of ours, just through Facebook. Ruby was commenting on her own glamorous party picture from when she went out on a girl's night, dancing. She then started going back and forth with another mom. I didn't know the other lady. Ruby was arguing about how all us moms should be going out and glamming up, and—"

"Oh no, she didn't," Ella interrupts me. "See that's why I don't like social media, Mia." She throws her hands above her head. "It's unrealistic."

"I couldn't agree more. Normally, I don't argue with anyone online, especially not knowing the person personally, but I felt I had to. Ruby was making this other mom, Trisha was her name, feel bad because she has no time to go out and party."

"Like what parent really does?" Ella says with annoyance kicking in. She lets out a guffaw. "So, what made you bring out the Teacher Savior thing?"

"When Ruby started trying to belittle me for sticking up for Trisha, I wrote that I am the Teacher Savior at my school, proving that *she* can't bring me down a couple pegs."

Ella bursts out laughing. "You finally used the title, and let it go to your head a little bit." She continues to laugh. "Well, in this instance anyway. What's funny is that this Ruby doesn't even know what a Teacher Savior is, since it's a made up title."

I make a funny face and shrug my shoulders, because I know she's right.

"I love that you stood up for Trisha, though, but you see how people argue online and they don't even know who they're arguing with. It's all fake. There's a reason online bullying and trolling is so big these days. They find it easy to go after someone without having to face them in person."

She shakes her head side to side, angry. Her shiny black Egyptian Goddess hair and tan skin glisten against the sunlight pouring in through the window at our table. Somehow, even Mad Ella seems to keep her elegant composure.

I don't know how she does it. When I'm mad, I get all beet-red and huffy. My blood pressure rises, making me feel like lava is flowing throughout my veins. I strive to be more like Ella, and keep myself composed, for the most part, which will do me a world of good.

"I know, it's terrible," I reply, shaking my head too.

"Well, don't go making this a habit with getting someone all riled up, because you're sticking up for a random person, you don't even know, online.

I don't want to have to find someone and give them the beat down for messing with you."

She reaches across the table and pats my hand, then chuckles. "Besides, you don't even know if that individual you're defending is real. Fake accounts are made all the time, just to create drama situations."

I sharply nod. "You're right, because in the school group I started for anti-cyber bullying, that exact thing happened to Mrs. Write. She shared her experience with a group of fifth graders. Some hacker actually made a fake account using her info, but with a slight change."

Ella closes her eyes and sighs. "See, things like that happen all the time. I've broken away from social media a lot lately. Besides, it was getting to a point of distracting me from Marcus."

"Yeah, me too. After that Ruby incident, I realized more of a break was needed, and that type of aggravation takes my mind away from Cody too."

We nod at each other and chat for a bit more while finishing our blueberry muffins. We then leave to go home and get some chores done before picking up the kids. Normally, Ella and I will see if one of the teachers needs help, or if the school's administration team can use an extra set of hands for an event coming up, but today we decide not to.

They all appreciate our time, but the fact we aren't hearing back from the principal about our concern with the new dropping off procedure is a little annoying. After entering the house, I take Caesar in the backyard to play ball. This quality time allows me to think with the peace and quiet of the still air and beautiful day.

I get envious scrolling through pictures and posts on, not only Facebook, but also Instagram and Twitter.

My life involves running around after Cody and Caesar, picking up messes of everything from spilled food to poop. Constant dog training and playing teacher with Cody's homework takes up a large chunk of what's supposed to be free time for me.

I'm going nonstop all day. I then end up feeling bad after scrolling through social media pages, because I don't have the time to do extra primping and enjoy late party nights like I used to when I was younger. This only makes me feel frumpy and not my best self.

Seeing others out, dressing up and partying brings me down at times, knowing the fact that a lot of them are parents doesn't help, and I think, *what am I doing wrong?* I mean, I don't even get to have a sick day, or take a vacation day to rest for myself.

At times, I think if those parents can do it, so can I. Time just never presents itself to allow for it in my situation.

Ella repeatedly makes it a point to say that women will put on a nice dress and makeup for the sole purpose of taking a picture for their social media accounts. Making it look like they are going out and living it up, when those women are really staying home with daily chores just like her and me.

Of course, many people go out and have great times, but that might be all those individuals post, so their life always seems fun.

No one's life is perfect, no matter what they post, I remind myself, which I tend to forget sometimes. And that is mostly why I've cut back on keeping up with social media.

As I throw the ball for Caesar once again, I gaze up into the sky, vowing to not let anyone else dictate how I feel about my life. Everyone is different, and I have a pretty darn good life, hectic as it is. Caesar runs, grabs the ball, and brings it back, and I throw it again. We keep repeating this. He'll tire, eventually.

Ah, pre-social media: the simple life.

As Caesar and I slowdown in playing, I confirm my vow of not envying others through their actions. I love all the new improvements in staying connected nowadays, but I do often miss the simplicity of life, pre-computers, tablets, IPhones, etc.

Even toys nowadays seem like they have a booklet of instructions with how to put together and use; making assembly more complicated. I can hold my own with a lot of technology and figuring how to work things, but my six-year-old teaches me so much.

Never did I think I will be going to my child to ask how to use something. I'm the mom, aren't I the one supposed to be teaching here? As the years pass, everything I continue to learn from Cody are breaths of fresh air. However, observing other parents, mainly when taking Cody to our community pool and out to dinner, worries me a bit.

Pool outings are, for the most part, family events, as with going out to dinner. There are opportunities to learn from your kids and spend quality family time. Have fun with them. I see a lot of parents sitting glued to their phone, scrolling, while their children are in the pool.

And what's worse, the countless times I witness how parents, and children alike, will each be on their own phone at a restaurant table. No talking, laughing, or communicating. The only communication going on is with the screen in front of them.

At the pool I'll hear, "Mommy, look! Look at this. Mommy, look now!" One child shouts before doing summersaults in the water.

"Very good," the mother replies without once looking up from her phone. She, among sporadic mothers and fathers, actually don't put their phones down till it's time to leave.

This is seen a lot at the pool, and I'm left wondering how far gone is humanity. Social media is mostly the culprit and has taken over the world, and I'm not quite sure it's in a good way. Sure, it helps us to stay connected with people near and far, but social media has also created disconnect within real-life moments, memories. As people scroll through news feeds and profiles, they're missing out on what's going on right in front of them.

Making every attempt to be up front and present in mothering is a place of high importance for me, thus confirming taking a step back from my accounts. Aside from my mommy breaks via the escape room and toilet closet, and phone time right before I go to sleep in bed, I make it a priority to pay attention to family and friends in person, in 'real-life'.

After school, I have Cody doing his homework in his room, and give him a snack to munch on. Will's working on a big website project in the office upstairs. And Caesar is napping in his crate, worn out from this afternoon of playing ball.

The busyness will be kept down for a small mom's group get-together at my house. Another emergency meeting I feel is necessary, following my life-reflecting moment in the backyard today. We moms need to all be reminded of the dangers of scrolling through post after post on social media. It can get us down, and also disconnect us from reality.

I know that Tamara specifically falls prey to being envious, especially with the Kardashian family. She really does keep up with the Kardashians. I feel that is where she gets most of her confident personality and poise from, and that's great, because those are wonderful attributes in life.

But she stresses when dressing up doesn't happen just right, or a look she's going for doesn't turn out perfect, and all mostly due to her motherhood challenges. Lucky for me, most of the group can make it to the meeting, including Tamara.

"You cannot base your life off Kim, Tamara." I wave my hand in the air, not getting through to her. She keeps arguing that just by following Kim Kardashian (mostly, she follows her over any of the other Kardashians), you're not given a false impression, only tips to go by, and ways to work on.

"This may be some of the case, but it's not healthy to stick so close to another's actions, especially someone you don't even know personally, and worry you aren't like them. The percentage of Kim's out there is minuet," I say to try and get her to see where I'm coming from. This is envy to the extreme.

"I don't base my life after her, *Mia*." Tamara does that singsong voice again when she says my name, and continues, "I admire Kim's ways, that's all. She's confident, beautiful, and has everything."

Ella chimes in, the only other mom who does. Tamara probably intimidates most of the other moms. "That's just it, Tamara, the Kardashians have everything. Full-time nannies, chefs, housekeepers, personal assistants, drivers, and anything else you can think of. Of course, they look beautiful—"

"I know. They have the money to pay for all that, and—" Tamara starts to talk over Ella, but doesn't get very far.

"Let me finish," Ella cut her off. "Tamara, you get discouraged because an outfit gets messed, or you don't have enough time for a full face of makeup. With all the help Kim, for example, gets, she has time to glam up, or time for someone else to glam her up."

She holds out her hands, palms facing outward, to calm down the situation. "I'm only saying, we're only saying," Ella looks over at me, "we care about you, and want you to be happy. Not sad because another parent you don't even know always looks put together, and doesn't deal with all that you do."

"Even Kim, and all the Kardashians, have problems, too. Maybe it doesn't seem like it, but they do. Everyone does, only in different ways," I realistically say.

Tamara quickly transforms from anger to tears welling up in her eyes, showing a look of appreciation for us. Her tears aren't happy ones. "Motherhood is so hard sometimes." Tamara tries holding back her sobs.

Clearly, she has bottled up her feelings over time. "I love Giselle more than anything in this world, but I feel like I've lost myself somewhere along the way."

I get up to go sit next to her. "We all feel that way, Tamara." I place my arm around her shoulders to console her. The rest of the moms nod in agreement.

For the first time ever, Tamara is showing a vulnerable side. She's the consistent spunky, confident, opinionated, well-put-together one. At least the best put-together from the rest of the group, that is. Shiny darker-black skin, her hair is silky and shiny to match her complexion, all small curls. Anyone can tell she takes good care of herself. But at what cost, is what I'm now realizing.

"Derek doesn't really help me that much either," she confides in us, another first for her.

"Neither does Will." I bow my head, looking down at the ground. "I see the back of Will's head more than anything as he runs off avoiding messes, or tantrums."

"At least you have a nice view." Audrey smirked to herself. She immediately put her hand in front of her mouth. Obviously not meaning to say that out loud.

I peer at Audrey through the side of my eyes. Feeling annoyance rising up, since this isn't the first time she's made a snippet of a comment about Will and his good looks. Sometimes, I think that Audrey is overly confident with her beautiful classic Asian features, and sophisticated personality. She tries to attract Will when we're all together. It's more than obvious to me.

Ella shoots her an irritated glance, knowing what I know. She then turns back to Tamara, adding, "Motherhood isn't easy. If it were easy, fathers would do it."

Her comment breaks my Audrey gaze, making me giggle, and causes Tamara to laugh. We all end up belly laughing, especially me. I know, we all do, Ella gets that line from the show *Golden Girls*. Dorothy says that during one late-night talking session when her, Blanche, Rose, and Sophia are sitting at the kitchen table discussing motherhood. Of course, while eating cheesecake.

"That's why I called this emergency meeting." I look to each mom sitting around me. "Being a mom is difficult. Why do you think we talk to ourselves, and have our roller coaster of emotions? Today, I thought about how social media is thrown into the mix, now more than ever, and it bothered me."

"Looking at people's lives and what they choose to show. Mostly filtering out the bad and the ugly, showing only the good on their accounts. We envy what we don't have. I think by distancing a little from social media would do a world of good for us."

"Yes, I think so, too!" Kristin agrees right away.

"Here. Here." Joanne flings her hand outward, nodding that she feels the same.

"You know I'm all for it." Ella then exclaims matter of fact. "That's why we have our mom's group. Real-life connections. Seeing the similar struggles in person, up front and center. Not basing our mothering off things only seen on social media!"

"Right!" Tamara jumps right in and cheers. "Mia, tell me more about your escape room. I have an extra room in my house, and I'm thinking of transforming it. That might be just what I need."

"Yes, ma'am!" I am elated to share what works for me with any mom, especially Tamara. She's been a tough nut to crack, and now I finally feel she is one hundred percent open to the group.

Our gathering came to an end. The ladies start to walk out, chatting to each other as they leave. And now it's time for me to make sure Cody and Caesar are prepared for nighttime.

Seems they're turning into werewolves or something the way I need to get ready for nightfall. I chuckle.

They both really do act like a werewolf when it's dark out, come to think of it, not far off from the horror movie scenario. My eyes widen. I really do live in a scary movie. Shivers run down my spine as I head upstairs to Cody's room.

After everyone goes to bed, I scoot down to my escape room, tip toeing, and lock the door behind me. Intent on listening for any odd sounds of transformation from normal to beast.

Nothing.

"Mia, you seriously need to lay off the horror movies. Stop scaring yourself," I say to my reflection in the mirror hanging above one of the couches. I breathe out a stream of air.

I gasp and jump when I hear a loud boom coming from down the hall. Hearing Caesar scooting his bone around in his crate makes me know the noise had just been him playing with his extra-large Nylabone. He drops it again with a huge thud.

Will took him on a long walk while I had the mom's meeting. He should be tired. I huff in exasperation hearing an even louder thud, but relief overcomes me that the noise is coming from him, and not a werewolf.

Grabbing a cold eye mask from my mini fridge, I plop down on one of the couches. I close my eyes, adjust the mask, and soothe my sinister-imagination nerves.

I think, *hang in there, Mia, morning will come soon enough.*

Chapter 23
Dog Mom

Every day life's full, no matter what, since becoming a mother to Cody, and then with Caesar, my life quickly set into overload.

My Dalmatian continuously matures, and he's a wonderful dog at three years old. But days are jam-packed with chores to do, and a lot is for Caesar, but not as much now as with his puppy stage.

I remember potty training as only the tip of the iceberg. A very important tip to overcome, but just the start of raising him.

Will and Cody pleaded their case the night the idea of getting a dog was presented to me. Of course, they won. Rarely when there's two against one, the one wins.

"Okay." An exasperated sigh escaped. I shrugged. "What kind of dog are you thinking?"

"A Dalmatian puppy!" Will said enthusiastically.

"Where did you get an idea for Dalmatians?" Puzzled at first, but then quickly realized it was from the movie, 101 Dalmatians.

"The movie. So cute!" Cody jumped right in.

In that moment, I remembered seeing on the news that a lot of Dalmatian puppies had turned up in animal shelters after the non-animated 101 Dalmatians movie came out. Supposedly, many people bought the puppy because they were so adorable in the movie, then discovered how much work was involved with a Dalmatian, let alone a newborn one. Apparently, even repeat dog owners couldn't handle the vivacious breed.

I then started to research Dalmatians a bit after the news segment. I loved learning about dogs, since I've always been a dog lover. There's no secret about puppies being an abundance of work, but I read Dalmatians were a very stubborn breed, needing a lot of obedience training. And having extremely high energy to boot.

Will and Cody kept it up, and kept it up, till I finally gave in. This reminded me of all the years of repeating things over and over, and I'm mainly referring to my husband.

You can do this, Mia. You're no stranger to dogs, and you can figure Dalmatians out, *I convinced myself.*

Within a couple of months, Caesar came home. And the fun began for me.

Potty training, teething, obedience, discipline, feeding, grooming, all fell on my time. Sure, the first couple of weeks everyone pitched in, but then gradually, Will was 'too busy', and Cody sprinted off being a kid. Playing with Caesar eventually became my duty as well.

A new imaginary hat had to be made for all these extra duties. I named it Animal Extraordinaire. The title made me feel very expertise.

One thing the Animal Extraordinaire hat couldn't exactly master had been the teething stage with mouthing our hands. I watched videos, I talked to Caesar's breeder, I read articles on the subject, and tried all suggestions. Alas, nothing worked.

Great, I have a robotic dog. Programmed to be immune to anything preventing his flying mouth. *I sat and marveled in a daze while removing my hands from sharp baby teeth.*

"Ouch! Caesar, no bite!" I said in a stern tone.

I found the teething stage the hardest. I couldn't help but get frustrated with the puppy stage in general, for that matter. And, it's not like this was my first rodeo with a puppy, or my second, or third. I've had numerous puppies since a kid.

Thank goodness, one piece of advice worked from all the hours I spent reading up on the wonders of these young years. You must take time out for yourself. Everyone gets frustrated at some point with puppies, and you need to walk away, and take deep breaths—essential.

I headed to my escape room more often than not. Plopped down on the couch. Talked to myself. This was pretty much the order of things when I took a break from puppyhood. After locking the door, occasionally I would throw my imaginary Animal Extraordinaire hat down on the floor, and shout in its direction, "You're NOT working!" My voice did this singsong thing.

I talk to my imaginary hats often. Ella worries about this, but I assure her there's nothing to worry about. It's not like the hats answer me back, or anything. Well, not all the time anyway.

"Of course, Will is returning emails right when Caesar peed on the floor, runs amuck after stepping in the pee, then nips my toes as he rushes past, skidding under my grabbing hands." I cringed, imagining the sideshow all over again. I barely caught a glimpse of Will's back as he hastily rounded the corner and up the stairs. Away from the fiasco.

After my dog-mom moment, and having mopped the floors, I looked at Caesar in his crate. He wagged his tail. All anger disappeared, for the time being, as I watched my happy, loving puppy.

In hindsight, I really should have started a dog mom's group. We needed support just as with children. Although several of the moms in my group had dogs, so it was only natural we brought up pet issues too.

When the teen puppy stage started, Caesar loved to talk back and do things he knew not to. This needed to be corrected, and fast. This issue would make or break my goal in finding a better dog motherhood routine with him.

One day, Caesar turned right around in front of me and grabbed one of my shoes in his mouth, after I had just disciplined him for already being naughty. He didn't take well to being told not to do something. Sounds much like human teenagers, if you asked me. This stage had not been fun.

Caesar's mood swings kicked in then with testosterone fuel. And talking back would ensue to try and show that he's the boss. I stood my ground, and prevailed.

That's right, you're the boss, Mia. And don't you forget it, *I asserted myself.*

Of course, Caesar didn't let this go right away, he tried his antics other times, but I never gave in. Eventually, he stopped trying to be set on getting his way.

Overall, Caesar is the most loving dog, and very happy. The key to being a dog mom is sticking with the different stages, because they do get better.

Meanwhile, my fake potted plant in the living room takes another hit. Dried moss strewn all over. Caesar's nowhere to be found, except for a trail of plant filler leading me right to him sitting in the hallway.

He licks his paws, innocent enough. Wags his tail happily when he sees me coming, like he can never do wrong. But a small piece of moss hangs from the side of his mouth, giving him away as the culprit. I place my hands on my hips, and tap one foot. My mouth lifts to one side.

Detective Mia always gets her man, in this case, her dog.

I glance up from Caesar only to see Will's back once again skating around the corner and out of sight. Away from any possibility of seeing the mess.

Thank you, Francesca, for not making Will clean up after himself when growing up, I think, disgruntled at my mother-in-law.

Maybe a few dog dad lessons are needed for him. I huff, exhaling a huge sigh.

Chapter 24
Re-Gifting Personal Belongings

The holiday months roll in fast, and my days fill up with preparing for them. Big dinners, school breaks, winter activities, and the legendary challenge of what gift to buy for whom. Presents are never the focal point for the holidays in my family, but they are a tradition.

I love receiving a surprise. Something special given to me to let me know I'm being thought of, either at a holiday, or just because. The 'just because' gifts are the best, because those are given when least expected. In my opinion, I'll take the unexpected notion over anything else, any day.

My fellow moms and I have more than usual insanity problems during the holidays. But nothing makes us laugh harder in our group gatherings than the bombshells we receive from our children, where re-gifting comes into play.

I alone have my fair share of moments where my belongings go missing. And no, I'm not referring to someone stealing. I'm talking about not being able to find personal items, and then they slowly turn up at some point in packages from Cody. He re-gifts my stuff back to me.

Honestly, my biggest help in motherhood is talking to another mom, occasionally a dad. I know quite a few stay-at-home dads who go through the hectic every day twenty-four-seven challenges too. How our stories are so similar.

Comfort comes in all forms, and parent support doesn't fall short in comforting when talking to each other. Sharing experiences. The struggle is real, and we need a nice familiarity.

Talk to a fellow mom. Join us and you can't go wrong. I came up with this slogan for next year's recruiting session to recruit new moms into our group. I will even bring this gifting phenomenon up to a stranger, a mother, mostly.

"Now, let me ask you, have you ever seen your things go missing over the years? Where you have looked everywhere, and just couldn't find them? No matter how many places you've searched," I asked her.

Like I often say, I teeter on the sanity line at times. I can come across a bit weird, but do mean well though. Wanting to have conversations of interesting mom adventures. I just should rethink how I start a conversation with a stranger. My friends already know about my weirdness, someone new might just call the cops on me one day.

Christmas morning arrives and I jump out of bed to start the coffee. Will and I need that first cup to jolt our day into action. As the sun rises, I stare at our Christmas tree, listening to the coffee brewing. Smelling the aroma of fresh coffee perks me right up. The tree is lovely and festive decorated with glistening ornaments, garland, and a sparkling topper. An extra-large red and white tree skirt adorns the base.

Through the last couple of weeks, packages pop up under the tree every so often in brightly colored Christmas paper. Making the tradition even more colorful and uplifting. A glowing sight.

notes had also vanished. Then I started to panic of what I would do without all of my notepads.

I had to run to the store to buy new ones. Hair disheveled and all. As I walked at a brisk pace through the store's sliding glass doors, Walgreens this time, not Walmart (still had been recovering from the multiple fiascoes from a few months back), I noticed I hadn't even changed my slippers for shoes before I left the house in a rush.

"Ah!" I heard myself say out loud. I jolted to a stop. My eyes flitted down to make sure I was at least dressed. "Thank goodness." I breathed out a sigh of relief when I saw the pants of my pajamas on. I smoothed out my pajama top that read: Be Kind or Be Quiet.

And where oh where has my favorite charm bracelet disappeared? *I searched all my jewelry drawers. No use.*

"Has my home all of a sudden become a house of magic?" I asked myself.
Belongings seemed to have disappeared faster than I could say magic. Leaving me to vaguely wonder if I've finally gone mad. Face it, a mom's life could make a woman feel that way, a lot. Going mad was a definite possibility.
However, I held onto my sanity cap a little while longer, because the result explained all the mysterious vanishing.

Family arrives early. Cody is raring to go and dives right into present unveiling. We don't waste any time. Names are written on cute Santa Claus, snowman, and reindeer tags—to and from. We all sit around the Christmas tree, undoing ribbon and wrapping paper.

I decide to first open up a gift from Cody. A small square box. I take off the lid, slow. Lo and behold in the box sits… "My charm bracelet!" I shout.

My attention moves to Cody's grandparents, aunts and uncles, and my husband, all opening something from my smiling boy. Each package is shaped very differently from the other.

Plastic bowls, paperclips, notepads, my favorite spatula and salad utensils are now being unearthed. All from Cody. He spread out gifts to look as though he's giving more by splitting the notepads in half, and dividing up the paper clips between each person.

That is where everything went! An *ah-ha* thought floods my mind.

Looking over at him, he has such an excited and pleased expression, watching his family discover what they're receiving. This in itself causes me not to say anything but, "Thank you, sweetheart. I love it."

Now, I know I'm not insane, and the house is not turning into a magic zone. My belongings are re-gifted.

Through shared experiences, young children only want to join in with giving gifts, too. But with no job, or car to drive (no, the kid motorized Cadillac Escalade or the Power Wheels Jeep doesn't count), they have no way to buy surprise presents.

Clearly, kids go into drawers around the house and grab items to wrap. Maybe they're not items they buy, but they most definitely *are* a surprise.

Re-gifting is a subject I hear about, and also from before I became a mother, parents would talk about this. Stories I found endearing pre-motherhood. Not entirely sure I believed it at the time, but I always thought the idea to be sweet.

Turns out children do re-gift, and it is very real, not mythical as I'd once thought. Now, it's happening to me, being my favorite moment to-date. I realize Cody is now at a growing up point where he wants to participate in the gift of giving, to make others happy.

Being kids will do humorous acts repeatedly to get laughter, giving presents fits right in with wanting to spread the cheer. The giddiness and smiles that come along with unwrapping a gift is just a different form of seeing happiness.

After Christmas dinner, while Cody's preoccupied with his new toys, I walk around, collecting my various items. This is no small task, let me tell you. The plastic bowls alone, I have to go to four different people to get my complete set back. We all chuckle and smile, knowing the kindness and thoughtfulness behind his gifts.

Kids really do the darndest things.

Even Will's mother, Francesca, is laughing, and that is not a sight we see often from her. I like to refer to Francesca as my Marie, from *Everybody Loves Raymond.* She even resembles her. Short Italian stature, makeup always done, and she has short blonde hair, styled in a poof formation.

At least this Christmas, my mother-in-law is not being so critical of me.

"Mia, dear, the dishes are piling up in the kitchen. Is that how you intended it?" Francesca peeks around the kitchen corner, smiling in an over-exaggerated sweet way.

Oops, spoke too soon, Mia. She's at it again. I retract my thoughts from earlier.

"No, Francesca, that's not how I intended it, but I'll get to the dishes in a minute after organizing Cody's gifts here." I continue stacking his presents of toys and games.

"Oh, okay, dear. I think I better start cleaning. It looks like you aren't nearly done straitening up, by the looks of things." She smiles in the same way again, overly sweet.

Francesca always makes her point clear without coming right out and saying it. Even her compliments have a hidden meaning of ways to improve behind them. My very own Marie Barone.

"I'm actually almost done, thank you." I smile back, mirroring her.

She shrugs. "Whatever, dear. You're trying to organize, and that's what counts. I'll start washing anyway." Francesca spins around to retreat back in the kitchen, but stops to look over her shoulder. She flicks her hand in the air, and says, "Don't worry, I'll do a once-over in here after the kitchen."

I start picking up a couple more things, mumbling in frustration, "Why does she always do this, so passive aggressive. You want a perfect house, well lady, there isn't one."

At least she doesn't live across the street like Marie does in the show. Ending on that positive note helps me to continue straightening up. My way. I giggle periodically with Cody, as he tries out a new game.

Will catches my attention with an apologetic smile hearing his mom talk. He finally realizes she does make critical comments in a roundabout way. I grin back in a Marie, I mean Francesca, manner—wide and sweet.

Chapter 25
The Package is What Counts

I love watching Cody open his gifts, and not just on Christmas.

The excitement. The smile. His race of tearing the colorful paper off to get to the treasure underneath; the box. Yes, it's all about the box. Up until fairly recently, the only thing that interests Cody are what encases the present itself. This year, he actually wants the contents in the packaging to play with. Plus the box.

Till this Christmas, seeing a box underneath wrapping paper was the only thing that thrilled him. The apple of Cody's eye—the promise of countless hours of play with the box. Forget about the actual toy.

Shocker for Will and I to witness.

I guess all the years buying infant and toddler presents were really just for me. Those stages are my personal favorites in shopping. Merchandise for these young age-ranges are cute and cuddly. Honestly bringing out the kid in me.

The bouncy jumpers and playmat scenes have bright fun colors. The playhouses and mini kitchens do, too, along with number and letter puzzles. Bath toys and bath books bring out great imagination in the sudsy water. The teddy bears and Disney movie character stuffed animals are my favorite.

Will says to me as soon as I walk in the door on most shopping days, "Cody does not need any more stuffed animals. Don't keep buying them."

"He needs them." I will retort, standing my ground. My expression as strict as it can get.

"No. You want them," he'll tell me back, and point an index finger in my direction.

He's right. Cody hardly plays with stuffed animals, never has, but I play with them. And love it. So really, I only use Cody as a cover to buy cute, squishy, and fluffy toys.

Sometimes, I'll go in his closet, where the piled goods are, and take a few animals to my escape room. Then I'll have a kid moment, making my area playful, instead of the many de-stressing sessions that go on in there. Over on the mini kitchen counter, I keep dark chocolate bars in stock.

I then have one with playtime, making for a real childhood-type scenario. I find this key in creating mommy happiness to continue on with my daily motherhood routine. Have fun like a kid! Adults, mainly moms, forget to lightheartedly play like their young ones do. Chores catch up to us, consuming our days, dragging moms down.

Cody's bath time also creates fun with bath books. How great is it to read in the water without worrying about getting the book wet and ruining it? You're actually supposed to soak them. Added bonus, they are squishy, too (Come to think of it, I really do love squeezing things, maybe more of a de-stresser than I think). Also, the puffy pages of the water book change color going from dry to wet.

However, I do have a memory of an odd realization about these books.

After the first night I brought a bath book home, and Cody played with it in the tub, he then started putting other books of his into the bathtub. He thought that they could all go in the water.

One night, I started running the water for bath time, meanwhile Cody played in his playroom until his bath was ready. I turned around to grab a towel from the closet, only to turn back and see him standing at the tub, dropping regular books in the suds.

I ended up drying out four hardback books that night. One of which had been 101 Dalmatians. Wasn't too happy about that one. If I'd known how Cody would have perceived all reading material as being waterproof, I would have explained the difference beforehand.

"Some can go in the water, but most cannot. Please ask mom before putting something in the bathtub," I said pulling out the four soaked hardback books.

"Okay, Mommy," Cody responded, smiling.

Ah, the innocence of little ones, *I thought in adoration. I knew I couldn't be mad at him, because I didn't foresee needing to teach him this beforehand. Learned this lesson the hard way. Those books were never the same again.*

I feel the need to pass this bit of newfound knowledge on to fellow parents.

The art of giving at this young age has proven to be interesting throughout the years, and it's not only because of re-gifting. Cody will unwrap a present Will and I get him only to push the contents to the side.

The box or bubble wrap quickly takes precedence over the gift itself. Even when the flashing, lots of buttons to push, Leap Frog Laptop is unveiled, the outer casing is what counts.

Believe me, at many times I'll ask myself, *Mia, why did I pay so much money for that? All I needed to do was just put bubble wrap in a box and wrap it.*

We spend a decent amount of money on things like a fort house. But no, Cody doesn't want to use the fort house as his imaginary surrounding. He wants to make the box the fort came in into his playful structure instead. The packaging being the star.

After catching on to what Cody truly enjoys, I've started bringing home random large boxes to play with, making me all of a sudden mother of the year. Incidentally, this saves Will and me money as well. The price of several packing boxes is pennies compared to big fancy playhouses. Everybody wins.

Throughout the years of watching Cody open his gifts I have no choice but to just sit back in amazement. The simplistic nature of the packaging attraction is very strange. Many times, I feel like I live in the craziest world of non-fiction stories. Borderline horror actions only add to this feeling.

What I do next is make time for *me* to be a kid again. I push all the buttons on the not-paid-attention-to Leap Frog laptop. I pretend to bake in the ignored easy bake oven. Then I grab my husband's hand and drag him to the outside playhouse like a schoolgirl does with a boy she likes. We throw our hands in the air, sliding down the yellow slide attached to the disregarded playhouse, shouting, "Weeee!" all the way down.

Who says *we* can't enjoy Cody's gifts while he's off to the side building forts and houses out of empty boxing? I say to let the adult stresses momentarily fly out the window, and simply play.

Chapter 26
Mommy's Sick Day

What winter month will be complete without a slight cold, and hopefully not worse with the flu? I hardly get sick. Knock on wood. Cody usually gets some sort of bug from school, and Will may or may not catch it. If Cody does come down with the sniffles or coughing, I know to start my usual disinfecting blast.

After all, when one comes home sick, it typically spreads throughout the entire house. My imaginary maid hat goes right on, and I get to work. In the big picture of motherhood, this hat is probably worn the most, out of any of the other hats.

Organizing, tidying up, and scrubbing every surface in the house, including Cody, Caesar, and occasionally Will (he can create the biggest mess of all), I'm mostly a twenty-four-seven maid.

Work your magic, Maid Mia.

I clean all year round, but when one of us is sick, again it mostly isn't me (mothers just tend to keep on going, and not let any little thing stop them—Energizer Bunnies!), my house is consumed with citrus and linen, and antibacterial aromas. Those are personal favorite scents of mine.

I go over the entire house, twice.

I say that *I* clean and disinfect the house, because I can't count on Will to help. If he feels under the weather with a runny nose, or slight cough, he's lying in bed like the world's about to end. If I'll do that every time my nose starts to run, or my throat feels a little bit scratchy, nothing will ever get done.

Moms really are hardcore. What would the world be without us? Oh, that's right, there wouldn't be a human population, that's what.

Envisioning my superwoman stance, I think, *there's a reason why women were chosen to give birth—we are a bad ass creature, that's why.*

I shudder to think how my husband would act if he got to go on the pregnancy venture. And I turn everything he once said to me during pregnancy back on him. It wouldn't be a very pleasant nine months, for anyone. At least I adapt, use my womanly strength, and overcome, especially with overcoming my bruised ribs from Cody kicking in the womb.

Well, this morning, I find myself waking up with a sore throat and a runny nose. Nothing more serious than that, but I feel weak trying to get out of bed, so I flop right back down.

Oh no, Mia. Now what do I do? There is so much to do today! Worry sets in.

Even though Will is a great husband and father when it comes right down to it, maybe not very empathetic toward me a lot of times, but he is pretty awesome, he still doesn't help out all that much. Especially, he's not eager to help with Caesar and his highly energetic stubborn ways.

"Will," I croak out. Him lying next to me.

"Hum?" He groans.

"I don't feel well." My words barely come out while patting his arm.

He sits right up, appearing concerned at first, then scared second. His expression shows he knows what I'm going to say next.

"I need your help today with Cody and Caesar," I whisper, placing the back of my hand against my forehead. *No fever, thank goodness.*

"Are you sure? When you get up and start moving around, you'll feel much better." Will motions me to sit up. "Just rub some dirt on it, and shake it off," he jokes, trying to scramble his way out of the inevitable.

I shake my head. He let out a huge sigh, knowing he'll need to tend to Cody, who is now calling out for me. And Caesar starts to whine from downstairs.

Honestly, why do most men panic if they have to help out more around the house? *They aren't used to it in the first place, that's why,* Detective Mia answers. *There are a lot of Francesca's in the world.*

Will half-smiles in my direction as he gets up and dresses. He kisses my forehead and leaves the room. After drinking a good amount of warm water with lemon in it, my throat doesn't feel as sore at least.

"Honey," I call the best I can from the top of the steps. "Could you please get me a bottle of DayQuil and a bag of cough drops from the store?"

"I'm watching everyone. Can't *you* go to the store?" His voice is faint coming all the way from the living room, but I can still hear the annoyance in it.

"Really? This is what I do every single day. It's no cake walk, but *I* seem to manage," I mumble under my breath. "Everyone, like he's watching a whole team of kids, or something. Plus it's only ten o'clock. He's been watching them not even for two hours." I scoff, turning on my heel.

I don't even respond to his uncaring reply, and go right back to lay down in bed. Yanking the covers back over my body, I'm irritated.

Will appears in the doorway seconds later, leaning against the wall. "I just put Caesar in his crate. Cody and I will go to the store. Sorry, they both weren't listening, and—" He brings his hand to his forehead, palm facing inward, and rubs, cringing. Then he drags his hand down his five o'clock shadow. "I don't know how you do it, Mia."

I take that as a small apology for being insensitive moments ago.

"I don't know how at times either. I do the best I can, I guess." A smile returns in my expression.

It's the imaginary hats that save me most the time, giving me my boosts. I grin inside.

A little over an hour passes since Will and Cody left for the store. Then I hear the garage door open. The sound of Cody wailing is clear as a bell.

Jumping out of bed, my first thought is he's hurt. The crying gets louder and louder as I hurry down the steps. Even not feeling well, maternal instincts kick in, giving me whatever push I need.

"What's wrong?" I rush over to Cody. Falling to my knees, checking him over, then looking at Will.

"He's fine," Will says in full exasperation mode. Sighing and huffing. "He wanted to get you a bracelet in a store window, but I told him it was really expensive. But we could get something else for you though."

Tears continue to stream down Cody's cheeks, falling onto the kitchen floor. His face looks absolutely beet-red. Not with anger, but with extreme sadness.

A slight laugh escapes me, because I now know the temper tantrum is all about buying me something, and not some catastrophic event. By the looks of Cody, one would think he's being tortured. I've been in this type of situation before. And for some reason, it seems funny to me with how Will's reacting.

"Don't laugh, I have a splitting headache." My six-foot-five, as masculine as they come, husband scrunches his eyes shut. Fatherhood gets to the toughest. But even he can't help letting out a snicker.

Encounters with children make life feel absurd and unreal at any given moment, and parenthood turns on a dime.

Cody's tears start to subside as he watches Will reach for the store's bags with the remedies inside to help make me feel better. Then Will bends down behind the kitchen counter and produces a small blue bag.

Tiffany's! My eyes fly open.

"We bought you a tiny get well gift. You do so much. I've just been taking care of things for a half of day, and I'm already exhausted." He holds out the bag, and adds, "I appreciate all you do."

My mouth pulls up in a slow smile. "Oh, thank you both." I take the extended bright blue bag, kissing both Will and Cody.

I reach inside and pull out a long slender blue box with a white ribbon. Inside is a fourteen-carat white-gold rope necklace. A heart pendant is dangling at the end with a tiny diamond chip resting at the top of the heart.

"It's absolutely beautiful. I can't tell you how much I appreciate this." I motion Will to clasp the necklace at the nape of my neck. "Incidentally, was the bracelet in the Tiffany's store window?" I question, lifting one of my eyebrows (I get this rare talent from my maternal grandfather). Everyone knows how expensive everything is in Tiffany's.

"Yes, it was fifty thousand dollars." He starts to laugh, glancing down at Cody, who I can tell still doesn't understand why his dad would not buy the bracelet. I mock being in shock to over exaggerate, showing how much money that is.

Kneeling back down, I say in a soft voice, "Cody that is too much money to spend on Mommy just for being sick. Fifty thousand dollars is a lot of money in general." I turn to Will, and add, "Now for my birthday, or our anniversary, maybe it's more appropriate."

I wink and smile at him, signaling I'm making a joke. Too exorbitant of a gift. I mean, I'm not saying I will be mad if by chance, I happen to open a Tiffany's box in the future, and the bracelet is inside.

"I know it's expensive, Mom, but it was pretty, like you." Cody slowly wipes his eyes, holding back a sob.

My heart melts into a pool of butter, and all of a sudden, I don't even feel sick anymore. I want to just hug him and play whatever he wants. I'm not back to normal yet, but his compliment gives me a burst of energy.

Wow, Tiffany's, I should get sick more often. I giggle at the thought later that night, climbing into bed, ready to catch up on rest.

Chapter 27
Two Children in One

Winter break is over in a flash. Time to head back to school, and learning is in session once again. Big tests will be prepared for, and parent-teacher conferences are on the horizon.

Cody is on his best behavior with teachers, and other parents. Strangers even come up to me saying how sweet he is. I'll look over at my four-foot tall wonder, pondering where all this is coming from.

I strive to make sure he behaves in public, in fact, I've had long conversations with him about the behaving issue. But when at home, not much alludes to exceptional behavior outside of the house. A day here, a day there, comments are made about the caring, friendship, and respect Cody shows. I do see sporadic moments from him in school by volunteering.

I must be doing something right, I think.

If you throw enough mud against the wall, some of it's bound to stick. A good portion of our talks do stick, and the proof shows when I'm rewarded with temporary glimpses into Cody's adulthood. Of course, while wading through the Amazon rainforests of the hectic stages of childhood.

Basically, my conclusion is I have two children in one. At home, Cody is a whirlwind of who knows what. In public, he's the pillar of a good example. Talk about getting mothering whiplash. Hopefully, a visit to the chiropractor won't be needed.

I'll say to friends or other parent acquaintances of how wonderful their son or daughter is. Especially by volunteering, I work with many students.

"How well behaved and polite."

"How sweet and understanding."

I'm thinking that many of those mothers and fathers go home, asking themselves the same exact thing I do. *Is this the same child we're talking about?*

Parents tell me often, "This is not how my little one always acts, you know." Then going on to add, "Boy, you should see *her* at home," or, "*He* is completely different in the house with running, screaming, and demanding."

My eyes widen in disbelief, because the student I know doesn't show even the slightest glimmer of that behavior. I don't like to say this, but I'm kind of glad hearing these statements. Listening to others about two children in one makes me feel a whole lot better. A temporary sense of calm flows over me— I'm not alone, and the struggle *is* real.

In fact, I saw an interesting video the other day on how scientists did a study on children's actions around their mothers and then documented how they acted around other adults in their life. Eight hundred percent. Worse. Yes, you are reading that right.

The studies show children are eight hundred percent worse with their mothers than anyone else. This explains so much, and is proof showing the reality of supermoms, everywhere. Dragging a hand down my face in utter exhaustion, I figure I'll keep that number in my memory bank for the next time an explanation is needed for Cody's outbursts with me.

It's a challenge.

A week passes since starting school, giving teachers time to pull the student's grades together with their testing scores. Classroom behaviors have already been logged from over the first half of the school year.

Cody and I walk through the front door, returning home from a long day of me volunteering, and having our parent/teacher conference after school. Closing the door behind us, I take extra notice, obviously he has not done what I'd asked earlier of him in the week—clean up his toys.

Opening his bedroom door, the room is a mess. Not cleaning his room either. Heck, his clothes don't even make it into the laundry hamper, which *is* right next to the pile of clothing on the floor.

Big sigh.

A long exhale escapes me as I turn on my heel to head into the office, where papers are scattered everywhere on the desk. Will clearly doesn't organize either, even though I ask him quite often. Not only does my son not attempt to clean up, but neither does my other half.

Now I know where Cody gets his lack of organization—my husband. That's my firm place of blame, and I'm going to stick to it. I head out of the paper pit and straight downstairs to the kitchen.

Running and shouting begins overhead. "I'm Godzilla! Rooooaaarrr!" Caesar's four paws are rapidly following Cody, pounding. Evidently, the talk about doing homework as soon as we get home isn't sinking in.

I decide to slump down into one of the chairs at the kitchen table. Overtiredness sets in from my constant battle with getting everyone to pitch in and help with the chores and homework. It seems to be all lost in vain.

The memory from today's conference comes back with how well Cody does in school.

"He shares his supplies with his classmates, and really focuses on tasks nicely, and is respectful with always raising his hand. I'm also happy with his grades. Cody is very smart, and an excellent student," Ms. Dorsey stated everything with a glisten in her eyes. Obviously, this was a proud student-bragging moment for her.

Pride hit me with knowing my son has been succeeding in school.

"That's so good to hear." A permanent smile spreads across my face.

But why he is so different at home than in school? Wait, is this my child? I had thought.

Cody sat quietly by my side as his teacher continued our conference. Pride turned to confusion. I didn't let anything show, of course. I wouldn't want his teacher to think anything other than the great thoughts she did.

She then added, "I don't know if you know this, but Cody is one of the most loyal and kind friends I've seen interacting with others."

"Really?"

"Yes. The other day, I was assigning environments for our second semester big project." Ms. Dorsey paused to ask, "Remember when you were volunteering that one day, and I had the kids pick an environment out of a hat?"

"I do remember. Cody wanted the ocean so badly, and was thrilled when he picked that piece of paper out with ocean written on it."

We laughed, both looking at Cody, who sat next to me, smiling wide-eyed.

"Well, his friend Liam got the desert. He wanted the ocean too, but I only had four pieces of paper in the hat with ocean written on them. Cody came up to me later in the afternoon almost in tears." She paused, giving Cody a warm

smile. "I asked him what was wrong, and he then asked me if he could trade his ocean paper with Liam, and he'll take the desert."

"Liam was really sad," Cody said. "I wanted him to be happy."

"I know you did. And that was so sweet," Ms. Dorsey said to him. "But you need to be happy too, Cody. It's nice to think of others, but it's okay to be happy with what you get also."

He nodded as she let out a faint chuckle, continuing, "Cody kept it up, and didn't want to give up on trading. He was genuinely sad for Liam. So, I made an exception and gave Liam the ocean environment for his project."

"That was sure nice of you." I smiled.

"What can I say? I want my students to be happy too. And Cody was making a good case." She laughed, and so did we.

Leaving school, I smiled, so proud of my son and his heart.

I uncover the best things from others, and have sneak peaks of what a compassionate child I have. He'll do just fine in life, outside the house.

***

Nothing gets done the first time I ask, well actually the third, four, or tenth time either. But at school, or at a friend's house, when someone other than me asks Cody to do something, no questions asked, he'll hop right to it. This is because I'm witness to the fact that I have two children in one.

And from all things I read in articles and on social media, and hear from my fellow moms, this is completely normal. Children are in their comfort zone at home. They can be their natural selves. In a way, that makes me feel a little better, knowing that Cody is at ease in our house, but in a way not entirely better.

There needs to be a happy medium. I'm not reaching for the stars here, I contemplate almost daily, and shake my head. *Or am I? Eight hundred percent, Mia. Scientists say eight hundred percent. Worse,* I remind myself.

I know I actually am trying to reach too far up, because this behavior appears to be the law of nature with young ones. But hey, I can at least dream of a content middle ground.

My thought process is that my own son should want to help at home the most. We are the ones doing the most for him, caring the most for him. But no, it's the other way around apparently. Don't get me wrong, I'm glad he proves to be a good example out in public, it is a direct reflection of my mothering after all. Proof some of my respect talks stick. However, that behavior needs to be shown most of the time in the house as well.

I put on my Detective Mia hat to investigate this issue. Not finding anything conclusive in solving my daily challenge, but enough to work toward being satisfied. And sometimes that is enough.

I find columns explaining how parents should feel good about their children being in his or her comfort zone at home, because this trait is very common. I felt more at ease, knowing my struggle is out there *and* in print.

Each column had been written by some sort of expert in child psychology, parents themselves, which makes me sit up and take notice. One column does stand out to me though, from a man psychologist, the writer, leaving it up in the air if he is a father himself. And if he is experiencing his advice firsthand, or just studying facts from work or from books he read in college.

Did that expert experience the horrors behind closed doors? Try feeling good then. My feelings are that you need to go through something to truly be able to talk about it. I decide to pay more attention to the columns I read from someone who states they are a parent. Makes me feel a connection to them.

More investigation needs to be done on my off time from mothering and being the Teacher Savior. Title still not going to my head, but love to think about it.

I decide that this comfort-zone-thing can be overrated. I guess it's one of my internal struggles; to be comfortable or not to be comfortable? That is the question. Balancing that fine line of motherhood sanity. I want to be at my best every day. That needs to play a factor in there *somewhere*. I'm not reaching for the stars here.

I tell mothers and fathers not to worry when we talk about this. "I am right there with you sitting down in utter bewilderment, wondering where my child from school has gone. It's crystal clear we all have two children in one. One is left at school, and one is at home with us—the comfortable one."

At the kitchen table, my eyes shift up toward the ceiling at the second floor.

"Godzilla is destroying the rooms!" Cody shouts.

Feet and paws pound on the second floor in loud booms.

A long sigh escapes. My eyes slowly close. *This is being comfortable.*

Chapter 28
The Power of No

"Time for homework!" I shout over the roars and pounding, standing at the base of the steps.

Cody emerges with Caesar at the top of the staircase. Caesar has on his Halloween superhero costume from last year. "No, I'm not doing my homework now, and you can't make me." He spins around to head back to his playroom. "Caesar hasn't saved the house yet from Godzilla," he informs from over his shoulder.

"Stop right there, mister. You—"

Cody interrupts me, raising his voice, "I'm busy!"

"Busy playing," I mumble, and add in a louder voice, "I'll call Ms. Dorsey!" Oops, a threat slips out. Well, maybe not. I *am* supposed to let her know if I'll be volunteering tomorrow, anyway.

"Just stating a fact, Mia," I say to myself out loud. *How he perceives it is entirely up to him.* I sharply nod.

"No, you won't, Mom. Do not call her!" Cody stalks halfway down the stairs. Face now set to angry mode. His brows crease almost as one.

"Listen, just please do your homework to keep your grades up. Movie directors had to do their homework, so they could get their college degree. I'm trying to help you."

His anger now softens.

There, Mia, you've used his way of thinking to steer away from threats.

"Okay, but after I finish playing. Fifteen minutes." He starts the bartering process.

I huff, and give in, slightly. "Ten minutes only, then get to work. You can play again after homework."

"Okay, ten minutes." Cody smiles, wide, and runs back up the stairs to Caesar to continue their role-play of Godzilla and the superhero.

I stride back to the kitchen, confident. Proud with recovering fast from using a possible threat, but end up stopping in my tracks. *Oh no, you just negotiated.* Hand slap to the forehead moment. I said I'll never do it, but here I am *again.*

"Cody, it's been ten minutes," I call upstairs. "Time for homework."

"No, five more minutes, Mom!" He yells from his playroom.

Now, we are right back to our bedtime routine with five more minutes. I practically sprint to my escape room for quiet time. I need to think before I'm driven insane for the day.

No is one of the first words I used when becoming a mother. I try to divert away from this word, as to not be on the negative side. It's so hard, let me tell you.

There are parenting classes out there, teaching how to parent more effectively. One of the main lessons they teach is how to avoid the overuse of no (I've researched the classes and their 'curriculum'). The teacher shows how to use different techniques in getting a point across when not to do something.

Must be useful. I just haven't taken the final plunge in signing up for parenting classes. Even though I'm sure I can benefit from them, I'm not all that eager to be a student in a classroom again. Been there, done that. Volunteering in school only, for me.

I wing it with motherhood, using the best common sense and maternal instincts I have.

And how has that been working out for you, Mia? I often joke with myself.

I suppose trying not to say the powerful word of no will be more effective in positive development. My thinking is that Cody will hear it on the streets anyway, so why shelter it from him now.

On the other hand, another reason not to say this all the time is that he will grow up always using it as a go-to word. I want Cody to problem solve in a more effective way than solely saying, "No." Possibly being more polite in the process.

Can definitely go for extra politeness. Can't we all?

School shows him better methodical ways than just flat out saying no, which helps me in the long run. Can't say it enough, God bless our teachers.

All else aside, I believe in the grand scheme of things as long as Cody grows up doing good, and treating others well, my mothering skills have worked.

Just like with schooling—debating whether to send children to private or public school, choices will really depend on the individual child. They'll eventually decide how to apply themselves in life. As the same with parenting classes, if they will work or not solely depends on the individual parent, in my opinion, and if they exercise their newly-learned information, or not.

I'm determined to try my best and give good examples, knowing there is "no" guarantee. And when my son utilizes this word too much, as how he just did right now with the homework thing, driving me crazy, I know it's myself to hold responsible.

Again, I can slap myself on the head at this point. By now, I'd think there'd be a permanent handprint on my forehead. *Motherhood.* Big. Long. Sigh.

From time to time, when Cody opens a door for a person going in a store, all is forgotten. I smile and realize I'm doing an okay job, and to stop being so hard on myself.

No is such an easy word to repeat. *Yes* is easy too, but yes is not nearly as fun to say than its antonym. To Cody, no simply means he doesn't want to do something, meaning the possibility of getting out of a chore. Also to get out of homework, like today.

Looking on the upside, there can be worse things repeated. The other day, he hears me complaining about Uncle Tony, or letting the S bomb slip out when stubbing my toe two nights ago, all can be repeated. And maybe those things are, which that will then fall under TMI stories being released to others.

I'll then be forced into my default mode of making a beeline for the nearest exit door. Maybe my little Myna bird only repeating *no* doesn't seem so bad now.

I'm positive there's a child detective-like strategy behind the use of this most popular word, which is still unbeknownst to adults. Children may have secretly band together using modern-day technology. Creating a high-tech device to avoid a grown-up from finding out certain reasons behind their actions. In theory, saying this word might be all part of a genius reverse psychology plan that has not yet been uprooted.

Everyone constantly says how today's children are much smarter than they were fifty years ago. This is true, especially with all the technology available to them.

But how much smarter, is the question? I often think.

Maybe clever in the sense that Cody figures out a way to get me to say no as much as I can, in turn getting his way in the end. If I think about it, how many times do I stand firm with not getting a certain item, but in the same breath, agree to something else. This saves an argument and sanity on my part. It also gets him what he probably wants in the first place.

Aim high to make the original desired purchase seem appealing. Intelligent to seal-the-deal. Sounds a lot like negotiating, too. The game of wheel-and-deal to all intents and purposes is linked to saying no. How revolutionary.

"No sweetheart, the King Ghidorah S.H Monsterarts is way too expensive. But the Bandai Vinyl King Ghidorah is only a tenth of the price. Plus, it looks exactly the same. How about that?" I suggested, looking down at Cody.

"No honey, you cannot get that expensive robot that just came out, but how about a dinosaur Lego set? It's really cool, and a lot less money. Besides, you get to build, and that's your favorite," I said another time.

Building creates focus and good problem solving for kids. I'll lean toward Lego's and STEM products any day. Telling the moms in my group to simply buy a theme their child's interested in, and now learning is combined with playing.

It's all about dinosaurs or Godzilla with Cody, so I work with those. Most of the time, I just plain think that my little genius uses the power in *no* more often to blame me in the long run.

The other day after school, Cody was in a bad mood when we got home. He wanted to play on the school's playground after the bell rang at the end of the day. We needed to leave for an appointment, so I told him we couldn't stay.

"No, I won't do my chores. No, I won't clean up. And no, I won't shower," Cody yelled at me. He stalked up the stairs.

"Why do you constantly say no? Why can't you say yes more often?" I asked.

"You always say no to me, and only say yes sometimes, so I can do the same thing." He turned around in mid-step, and glared. His eyes tried to pierce into mine as if he had a ray that could stun me.

"No, you can't do the same thing, I am the parent. I can't just let you do whatever you want. I have to teach you."

"You taught me to say no."

And bam, there it was. He had only stated the truth. I basically did teach him this. I let out an exasperated huff.

I can't let him run amuck without me ever stopping him. Cody's too smart for his own good. He found a way to turn the tables, making me the one held accountable for him not doing more. Thus letting me know why he didn't utilize yes more often—I've taught him no through my overuse of it. This was brilliant and very adult-like strategic thinking.

I'm being duped by my own son.

These scenarios don't happen all the time, but if I stop and think about it, they happen enough.

The power in the word no is endless. It keeps Cody safe. It stops him from getting what he wants all the time. Or delaying gratification to something else. But I'm starting to assess many instances, concluding he's more planned out than he leads on to be.

Maybe even harping on the same subject with repeating interests combined with getting me to say no will actually get me to say yes to something else. This is psychology at its finest. I'm worn out just thinking about it. I need to go lie down, rest, and place a cool towel on my hypothetical hand-printed forehead.

Having snapped out of a use-of-no trance, quietness fills the house. "What is he up to?" I leave my escape room and head upstairs.

"Cody? Where are you?" I ask.

"In my room," he replies from behind his closed bedroom door.

I knock. "May I come in?"

Surprise hits me upon opening the door, seeing his school workbook open and pencil writing in progress.

In this moment, I realize solutions aren't always seen in black and white, but in the knowledge of taking five. Leaving an argument, or what's about to become an argument.

My escape room quietness, or my toilet closet retreat, provides the exact mental break I need for myself, and for my son alike. Sometimes, solutions are right in front of my eyes without the detective work being done.

Chapter 29
The Shower Controversy

Shower, or not to shower—a repeat dilemma every day. Who knew taking a shower can even be a question, but in motherhood, it is a long drawn out debate.

I can't comprehend why my child won't want to shower, especially after spending all day in school. Running around on the playground, getting all hot and sticky. This baffles me. To my astonishment, and many more like-minded parents, showers create arguments just as jaw-dropping and confusingly frustrating as a political debate.

Add to my daily question list: Should I save an argument, and pick my battles today? Do I save my energy for the bedtime controversy, or the 'you're-eating-too-much-candy' talk? Should I tightrope the thin line of parenting, or not?

Face it, shower time is not the easiest. Granted, not every time's challenging. There are those days my little dirty one actually wants to get clean. But those days are far and few between.

To me, it's a no brainier. There's nothing like a nice hot cascade of water pouring over me to wash and steam away the stresses from a daunting day. Especially on days like today with volunteering, a parent conference, and then having the argument after with doing homework.

I do try and think back to being a kid myself, and if I despised showers as well. I really don't remember, but I probably did at that age. And kids' most likely think, by taking a break in playing to clean up, they'll miss out on an important event.

A delivery might arrive, or their mom hides a few of their belongings when cleaning the house. At this age range, common rationality is; it's best not to take a shower to avoid missing out.

I'm sure being in school all day also plays a factor in Cody's decisions. After all, he does not play with his toys ALL day long. Now that he's home and able to play, *I* am telling him to do homework and shower—chores. This takes all of only fifteen minutes, the shower part, anyway. Getting him clean is considered unimportant compared to playing, and he thinks he'll be losing valuable time.

An argument begins the minute I mention a shower. What a catastrophe over a matter that's so small.

"Okay big guy, time to shower. I let you play after your homework. Now you have to get cleaned up." I enter Cody's playroom.

"Playing is more important," he replies without looking up from his train set.

"Don't you want to get clean? Don't you want to feel fresh?" I ask, smiling.

"I feel clean. You just don't want me to play, do you?" Cody tilts his head to one side, now staring at me. Almost as if he's challenging me to dare answer him. Amazing how much he and Caesar are exactly alike. Caesar does the same thing. They must learn from each other—partners in crime.

Challenge accepted, but with an understanding approach. "I didn't say that. I'm glad you like playing, and using your imagination. But you've been in school the entire day and on the floor in your classroom. You've been in the grass and all over on the playground. I'm helping you to be at your best, to feel refreshed for even more playing time. You need to wash everything, so please take a shower now."

"I'm going to draw now." He stands straight up, like he doesn't hear a word I'm saying, and marches over to grab plain paper and a pencil.

In one ear and out the other. Mia, stand firm. "Cody, you can draw after your shower."

"You don't like my drawings, do you? Huh? You don't think they're important." He slams his hands down on his hips.

"What are you talking about? I love your drawings. This is not about drawing or playing. This is about washing up after a long day. Stop arguing! You would have been done by now." I wave a hand in the air in exasperation.

"You don't want me to draw anymore, do you?" He grins as his mouth pulls up to one side.

I throw both my hands up. This is obviously getting nowhere, fast. Also my cue to take another five. I turn on my heel. On the way out of the room, I murmur under my breath, "I'll put the sleeping bag outside. You can sleep in that on the dirty ground if you don't want to shower. You tell me no—well, no sleeping in a comfortable clean bed then."

My words trail off, heated. I pass Will in the office. He's conveniently pretending not to hear any of the argument. Being only down the hall from us, I know he just doesn't want to get involved, this time anyway. Will's probably sitting in the office, making more of a mess with strewing papers around and picking his nose.

Today, my frustration seems like it's mounting, and now the shower debate is the last straw. I have a couple more choice words for Will, too, as I stalk down the stairs.

"I'll throw out an extra sleeping bag for you, too, tonight. You both are dirty and can sleep in the backyard. How do you like that one?" I say under my breath. Both my arms wave in the air, side to side, like a mad woman on the loose, overly-angry at this point. I march right back into my escape room to start my relaxation breathing exercises.

Inhale through my nose. *One, two, three, four, five.*

Long exhale through my mouth. *One, two, three, four, five.*

Repeat.

I do this for five minutes, and feel relief envelop me.

Words are put in my mouth from time to time just like with this shower debate, and words that would never even cross my mind.

What just happened? I think.

How can such young little people be so quick and smart? He somehow thinks to turn this shower business into some form of guilt. Isn't that something I'll see from a presidential candidate firing false statements? Or from my mother-in-law?

The answer's simple to my plethora of questions—children are underestimated. They are tiny individuals who are not given enough credit for their exuberant thriving minds in figuring ways around a situation.

Cody is six going on twenty-six.

I sit back against my plush couch, hug a fluffy soft square pillow, and wonder what to do as a mom. Again, I have to choose my battles. I have learned over the years to do this. But a question does bear close attention. Am I choosing my battles, or is Cody really choosing his arguments?

I take a slow sip of wine. With my eye mask on to soothe my eyes, I feel in more of a relaxed state, to now think.

Multiple times, we go back and forth about doing certain things, and oddly enough, he gives in pretty quickly. Those moments, no arguing is involved. As opposed to times he'll keep it up until I give in, or give up. I examine scenarios over in my mind. Realizing while I decide on what battles to pick, Cody is doing the same. Only with what arguments to choose.

Ah-ha!

The result—I might just have to suck it up and wade through these younger years. In order to keep my stress level down, I shouldn't argue this every day. Cody's pediatrician once told me that it's not good for children to shower every single day as it is, especially with the dry air in Las Vegas.

"Every three days is just fine, combined with Cetaphil or Cera V for moisture protection, you will actually be doing Cody some good," Dr. Stewart explains to a worrisome me, then adds, "We live in the desert, put any constant showering quarrels to the side. Save yourself the anguish, Mia."

I remember not feeling so tense leaving that doctor's visit, but how quickly I slip back into my old ways. I really need to remind myself of what he said. Save myself the battles.

Besides, I know when Cody's a teenager, he will take more than enough showers to hopefully scrub off the entire extra childhood dirt.

Teenagers are completely night and day from younger years. You literally need to pull teens away from taking too many showers. That is not healthy either. Over-washing keeps good bacteria away, which we need to be well. Only when younger, we need to push kids toward the shower.

It's all in the different stages of maturing. Teenagers are hormone-ravaged as they go through the desires of puberty. They want to look good and smell good to attract a boyfriend or girlfriend. On the other hand, small kids have only one thing on their mind when it comes to the laws of attraction—boys have cooties, girls have cooties. I went through all this growing up.

Although to this day, I'm not wholly convinced that men don't have cooties. I admit I set that idea aside for a point and time, or else how did Cody come about. But this realization pops up every now and again. I do think men haven't lost their cooties completely from boyhood.

An image from awhile back comes to mind of the man getting out of his Hummer, picking his nose in the grocery store parking lot. *Ew.* I get a shiver just thinking about it.

The thought of needing to smell good, and appear clean, isn't all that important at Cody's age. This will naturally fade becoming older. Then he will most likely want to use cologne on top of showering frequently, similar to my nephew-in-law, Cayden, but hopefully not as potent.

Will's nephew came for a visit one time when he was in middle school. He had a newfound love for cologne that could be smelled a mile away. Way too much was used. I thought that Will's brother and sister-in-law probably didn't educate him on the saying, a little goes a long way.

The cologne was on his backpack, clothes, him, and everything he touched in the house. Cayden told us one night of how he wished he had a girlfriend in every class. Needless to say, he was going through puberty, and basically girl-crazed. Probably having thought, the more cologne he puts on, the more girls would be attracted to him.

Not with that much, *I thought.* The poor girl will be overcome by the vapors.

I encouraged Will to say something to his nephew, since he was the uncle, and a man with experience. I saw this as a good life-teaching moment for him, where Uncle and Nephew could have some extra bonding time.

But Will didn't talk to Cayden during the trip, thinking this advice should come from Dominic and Leila, his brother and sister-in-law. I saw his point, but I figured if they hadn't said anything by now, about less is more, they probably wouldn't.

Maybe him and his wife are passed out from the cloud of fumes in the house, and can't coherently tell Cayden. *The reality hit me of the possibility.* Someone should check on them!

I texted Leila, to say hi with nothing else, just to see that she responded.
She sent me a text back almost immediately.
Hi, Mia. Is everything okay?
Phew! *I thought, relieved.*
Yes, everything is fine. Just checking in.
Oh, okay. How is Cayden? Is he behaving?
He's fine. He had fun!

Good to hear. Thought something might be wrong. Thanks again for having him!

Anytime!

I withheld a little information. Everything was fine, except my house may never smell the same again. I felt relieved and irritated all at the same time— Dominic and Leila turned out to be fine, but on the other hand, truly hadn't talked with their son about the cologne over-usage. They couldn't have, or else he just didn't listen.

Long after he went home, as I suspected, the aroma lingered, which would have been semi-fine, except for the fact that I didn't care for the smell of Cayden's cologne at all.

Overall, I can't believe that a showering controversy is even a thing. I'm wading through this one the cleanest way I can.

Tomorrow is a new day.

Chapter 30
Traveling with Kids

Even though I play like I'm an actual detective to find better solutions to my days running smoother, my life is pretty much hectic. Par for the course of motherhood. Detective Mia back on the job.

For the most part due to the ongoing stupor I'm in, I ask myself often, *when aren't vacations needed?*

Work, home, mothering duties, life in general gets busy and stressful. Chances to take a vacation do not come easy. My husband must coordinate completing web projects around time off, finding breaks in the annual school calendar, and money, oh boy, that's the biggest vacation-stopper right there. Life somehow finds a way to take a lot of funding, even that holiday bundle of cash we set aside months ago. Going, going, gone.

Especially when things in the house need to be fixed, like broken appliances. Those usually break in three's. That's a lovely old wives' tale, mostly coming true.

Darn breaking in three's.

It's not like the past few days aren't challenging me enough. Or those projects I've been helping Cody with for school, which are supposed to be done by tomorrow aren't hard either. I now have to fix entities in our house on top of everything, and spend a pretty penny on them.

Not to mention how I dread scheduling service appointments—a four to six hour window a person needs to be waiting at home.

At the kitchen table, I sit anxiously. Pen tapping on my post it notepad. One leg crosses over the other and nervously shakes while trying to organize someone to come out and repair my recently broken oven. Cody's at school, and I'm not volunteering today, so I'm using this time to organize with the appliance company.

"You mean to tell me you can't give a more exact time?" I ask the company's receptionist. I'm more frustrated than not. "My day doesn't consist of twiddling my thumbs, you know, hoping someone will suddenly pop by to entertain me. I'm an on-the-go mom."

A lovely woman is on the other end. It's not her fault, and I really don't want to take my being angry out on her. It's the company she works for, and all the other companies who have the same protocols, fault.

I am pointing fingers here. Not proud of it, but angry mothers do that sort of thing.

"I understand, ma'am. I'm sorry for any inconvenience. It's the time of year. Right after the holidays, a lot of appliances seem to break down. Probably the extra cooking, and if ovens and stoves are older, they take a hit," the receptionist apologizes.

"I'm also the Teacher Savior at my son's school. They need me there, and—" I freeze. *Great job, Mia. She doesn't care what I do, nor does she know what the heck a Teacher Savior is. It's a made-up title; apparently now going to my head.*

I totally discredit myself in that moment, and slouch down underneath the table, thinking I'm hiding. From what, I have no idea. The receptionist is on the phone for goodness sake, she's not able to see me.

You're a piece of work. You know that, right? I cringe in thought at my oddness.

The lady clears her throat awkwardly on the other end, followed by a short amount of weird silence. After agreeing to a time, the call quickly ends. I then laugh, completely out of context.

Piled on top of appliance frustration are the outgrowing of Cody's clothes and shoes, or having to take the car in for servicing.

That night at dinner, I shout out, "That's it! We are taking a vacation. I don't care where, but we need to get out of here." My hands land down on the table. The daily busyness finally pulls me to the end of my rope.

Cody and Will just stare at me. I'm breathing heavily. The service appointment, broken oven, new clothes shopping, embarrassing myself with the Teacher Savior comment, all come down on me.

Then they both glance at each other and nod in agreement. "Yep, vacation time, here we come!" Will exclaims.

My big kid makes a funny face at my little kid, and we all start cracking up.

Putting on my imaginary travel agent's hat, I take a few moments to think about a good point I say to my fellow moms. *Who said a high-priced vacation is the only way to get away?* I need to take my own advice sometimes.

There are plenty of options I'll suggest to parents.

What better way to figure this out than reciting my own advice out loud? Alone in my old-faithful escape room. Will still doesn't understand the talking to myself thing. He views people talking to themselves as something must be wrong with them. Which is correct in some cases, but not mine. Obviously, he's not a mom, and can't understand the helpfulness of talking to oneself.

After dinner and cleaning the dishes, I then take the conversations for me, myself, and I, in private, along with my imaginary hats. I'm perfectly fine and normal in doing so.

"Isn't that right, Mia?"

"Yes it is, Mia."

"Thank you for saying that, Mia."

"You're very welcome, Mia," I say back at my reflection in the wall mirror across from my mini kitchen. I then wink back at the nice looking momma that still, for some reason, has her hair intact, and makeup still done well.

"Take a small trip, an inexpensive trip. If you have family or friends who work in hotels or in the airline business, ask for their employee discounts. If not, no problem, there are always websites like Priceline to get you places cheaper. Pack up the family and dog to take off and drive to a neighboring place."

"Set up a couple tents and sleeping bags in a state park. Fall asleep with the stars and sky as your roof." When I got done rambling off my vacation-mom speech, which this actually does happen on a regular basis, I get to work planning.

Stress doesn't entirely go away on vacations though. It's better, but not absent. Even with a small trip, ironically all of Cody's things need to be packed just the same as a big trip, only not as much in quantity. What helps me with packing for him is to make a list.

This is a great stress-reducer in trip preparation. Granted, the list gets a little smaller as he gets older. No more bottles, formula, diapers, burp cloths, bibs, pacifiers, baby bags, and the exorbitant amount of onesies for all the times he spit up, or pee leaking out of the diapers seem, or poop flooding upwards.

Been there, done that. Parents traveling with infants definitely have it the hardest. Hats off to you. The entire extra time spent packing is only half the battle. Traveling is the other half.

Cody is very easygoing on vacation, another one of my eyes in the storm. But with having worked in the hotel business before becoming a stay-at-home mom, I've seen the sights. I'm not just talking about family squabbles either.

I've called security for lingerie being worn as normal in hallways or in the lobby. And how could I forget the occasional naked human thrown out of their room by an upset spouse. They banged on the door in his or her birthday suit.

These rare times had me feeling sorry for the person thrown out. The embarrassment. But who knew what they had done, so could have been completely warranted. Vacation stress came in all forms. Hotel working life equaled colorful stories.

Upon arrival, almost daily, kids would pull their parents this way and that. "I want to go here." "No, I want to go there." "That's boring. I don't want to do that." "Let's go here instead."

On several occasions, a child threw a temper tantrum, throwing their body on the floor. Kicking and screaming echoed throughout the lobby.

One child specifically went absolutely rigid, stiffening like a piece of wood on the ground. The little girl's dad had to drag her partly toward the elevator. Halfway there, he was able to pick her up and slung her over his shoulder. The guests and employees stood around in shock at the spectacle.

At that moment, I wondered in amazement if that was what parents dealt with on a daily basis. Being Cody wasn't even an apple in my eye back then, I didn't know. And of course, that sort of scenario hadn't happened every day, I don't want to exaggerate here. Maybe every other day.

After arguing in the lobby for about thirty seconds, parents couldn't take the whining anymore. That's the precise moment one of them would say, "Stop it! We will do something for everyone. The next person who argues will lose their chance to pick what they want to do. Capiche?"

Quiet filled the vacation air. A stare down started to commence for about thirty more seconds. Parents sneered at the kids. They sneered right back. Next came a triumph expression on Mom and Dad's face.

Well that worked. Thank goodness. *Thoughts obviously written all over their expressions, letting out a recuperated sigh.*

Any arguing and disagreements weren't over, but they subsided for the time being.

Coincidentally, those types of actions reverted back to negotiation and threatening—an obvious reoccurring link to everything. Parents didn't want to do it, but before they knew it, the words came out of their mouths.

Now, it was time to enjoy the vacation.

When we go on a trip, everyone gets a chance to pick an activity. This is only fair; or else we might have well just gone on all separate vacations. A solo getaway is an idea that crosses my mind, once or twice. Okay, well actually pretty much every day.

Then at night, when Cody finally falls asleep from our exhausting adventures for the day, it's Mommy and Daddy time. Vacations aren't just for the whole family to have fun, but also for couple's enjoyment. I do have to encourage myself. *Come on, Mia. Muster up that energy for some extracurricular activities.*

Adults need this release. By the way, sex is a great stress reliever, not meant for just a trip, but any day of the week. Plus, it's been proven to be one of the best forms of exercise around. Win-win situation—stress reliever and working out combined in one. Getting two birds with one stone. Not my favorite saying, but true enough.

Making sure everyone has a good time is exhausting. So though, it's wonderful to give children a chance to experience new places and cultures, it's also a parenting whirlwind.

Returning back home can be nice also. Home is a familiar comfortable setting, and I have my own bed back. My own pillow to comfort me. A hotel bed, cabin beds, sleeping bags, wherever our trip takes us, sleeping just isn't the same.

However, things quickly go back to normal entering the front door from any trip. My turbo raptor runs in roaring as a dinosaur to his room. Will heads to the office, retiring to his computer for some work. I begin unpacking, apprehensive about getting back to my daily routine.

With catching up on laundry and household chores, it feels like I need a vacation from a vacation. Especially after getting Caesar, I have to pick him up at my parents where he has his own getaway.

After a walk down memory lane, I mark the vacation date for spring break in April on my calendar and head off to bed.

The alone time rejuvenated me. Sweet dreams await.

Chapter 31
Disney World Vacation

April doesn't come soon enough. We all need a break from our daily routine of motherhood, fatherhood, and studentville.

It's the first day of spring break, and we land in Orlando, Florida. I'm actually more excited than Will and Cody put together to go to Disney World. This vacation is my surprise pick.

We haven't splurged going anywhere in a long time, and with Will landing the lead graphic designer for a big marketing company, we're able to have this nice getaway. Cody hasn't been to Disney World yet, and Will went to Disney World as a child, like me, but hasn't gone back since.

"Honey, I'm just going to call my parents to see how Caesar's doing, then let's go to the park." I clap in all excitement, looking over at Will then to Cody. I unpack the last of our clothes at a quicker pace before calling.

They're on the floor in the living room of our hotel suite, performing a Jurassic World scene. First Cody roars, then Will roars back. They jump up together, grabbing a few of Cody's dinosaurs to finish the reenactment.

Only a few dinosaurs is an understatement considering he took an entire backpack full of them that he just had to have on the trip. I think more dinosaurs were packed than actual clothes. They're heavier to carry than clothing, too.

"Mom, too heavy," Cody told me at the airport earlier, shrugging his backpack off his shoulders. He put it on the ground.

At first, an instant terror flashback hit me from the first day of school; he ran in attempt to escape. This happened after saying the exact same thing and took his backpack off.

I dusted the memory off. This is a totally different situation.

"You wanted to bring all of those toys. I'm carrying enough as it is. My purse alone weighs a ton. You're strong, carry your backpack a little further please." I started putting the straps back over his shoulders.

"No!" Cody stomped his foot, and stiffened his arms, so I couldn't put the straps over each shoulder.

I let out a big huff after a stare down moment. Of course, Will is over buying himself Starbuck's precisely when Cody acts up.

That's his plan, Mia. Kids pick fights with moms more, thinking they'll get away with it, *Detective Mia chimes in.* Face it, you're a soft touch.

I knew she was right. I did end up giving in, mainly to avoid a meltdown, and I carried the backpack the rest of the way to the terminal. At least me having to shove my imaginary disappearing hat on was temporarily avoided, for the time being.

I blink a few times to take myself away from my airport trance, and gaze out of the living room's floor-to-ceiling glass doors. The view from our room is spectacular. We have a bird's eye view of the Magic Kingdom. The travel agent said the real treat is going to be at night when Cinderella's castle lights up. Very romantic sounding.

Besides aiming for a fun and carefree vacation while at Disney World and in Orlando, I also have the goal of making our time a bit romantic for Will and I. We lose some of the romance through our busy days. And arguing over small things doesn't ever help, but that's all part of marriage. Hence, needing time away from life in general.

I'm in my glory, riding the rides, visiting with Mickey, Minnie, and all the Disney characters, and eating foods from around the globe—surreal. Motioning for pictures at every chance I get. Epcot center is my personal favorite. Sharing experiences from many different countries. The diversity is a cultural experience in itself.

I'm a total foodie, loving to try a variety of cuisine, even though my tastes weren't always like this. I had my picky years of eating as a child, the very same as in the article from the Monell Center by Marcia Pelchat, and from the talks in our mom meetings.

All part of growing up, and now look at me; trying new food is a part of my life.

"Over there!" I shout, giddy, hopping up and down. "Chocolate covered bananas!" Finally, we find the cart I've been looking for. Chocolate covered bananas on a stick are my absolute favorite. I pull Will and Cody over to the cart with the big yellow and white awning.

"We'll have three chocolate covered bananas with nuts please," I say to the lady standing behind the counter.

"Sure, coming right up." She giggles, seeing my excited expression. "Here you go." She hands a banana to each of us.

"Look, a big poop with chunks, mom!" Cody blurts out, holding his banana.

My face transforms to horrification. I try not to look at the nice lady behind the counter. I know she hears Cody, because my eyes catch glances from people walking by. There are a ton of kids here with their parents, and I'm sure they've all had their little ones make gross comments, so I don't think too much about the passers-by.

I laugh nervously in the lady's direction. "Thank you," I mumble.

"Cody, you don't say things like that out in public. It's gross," I tell him as we walk away.

"Well, it's true, Mom. Look at it." He holds up his banana on a stick. And I have to admit, he's kind of right, but here's a teaching moment to try to make a good point.

All goes out the window when Will bends down to give him a high-five. "That's my boy."

First embarrassing statement of the vacation. Please let it be the last. And leave it to Will to encourage him. After all, they do bond with nose-picking. No surprise there. I cringe for a second, until I take my first bite, and then I'm suddenly in my glory eating.

Next, we walk through Disney's Animal Kingdom Theme Park after finishing our poops on a stick, as Cody gave them the official name. This appears to be his favorite out of the four Disney World Parks, until we got to the Donald's Dino Boat Bash ride. He cries and wails, because he says it reminds him of Caesar.

"I want to go home. I miss Caesar," Cody sobs, almost uncontrollably.

"Caesar is having a great time with grandma and grandpa. He's on vacation, too," Will says, and rubs Cody's back. "I'm sure he misses us, but he is loving a fun different change."

This appears to soothe my teary-eyed son, and he calms down. I stand and smile, watching both of them together. Will may not be helpful with day to day chores, but he sure is a good father.

Remember that for bedtime tonight, Mia, Sexy Mia speaks up, scrounging around in the mental dresser drawer for her imaginary erotic hat. *A good father is so hot!* Sexy Mia internally waves the role-play erotic hat in the air. *Found it!*

A meltdown is avoided, thanks to Will, and we continue right on with our fun-filled day. We flash a sideways glance to each other, thinking the same thing, it's best to switch to another of the four theme parks, to change the scenery up from animals. Cody stops crying, but he still sticks on missing his dog. We want to direct his mind away from Caesar, so he can continue having fun.

Our plan works as we stroll through Disney's Hollywood Studios. Mickey and Minnie's Runaway Railway, Toy Story Land, and a bit of Star Wars excitement. This distracts Cody and seems to create an all-new set of giggles. Especially now that we're sporting our mouse ears for headbands and our newly bought Disney T-shirts.

I think my motherhood routine began running smoother once figuring out that redirecting Cody's attention to something else when tantrums arise, works very well. Not all the time, but enough to save my sanity on several occasions.

After a long, but exciting, day, room service feels in order to relax and wind down. Cody eats his chicken nuggets, carrots and ranch, and fries, then conks out on the living room couch. His legs stretch out over our laps. Will and I start to doze, watching T.V. Daily life is busy and tiring, but so is going on vacations. Just a different type of being on-the-go.

Today, my four-foot-two inch son (Cody recently had a growth spurt) has not been the only one enjoying being a kid—his parents are, too. Disney World doesn't only have magic in the light shows and fireworks, but also in turning back time for adults to be kids again.

Going on all the rides, my favorite so far being Remy's Ratatouille Adventure (no surprise, involving a food theme), Will and I are laughing the most we have in months. Playing with Cody's unused Christmas gifts are the last belly-laughing moments I can remember.

Lesson for a better couple's relationship is to play like we are kids. Childhood fun and simplicity is what I find work for great stress relievers shared between the two of us.

Laughter brings people together, married, unmarried, friends and family. And I can't wait to laugh and play again tomorrow. We have four more days to enjoy our childhood years all over again, and create memories with our fun-loving son.

But first, I need to make time for the other adult stress reliever—sex.

Forcing my eyes open from dozing, I think back to Will calming Cody down in the Animal Theme Kingdom Park today. Not only did he look sexy in his worn-out faded jeans, tight muscle black T-shirt (later changed to the Disney shirt), and sexy spiked hair, but he also sends my blood racing with his good fathering moment.

I mentally pull out my imaginary erotic hat from my internal dresser drawer and put it on. "Honey, wake up." I nudge my hot husband beside me. "Let's go in the bedroom, and let Cody rest out here on the couch," I add. My mouth lifts from one side, grinning.

"Oh yes, baby, let's." He appears wide-awake now. He brushes his lips ever so soft against mine, and gets up. He tucks the sprawled out blanket snug around Cody and kisses him on his forehead. Cody's out like a light. Then, Will extends his hand to take mine.

Oh yes, Mia. He's a hot dad! I feel all tingly inside. *Tonight, I'm breaking out the Naughty Nurse outfit that I remembered to pack.*

I give Cody a kiss goodnight and grab Will's outreached hand, leading him into the bedroom for a night of nurses healing and his doctors fixing. Our suitcase has a little something for Will to wear, too. As we make love, the ten o'clock firework show blares in the distance.

Our bedroom drapes are open just enough to see the sparkling lights shooting up into the sky, then trickling down, coloring the darkness of the night outside. Each firework going off creates the exact romantic feel I want.

Almost like a personal, sweet, sexy, and fun, party being made just for the nurse and doctor, who are bringing a new meaning to the medical office, one thrust at a time.

Afterwards, I grin at the thought, lying in bed in pure exhaustion. A small amount of soreness sets in from the roughness I asked for. Let's just say we enjoyed the fireworks excitement to the fullest. I'm barely able to keep my eyes open, once again.

Chapter 32
Never Take Anything from Strangers

Our week's trip flies by way too fast. As the old saying goes; time flies when you're having fun. But we find ourselves back at the airport, like we never left it. Juggling carry-ons and Cody's toys, and my purse that weighs a ton. Moms somehow end up carrying all the family's belongings in her one bag. Sure, my purse starts out with room to spare, but winds up brimming over the top. There's no turning back once that happens.

Disney World's memories—all fantastic. The best part being the banana poop thing was the only embarrassing comment Cody made while on our trip, surprisingly. Which eliminated me having to exit stage right at every corner.

Will and I made the most of our nights, making this the best romantic getaway. The role-play nights I envisioned before leaving—nurse and doctor costumes weren't the only ones I packed. Superwoman and Superman. Also, firefighter and damsel in distress. I was the damsel, of course. Although, I would be a badass firefighter, too.

Role switch for the future, Mia. I'll be the one saving the day for the hot-trapped man. *Sexy Mia rose to attention, mouth parted.*

Last night, I was in a black teddy sleeping soundly on top of the bed, woken by this big strong firefighter rescuing me from a fire threatening the building. Turned out I was even hotter than the hypothetical fire, because my rescuer, A.K.A Will, took me right then and there.

When I stop to think about it, I really do pretend to be someone else a lot. Having different character roles in the bedroom, and my plethora of various imaginary career hats.

Variety is the spice of my life. It makes my world complete, I conclude.

We pick up Caesar on the way home from the airport. Tail wagging so vigorously that he ends up falling once. He gets a good behavior report from my parents; a huge relief for me. Caesar gets into plenty of mischief at home.

Needless to say, I hold my breath that he doesn't do the same when somewhere else. Again, I think it might just be a mom thing, like when Cody waits for Will to go and work, his combative side all of a sudden comes out.

Another two children in one type scenario, if I think about it. Two dogs in one.

Such is life, and motherhood.

Whenever a school break is over, I have the hardest time getting back into the swing of things. Especially when we have such an amazing break. The early school mornings, the daily chores, volunteering, and cleaning up the house in between everything else.

At hotels, housekeepers clean-up for you, and I can't get enough of that. Going out to dinner, or ordering room service, a whole kitchen and front-of-house staff cooks, picks up the dishes, and cleans them. I get used to that all too easily.

Now, I'm back at school, volunteering after an early typical morning of breakfast, clean up, dog duties, clean up, dressing and washing up, clean up. I'm already set in exasperation mode.

"Mia, are you okay?" Mr. Sherman asks, breaking me out of my still-on-vacation trance.

"Oh yes, sorry. I'm trying to get going here with these papers." I don't mean to, but I let out a yawn, not being able to help it.

"I had a hard time motivating myself to get to work this morning. All I did was sleep in over break." He chuckles before adding, "I was checking on you, since I saw you looking out the window for so long."

I hadn't even been aware I was doing that. "Thank you. Once I get started here, I'll be more awake." I smile.

"You're my Teacher Savior too, you know, along with everyone else's." The fifth grade teacher smiles at me from ear to ear. He then turns, returning back to his lesson.

Mr. Sherman had asked the admin staff for a volunteer's help today, specifically me. I'll be in Cody's class after lunch.

"He totally likes you, Mia," Ella had told me one morning during one of our weekly Starbucks breakfast visits. "Mr. Sherman keeps requesting your help, not mine, or any other volunteer who is on the list."

"One time I did get that feeling," I answered honestly. "But, I've always kept it totally professional." My shoulders shrugged up in confusion.

"That's just it, you're the hot mom keeping it professional, business-like woman that he can't have. Men like that sort of stuff." She winked at me. "You underestimate your whole package, Mia." Ella raised her eyebrows.

"Well, I'm married, and I've talked about Will with him several times, so maybe we're reading into all this wrong." I shook my head.

Ella swayed her exotic Egyptian head side to side. "Yep, he wants what he can't have." She giggled, then added, "Heck, you should be flattered, he's hot. Tall, gorgeous black smooth skin, muscles showing through his shirts, and a beautiful smile to boot." She grinned, wide.

I raised one of my eyebrows at her, dubiously.

"Hey, just because I'm married, doesn't mean I don't notice good-looking men." Ella nodded, matter of fact. "Mothers with young children have it all wrong, in my opinion. We do lose ourselves a little with all the responsibilities of raising kids, but not entirely like most moms think."

"What do you mean?" I questioned. Honestly, waiting with bated breath to hear the answer. Anything to make motherhood, especially womanhood, better, I'm all ears.

"Moms think, even though they are in their twenties and thirties, and into their forties, and older, because they are tired all the time, and generally don't have the energy to make themselves up, that their sex appeal is lost. Not so." Ella raised her forefinger in the air to make a point.

"Men find this attractive, especially single men like Mr. Sherman. The empathy and caring toward younger children is nurturing, and a man finds this endearing and basically, hot." She pursed her lips together, widening her large brown eyes. Ella looked up toward the ceiling, nodding playfully.

As I remember our conversation, I still don't think of it that way with appearing attractive.

Homework papers are almost done now. My mind grows increasingly more tired after grading two stacks of thirty stapled packets in each of the piles. I'm ready to go see my little munchkin. The room quickly gets dim as clouds roll in, covering the sun. I glance out the classroom's window.

Cody catches my attention. His class is out at recess. I smile, watching him and all his classmates running and playing ball.

My eyes move off to the side of the playground to an older man walking along the outside of the blacktop fence. A bit scruffy in appearance, wearing a long beige trench coat, which I think to be odd with the warm spring temperature outside. He looks over at all the kids as he's walking, and smiles every now and then.

Children at play are fun to watch, and I smile, seeing the man joyed.

"Last one." A small huff escapes me, closing the last packet, and placing the grading pen down on the table.

Mr. Sherman already finished his lesson with Math. He puts the cap back on the Expo dry erase marker, and smiles in my direction, mouthing the words thank you. I give him a quick smile, and gather my things. Making a glance out the window, I sling my over-stuffed purse onto my shoulder.

Cody's class is still outside, but so is the older man. This time walking along the fence in the opposite direction, watching the kids. He stops every couple of steps. I'm having to squint my eyes to see better pass the glare reflecting off the clouds.

His mouth starts to move, saying something, but what? Who is he talking to? I'm unsure. His arm waves toward the children playing, motioning a few to go over to him. Cody's one of them.

I stand up straight, feeling something horrible in the pit of my stomach. Ms. Dorsey's on the other side of the playground, helping a boy with his light pull-over jacket. The zipper looks to be stuck. Her back faces the older man.

"Mr. Sherman, please come here for a second," I say in his direction. My eyes never move off the man in the trench coat. My tone is urgent and stern.

Mr. Sherman rushes by my side in an instant. "What's wrong?" he asks, alarmed, and leans in to look out the window. Almost too close.

"The man, over there, something feels off." I point out the window in his direction.

Cody and one of his friends walks toward him. Now, he has something in his hand, and tries squeezing it through a hole in the fence.

"Radio Mr. Espinoza, to the kinder playground!" I shout without thinking, and sprint out of the room and down the hall. I need the campus monitor to help. No stranger should be trying to give any child anything.

Cody, I'm coming! Momma Bear, Mia, rises up, and not just for my son, but for all the kids.

"Ella! Ella!" I holler, passing the room she's volunteering in today.

My ears catch the sound of her tennis shoes running down the hall after me and out the door to the playground.

"Hey! What are you doing?" I scream at the man. I'm getting closer. "Cody! Kids! Get away now!"

My feet skid on the pavement, stopping in front of the children. A combination of being out of breath, upset, and scared all at the same time, makes my voice uncontrollably shaky, but it still doesn't waver from being stern.

"I was giving them stickers," he answers in a nonchalant way, then turns on his heel to walk away.

"You can't give children anything without adult consent!" I say, loud enough for him to hear, being he's put a large gap between us now, walking away at a quicker pace from the school.

I drag air into my laboring lungs, not knowing what to exactly say, other than, "Stop!" Mr. Espinoza needs to question him.

He doesn't respond, just walks even faster down the street.

This isn't right! Horror thoughts strike me.

"Mia! What's going on?" Ella asks out of breath, halting to a stop by my side. She looks alarmed, not seeing me like this before.

"The police are here!" Mr. Espinoza runs up with Ms. Dorsey by his side before I can answer Ella.

Sirens blaze around from the front of the school. One police car on one side, one on the other. The man tries to run through a yard across from us, but an officer on foot catches him. The terror is over. The man is in handcuffs, and children are safely scooted inside.

"What quick thinking, Mia. Thank you." Mr. Espinoza hugs me.

Ms. Dorsey wraps her arms around my shoulders and squeezes, tight. "Mia, thank you, too. I didn't notice him." Her voice starts to crack with emotions.

"We just need a statement from you, Mrs. Gaffolo," Officer Randolf tells me while opening his small notebook. We're sitting in the principal's office alongside the principal, assistant principal, and Mr. Espinoza, the campus monitor.

I explain to him the exact timeline of events, in detail. He jots down word for word. Just as Officer Randolf starts to leave, he spins around on his heel. "Ever consider a job in law enforcement?"

The officer's straight-lace expression tells me he's serious.

"I haven't, till now," I half-joked, but still jittery from what happened.

Officer Mia, at the ready. I add a new imaginary hat to my collection. Along with a personalized slogan. *Officer Mia will work right alongside Detective Mia kicking butt and taking names.* I envision me standing proud in a Sherlock Holmes detective outfit alongside another me, looking strict in a police uniform, badge and all.

I end up taking Cody home from school early, needing a break from the environment, and to have a heart to heart talk with my son. He doesn't quite understand why I acted in the way I did.

"Do you know why Mommy was yelling at that man today?" I sit down on the couch with Cody in our living room while he's eating a snack.

"No, but you always say you're kind of odd." He giggles.

This makes me laugh out loud, because he's right. Except I say that only when talking to myself, so he must overhear me. A hand firmly pressed to the forehead moment.

"Well, I yelled at him, because he was a stranger trying to give you and your friends something." I run my hand through Cody's soft brown hair. "You never take anything from a stranger. Okay?"

"He said he was only giving us stickers," he says, looking confused. Stickers seem normal to a six-year-old as being able to accept.

"True, but then he ran from the police, so I don't think they were only stickers he was trying to give you and your friends. Bad people invent crazy things to get to children. To be on the safe side, you never take anything from anyone you don't know, and always tell Mommy, Daddy, and someone that works at the school." I smile sweetly in hopes he semi-understands.

"Okay, deal." Cody reaches out his hand to shake on it. "I promise."

We shake hands and hug. My good boy, and proud mom moment.

The phone rings, startling me. I still haven't shaken the nerves from today's incident.

"Hello," I softly answer.

"Mia. Its Principal Shea," she starts to speak on the other end. "I just got off the phone with Officer Randolf, and you wouldn't believe what they found on those stickers." Her voice sounds nervous.

I instantly get a cold shiver running up and down my spine.

Chapter 33
Graduation Preparation

"LSD. The stickers were laced with the LSD drug," Principal Shea says on the quieter side. In disbelief, no doubt. She continues, "I've never had anything like this happen since I've been a principal or a teacher."

"What!" I practically shout. "I can't believe this. I've heard of this kind of thing happening before, but now—" My words trail off. A large lump of emotions well up in my throat. Tears prick at the corners of my eyes.

"I thank you, Mia, from the bottom of my heart for being so astute, and acting so fast," she tells me before we hang up.

In bed, I cry on Will's shoulder, letting all my emotions from the day out at once. Being a mother is undoubtedly the hardest job in the world. Protecting, scared, worried, happy, playful, sad, mad, and loving, whirl-winding around and around.

"It could have been Cody putting that sticker on his hand." I sob.

"But it wasn't." Will tilts my face up, so I can look into his eyes. "You know why that is?"

"Why?" I breathe out, tears falling down my cheeks.

"Because you are an amazing mom and volunteer." He places his lips on top of mine, and adds, "Plus the Teacher Savior wouldn't let anything happen to anyone." His lips part in a grin.

A laugh escapes me, holding back another sob. He's right.

I am the Teacher Savior! Envisioning myself standing as superwoman, with one small change, there's another me standing there too. Officer Mia.

Feeling a little better, I inch even closer into Will, hugging him tightly. My head nestles in the base of his neck. "You know what the officer said to me before leaving today?" I look up with a slight grin.

His bright green eyes meet the hazel in mine with amusement. "What?"

"He asked if I've ever considered a job in law enforcement."

Wills eyes light up an even brighter green. "Does this mean what I think it means?"

"Yup." I pause to search his gaze. "An officer outfit. I'll buy new black stilettos to go with it."

He exhales a long, and very slow, excited, breath of air. There's an undeniable twinkle in his eyes. I give a slow smile, and say, "I'll hang it right next to my Superhero Teacher Savior outfit."

"Will there be handcuffs?" Will asks. "Oh, please tell me there'll be handcuffs." He kisses my forehead. The sheet draping over our waists catches my attention. It's moving upwards with his growing erection.

My eyes grow wide before saying, "Yes, handcuffs, I think can be arranged." I wink up at him.

We smile at each other and snuggle in love.

***

Months go by without a hitch.

Like the older-creepy-criminal-man thing wouldn't be enough of an event, forever.

Graduation is fast approaching, and Ms. Dorsey is working diligently with the two other kindergarten teachers to put together a song melody for the students to rehearse for the graduation performance. They also ask Ella to help, being she's involved with the performance structure every year.

I'm helping the teachers by arranging the kids in line formation on the stage each afternoon before dismissal. They practice for about thirty minutes for what the teachers are planning, will be a span of two months to rehearse for the ceremony's performance.

"A couple months should be plenty of time to get the four songs down pat. Wouldn't you think?" Ms. Dorsey asks me, standing by my side, watching the student's read off the lyric sheets in their hands. She winces when several of them break into all different songs at different times. Not in unison like instructed to do.

Mr. Cheshire, the school's music teacher, plays the piano, stopping every now and then to make corrections for singing the right song. Mostly lack of being in harmony seems to be the only challenge.

"I think so." I nod, but honestly, unsure of my answer. Sixty children, ages five and six, don't have the most structure in attention span. Which is to be expected. Although, all the students have vastly improved by leaps and bounds since the first day of kindergarten.

Watching Cody singing, or at least attempting to sing, brings tears to my eyes. *He is growing up so fast. Volunteering to help with the graduation ceremony I knew was risky with the possibility of me being a ball of emotions.* The memory of my thoughts warning me comes back.

I decided to do it anyway. A tear falls down my cheek.

"You okay?" Ms. Dorsey asks with a wide smile.

"Yeah, just emotional, that's all," I respond, wiping a stray tear away.

"I totally understand. I've been through this twice with my two kids." She places her arm around my shoulders.

"Oh no, Charlie!" I gasp, having to rush to the stage. One of the boys is starting to break into dance and is about to fall.

"No messing around, Charlie!" Mrs. Jansen, one of the other kindergarten teachers, shouts from the back of the room. "We need to bring this routine together!"

I get to Charlie just in time, but as anyone would've predicted, a few more students begin joining in his dance. And now all three classes get in trouble, and all three teachers lead the students strictly back to their classrooms.

Oh well, tomorrow's a new day. I sigh. A chuckle escapes my mouth.

When arranging the magnets on the whiteboard back in class, I think of how funny it is to go from being emotional to being scared in a nanosecond. Back in the multipurpose room, tears form in my eyes watching Cody prepare for his graduation, but they quickly dry up sprinting over to Charlie to stop him from falling.

Then listening to the teachers upset with many of the students ignoring their instructions, I in turn felt a bit mad. Even at this young age, each boy and girl knows better by now with most of the school year behind them.

The next day, one o'clock rolls around, and we're all back in the multipurpose room, going over each song. This time adding in some hand movements to coincide with the music and lyrics, per Ella's outline.

"Guys, stop giggling," I whisper, standing on stage at the end of one of the rows. "You need to pay attention."

The few students who are laughing stop and face front.

Great! They listened to me. Proud Teacher Savior moment.

Another girl then breaks out into a burst of laughter, but holds a hand over her mouth. I can tell she isn't meaning to laugh, but she apparently finds something funny. And the source of comedy is not going away. A couple boys also try to suppress their fit of giggles.

I scan each row of students, but nothing seems to be out of the ordinary. The teachers in front of the stage don't notice as they concentrate on teaching the lines of the second song, On My Way. The first song's mastered, and proudly. Ella chooses Kindergarten Rock to start off the performance.

"Gets the crowd pumped and energized for the whole ceremony," she says, and sways her hips, mimicking a dance move.

Each teacher looks up once in a while from her music sheet, but not long enough to see the giggling. Mr. Cheshire, playing the piano, is also right by their side, so the giggles are being drowned out by the music.

Again, a different child starts in. *What is going on here?* I question, completely puzzled. The only thing now to do is walk between each row. Seeing if I can spot the culprit causing this laughter. Any out of the ordinary movements or chatter will tip me right off.

Top row, nothing.

Second to the top row, nothing.

But when I get to the third row down, a pungent smell hits me like a ton of bricks.

Farts! Smells like someone literally pooped their pants. And it's vile.

I mentally put on an imaginary HazMat suit.

I hear a few soft chuckles toward the end of the row, but the child can't be seen behind his or her classmates. I see only a few low-waving gestures being made from a tiny kindergartner. One foot in front of the other, I have to be careful squeezing between the rows of children, so I don't tumble and fall, like Charlie almost had.

Cody! My eyes grow to the size of small dinner plates when I zero in on the comical child. Pursing my lips tight in a thin line, I feel mad and embarrassed all at the same time.

Cody is making a pee-yew motion, then waving his hand to try and spread the fart smell. He freezes in an instant when he finally notices me.

"Mia, is everything okay?" Ms. Dorsey asks, calling up from the front of the stage.

Maybe she hasn't taken notice of the laughter from earlier, but now with an adult standing in the midst of the sea of children, she's noticing now. Mr. Cheshire stops playing the piano, and automatically, we can hear a pin drop. The faint escape of chuckles is clear.

"Everything okay?" she asks, again, then looks around at who's making noise. "Shh!" She holds her index finger over her mouth.

I freeze in place like an outlaw is holding me up. I want to run, feeling guilty that it's my child causing the commotion. "Uh, yes," I stutter, as Cody's face goes from an expression of *oh no, I just got caught,* to an, *oopsie, I made a mess,* look. "I need to borrow Cody for a minute," I think fast to answer. Then take his hand to lead him to the nearest bathroom.

Ms. Dorsey nods, then says, "Alright, the rest of us, eyes straight, and continue where we left off." She holds her hands up, ready to cue the kids with music.

"Cody, what were you doing?" I start, shrugging his pants down to do an underpants check.

He knows he's in trouble.

"I was farting a lot and wanted my friends to smell them. I like sharing," he then confesses. "I forced out some, and—"

I interrupt him, getting angry. "And poop came out instead. Oh, Cody, it's a mess."

Light-brown pudding-consistency sits in his briefs.

"You need to listen to the teachers, and not fool around," I say sternly. "Now look. I don't have an extra pair of underwear for you to change into."

"I'm sorry, Mom." Cody tilts his head down toward the bathroom floor.

All of a sudden, I feel bad for him. He had only been thinking about acting silly, and not meaning for anything to come out. "Let's just learn from this. Okay?"

"Okay," he agrees, but in a glum way.

"I'll tell Ms. Dorsey we need to go home early. But how are you going to sit down in the car?" I internally scan the car for any possible thing that we can use as a barrier between Cody's butt and the car seat.

Towels! I remember. *I have those extra towels in the trunk from when I brought Caesar to the dog park the other day.* A sense of relief overcomes me.

I know I forgot them in there, which I normally don't do. Dog park towels go straight to the wash when we get home. That day, in particular, had been extra busy, so naturally, I got sidetracked.

From this afternoon at graduation practice, I believe Cody learned a lesson about forcing out a fart, and that it might end badly. And I learn a lesson to always keep an extra set of towels in the car, and possibly a couple pairs of underwear, just in case. This will make possible future hiccups better for me, simultaneously saving my motherhood routine for the day.

There's quite a clean-up when we get home, needing to get Cody in the shower first and foremost. Two loads of laundry have to be done—one with Cody's clothes, and the other with the soiled towels from the car seat. The cover also has to be taken off the base of the seat.

And I'm doing a third load for that. The poop smell penetrates right through the towels and onto the cover. The car seat base even smells. A total defragmentation needs to happen, but for the likes of poop instead of the meaning for a computer.

Who knew acting funny can create such a stench.

Cody practices the graduation performance routine every day when he comes home. Not because I tell him to, but because he wants to. He's having so much fun, and has a sense of pride with being given such a tall order to fill. The ceremony performance is the biggest task for the kindergarten school year, and the most responsibility they've had in school.

The morning of the graduation comes up in a flash. Through all the rehearsals, the kids learn all four songs and the moves to go along with them.

"I'm not going to cry. I'm not going to cry," I chant, facing my reflection in the bathroom mirror.

Watery eyes start to happen. *Way to go, Mia. Haven't you noticed yet that when you tell yourself not to cry, you do the exact opposite and cry.* I admonish myself for not remembering that one small detail.

I take a tissue and dry each eye, and put eye drops in before fixing my makeup. Clear Eyes always has a way of not only eliminating red eyes, but also preventing them, for a bit anyway. It'll be long enough to last till after the formalities of awards and diplomas.

I make every attempt to void my head of all thoughts, and keep a steady focus on getting ready. Thankfully, Cody's already in school, and isn't seeing me emotional before the ceremony begins. He never likes to see me cry, and gets worried. He protects his momma. I want him to only think about the songs, and the cues he needs to remember for when certificates are handed out.

"Hi. It's eleven o'clock. You almost ready?" Will asks, peeking around the bathroom corner.

"Yep, be right there." I feign a smile.

"You alright?" He questions with concern in his expression.

The Clear Eyes worked. Why is he asking me this? I grow slightly annoyed, because if something is bothering me, and I'm not crying about it, but if Will asks me what's wrong, or are you okay—*I cry.*

As if on cue, the tears pour out. Right there with Clear Eyes in one hand, mascara in the other. *Like they'll do any good now,* I think, putting them both down on the counter a little harder than I want to. *Why do I always get so emotional? Toughen up, Mia!*

Will walks over and wraps his arms around me. "I know, this is hard for you." I turn to face him, nodding. He then adds, "Hey, I bet it's hard for most moms, superb mothers. You're not alone."

"Why aren't you emotional about this whole graduation-from-kindergarten thing?" I slant my head to the side, genuinely interested in his answer.

"I think fathers just handle things differently with emotions. Mothers take compassion and empathy to a whole new level." He pauses, and his piercing-green eyes twinkle as if in admiration. Then adding, "Plus, mothers carry their child for nine months, that bond must have something to do with the emotions."

I'm sure he's right.

"Hey, if being a mother was so easy, fathers would do it." Will grins down playfully at me.

I can't help but chuckle, not just because it's true, but also because I remember Ella making that exact same statement at our emergency mom's meeting a few months back. I repeat quite a few lines from *Golden Girls,* but Ella's line from the show is my favorite though. Will knows this.

"Come on, let's go." Will takes my hand to lead me out of the bathroom. I grab the Clear Eyes and mascara on the way out.

Before walking out the door, I also grab my imaginary large number-one foam finger. *Can't forget that to cheer Cody on.*

But I have an actual present with a stick number-one balloon taped to it. Figuring that will be a bit more discreet than a real giant foam finger. And less embarrassing for Cody, so I mentally bring the giant finger along instead of physically bringing it.

He has come to the stage of saying things like, "Mom, stop it, you're embarrassing me." When he sees his friends watching me give him a kiss before he heads into school.

I'm embarrassing him? I often think. *I couldn't even begin to count the multitude of humiliating moments he's put me through.*

All part of growing up, I guess. I went through that as a child, too.

But he's not getting out of hugs and kisses today with graduating. I nod sharply to myself in the passenger seat of the car.

"We'll be at school a little earlier. We can get good seats," Will states, driving off.

"We actually have our seats already in the front with Ella and Jamal. She had organized the ceremony's music and dance moves, so the kindergarten teachers asked them to attend as well," I say, trying to attempt a possible makeup fix in the mirror on the sun visor.

"Oh, excuse me, I forgot I was married to the Teacher Savior." He winks in my direction, then looks back at the road, adding, "You and Ella sure do a lot for the school. They are lucky to have you both."

I smile widely over at him in appreciation.

Chapter 34
Graduation Ceremony

The multipurpose room is flooded with parents, grandparents, guardians, and other close family members invited to come.

"Ella!" I wave through the crowd.

She and Jamal are already sitting in their seats in the front row, our seats are right next to them.

"Hey! It's a packed house." Ella laughs. "Par-tay." She twirls her hand in the air.

I can tell her mascara is smudged at the corner of her eyes. She must have been crying a little, too.

"The arrangement you came up with will make this a party for sure." I smile at her and then turn to Jamal. "Hey, how are you?"

"You know, hustlin' as usual. And tryin' to keep this one from cryin'." Jamal motions to Ella.

She nudges him playfully. "Well, this brings back memories from when Marcus graduated kindergarten. I can't help it."

"True." He nods, and folds his arms over his chest. He glances over my shoulder at Will. "Will, we gotta get these two toughened up." He laughs, as Will nods in agreement.

Jamal's voice is deep, and so is his laugh. He may look tough on the outside—tall, muscular, stern expressions mostly, and husky overall, but he's the nicest person on the inside. Jamal is kind of like a big teddy bear.

"Oh, that is sure my tough teddy bear," Ella will say adoringly when talking about him.

Ella rolls her eyes in my direction.

"I'd be on board with that." Will smirks at me.

"Shh! Here they come," I whisper.

In single-file formation, the kids walk in calmly. Ms. Dorsey is leading the three kindergarten classes from the front of the line.

For now, my tears are completely gone. Maybe it's the excitement, or the wondering if all will go as planned. Or maybe it's hoping Cody won't be one to act up and disturb the whole performance. I just never know. I really don't want to break out my imaginary disappearing hat. Not now, and not on such an important occasion.

Yesterday, we had a talk about proper behavior at the ceremony.

"Cody, no funny business at graduation. Okay?" I told him.

"Okay," he agreed very upbeat.

Cody looked excited for the upcoming day, as he should be. I was also thrilled, but a serious reminder needed to happen ever since that passing gas rehearsal time.

"That means no acting funny on the stage to get your friends to laugh, especially no forced farting." I felt the last part would particularly be important to remind him of.

Not wanting to do extra cleaning aside, I didn't want him to ruin the ceremony for everyone else. Cody has always been a good-hearted boy, but the comedian in him wanted to take over a lot. And not necessarily at the right time.

"No farting?" He questioned, looking up. He appeared in deep thought. "What happens if I have to fart? Do I hold it in? If I do, then a blaster will come out when I can't hold it anymore."

Only my son, and probably every other six-year-old boy, would think of stuff like that.

"If you feel you have to fart, Cody, then that's different. My point is no forced farts." An emphasis needed to be put on forced, since that's my main point in this conversation.

"Oh, that's a relief." He sighed. "I thought I was going to have to hold gas in till the end."

"You won't even have time to think of that anyway with concentrating on the songs and moves. Then you'll go right into awards and diplomas. You'll be too occupied with remembering what you're supposed to do."

My explanation seemed to do the trick, except I could tell he was thinking of something else. I could always tell when my pensive son has something swirling in his mind.

"What is it? I can tell the wheels are turning, Cody." My eyes widened, *imploring him to confess.*

"Boogers. What if I need to pick my nose on stage?" He smirked.

I pressed my hand firmly to my forehead. What is it with him and farting, *and picking his nose? If a general passer-by heard him talk, they would be grossed out. Not to mention wonder what that boy's mom must be teaching him. In that case, my imaginary disappearing hat would be shoved right back on.*

"I have an idea. Ask Ms. Dorsey if you can use the bathroom right before going to the multipurpose room. Grab a tissue, and you can pick your nose, so you won't feel you have to do it at graduation. Wash your hands, and return back to class. How's that for a plan?" I waited, watching him think it over.

"Good! That could work." Cody rose his index finger in the air.

"Mr. Cheshire, we're ready." Ms. Dorsey turns to the music teacher, signaling for the music to start.

He starts playing, and so the performance commences. The kindergartners are as cute as can be. All the hard work put in from everybody is paying off in utter perfection, and cuteness. In the audience, the adults and older siblings dance in their seats. Even Will and Jamal are moving to the beat. The show seems to fly by, ending as quickly as it begins.

The part I both look forward to and dread at the same time (for fear of uncontrollable waterworks), approaches—handing out the certificates.

Ms. Dorsey calls each student's name, one at a time, to get his or her diploma. My eyes begin to water, until what I hope won't happen, happens. Cody puts a finger in his nose, digging. Right in front of everyone. I cringe with closed eyes. My only thought was to run toward the exit door in the back of the room.

I reopen my eyes to see him wiping his finger on an antibacterial wipe from the travel packet I keep in his backpack. He must have thought to bring it with him.

"Cody Gaffolo," Ms. Dorsey calls him next.

He darts off in the other direction to throw the wipe in the trash before accepting the diploma. Ms. Dorsey motions to him to get back quickly. She lets out a nervous chuckle in the mic, and gives a half-smile to the audience.

All eyes are on the appearing-to-be-out-of-line boy. Then she adds to fill the silence till he gets to her, "My students will never litter. Good job, Cody."

He takes his diploma, and we clap, loudly, whistling for him that he's now a kindergarten graduate. I find myself to be a combination of extremely happy, sad, and wanting to vanish all at once. Plus I don't cry, mostly due to the fact of the nose-picking moment and it distracting me.

Apparently, Cody did not go to the bathroom beforehand like I told him to. I blow out a big huff.

We have opportunities to take pictures afterwards with the kindergarten teachers and administration staff on both the red carpets we set up. One red carpet flows along the stairs of the stage, where each student needs to walk down after accepting their certificates.

The second red carpet lay as we exit the multipurpose room and down the main hallway of the school. Gold ropes are lining both sides of the carpet, like at the Oscars, except the spotlight is for young children.

"What a year!" Ms. Dorsey exclaims, standing next to me. We both watch Principal Shea taking pictures with each graduate.

"Yes. It has been eventful in all ways, and many great things happened." I smile in her direction.

"Absolutely," Ms. Dorsey says before running to pick up an award a girl drops, but doesn't notice.

Will and Jamal are standing off to the side in a deep conversation about sports. Making sure not to be within the gold ropes, or on the red carpet with all the crowding. Ella's in the middle of it all, helping take photos of the graduates for the Hall of Fame case in the main office. There are only two weeks left of school, so pictures can at least be displayed for that length of time.

"Hi, Mia." Mr. Sherman walks up and stands by my side, catching me off guard. "Congratulations to Cody." His perfect white smile shines brightly at me.

"Oh, hi. Thank you." I smile back while watching Cody move up to take a picture with the principal and Ms. Dorsey.

"My kids are at specials right now, so I thought I would pop down to see the graduates all dressed up. I love this time." Mr. Sherman looks at the little boys and girls with their grad caps on.

"Oh, that is nice. The ceremony was great." I motion into the multipurpose room. The janitors are in full swing, cleaning up and folding chairs ready to stack them. I conveniently left out the part of Cody picking his nose in front of everybody.

"I bet." He nods. "Well, I have to get back to my classroom. Glad I got to see you."

"Have a good rest of the day," I say only that, and smile. That last part of what Mr. Sherman says feels off, so I decide to skip over it.

After the graduation ceremony, some family members and friends come over to our house and celebrate. The living room's decor has a few simple decorations for Cody's milestone. Several hors d'oeuvres are set up on the kitchen island in fancy serving dishes. Flutes of champagne for the adults, and flutes of cider for the kids, stand next to the platters.

"What was the whole Mr. Sherman thing about?" Ella coyly asks me at our small post-graduation get-together. "I saw him standing next to you." The corner of her mouth pulls to one side.

"Nothing, really." She raises her right eyebrow at my answer, not satisfied. I decide to add an explanation with the coaxing of her eyes, "Well, he said his students were at specials, and he wanted to see the kinders all dressed up for their special day, so he walked over."

Ella goes back to looking normal. "That's nice."

She's my best friend, so I continue in full disclosure, "One thing he said seemed kind of odd though." Glancing around, I see that no one's within earshot. Everyone mostly is in the living room, while Ella and I talk in the kitchen.

"No one's listening. Go on," she prompts, as eager as any girl about to receive gossip. Her chin rests on her intertwined fingers, elbows propping her up. Both large gold hoop earrings sway back and forth as Ella situates even more to concentrate on what I'm about to say.

I roll my eyes at her eagerness, and sigh. "It's not that big, so calm down."

She laughs. "Come on, you know what I already think, so I'm just waiting for affirmation that I'm right about him. Spill," Ella orders.

"Alright." A giggle escapes me. "Before Mr. Sherman walked away, he said that he was glad he got to see me. Sort of an odd thing to say, but maybe not. I do volunteer for him quite a bit."

"Confirmation right there." She nods her head up and down, very pleased with herself. An *ah-ha* expression shows on her face. "Yes, he requests help a lot, asking the admin to check if *you're* available. Mr. Sherman came down looking for *you*, not the graduates, as he first said."

"You think?" She nods yes to my question. "I did get a funny feeling, because no other teachers from other grade levels came to see the kids."

"Exactly, Mia. He totally has the hots for you." She chuckles, louder than she should have. I wave my hands, quieting her down. She adds, "Take it as a compliment, that's all."

"I guess, but I think next year, if Mr. Sherman asks for me to volunteer for him, I'll tell the office staff I can't. It might be a compliment for me, but I don't want to give him the wrong idea by continuing to be in his classroom. Besides, I want to concentrate on Cody's teacher, and his grade level teachers from now on, not other grade's tasks."

"That's a good idea, but I have had fun contemplating if I was right about him liking you." She winks one of her large brown eyes at me. Her thick dark eyeliner makes her look even more like an Egyptian Goddess today.

"Well, now you know, so the fun's over." I chuckle, and take another sip of my champagne.

Ella shrugs. "I did enjoy using my imaginary detective hat too. The one you suggested me to use sometimes."

"I suggested that for Marcus's situations though." I laugh.

"Dual purpose, Mia. I needed some detective work for Mr. Sherman just the same. I put it on to link together clues about him." My lips curl up to one side in a dubious expression as she adds, "Those imaginary hats really work, by the way."

"I told you."

We grin knowingly at each other. I'm positive she's thinking right along with me about the personal slogan we share between us. *Two moms on a mission to figure out motherhood solutions, one imaginary hat at a time.*

Chapter 35
Field Trip Fears

"Mia, you aren't the only one that can go on field trips, you know," Audrey says to me just before leaving our post-grad get-together. Her tone drips with annoyance.

"What are you talking about, Audrey?" I ask her, generally confused, since this is straight out of the blue.

"I saw you on the chaperone list for Shark Reef." She pauses, about to say something else, but instantly closes her mouth.

I tilt my head to the side, thinking, *that is a confidential list. Ms. Dorsey always hides her chaperone papers along with other private school information in her locked drawer.*

"Um, Audrey, *I* don't even know if I'm going. None of us parents received an email. How do *you* know?" This is a question that needs to be asked. I can sense this particular thing has been bothering her, from the way she's been acting lately. Only now I know the reason behind her actions.

"Never mind, but there are other moms who would like to go to Shark Reef, just so you know." And with those being her last words, she turns, smiles widely at Will, who's standing next to me, and leaves.

"What was that all about?" He asks me, closing the door behind her. "So what if the teacher picked you as a chaperone. What's the big deal?"

"I've told Ms. Dorsey to ask other parents before asking me who wants to go on field trips, because I'm with the kids so much as it is." I tap my finger to my chin. "I think Audrey must have been snooping through Ms. Dorsey's private drawers."

"But she usually keeps one in particular locked with all private information in it, including chaperone lists. Maybe she had forgotten to lock it when Audrey had volunteered in Cody's and Esmerelda's class yesterday."

"She could be jealous you're at school so much, and thinking the teacher might be playing favorites." Will kisses my forehead, and adds, "Or that we had reserved front row seats. That was definitely pretty cool, and she might be envious of that."

"Maybe, or she might have been trying to act tough in front of you. Audrey flirts with you, you know." I wolfishly grin.

"Does she? I've never noticed." He honestly looks at me, puzzled.

"It's a woman thing to pick up on those type of slight gestures." I hoist myself up on my tiptoes to give him a kiss. "That's a compliment though. I know I have a hot husband."

He laughs, kissing me back. "I thought you two were friends."

"We are. I mean, I was the one who organized a painting party for her house when her kids got in the arts and crafts drawer, taking the paint, and turning white walls into a rainbow of colors." I shrug.

"Don't let it bother you. You can't please everybody, except—"

Jamal interrupts Will, "Sorry, but your dog got into the chicken skewers, and is eatin' them, and throwin' them in the air."

I don't hesitate with taking off running toward the kitchen, eyes as big as saucers. Sure enough, there's Caesar hopping up onto his hind legs, grabbing the chicken after every hop.

"Caesar, no!" My stern voice scares him to a halt. He darts away, but not before taking another skewer in his teeth.

I run after him. Will tries to corner him. But Caesar is lightning fast. Cody teeters back and forth on the couch, laughing as he watches us move this way and that. He laughs so hard, he propels himself backward on the couch. What started out as a fancy, relaxing party, is ending up in a huge fiasco.

After the last guest leaves, I begin cleaning up the spots of sauce drippings from the chicken skewers. When Caesar defiantly went running all over the house with them, he made a mess. He's lying in his crate, looking at what I'm doing. I'm sure a show for him with me spraying, scrubbing, and talking to myself.

"It's either Cody or Caesar creating a scene. Why can't I just have one week of them both being good? *Why?*" I question out loud, trying to keep my temper and sanity in check.

At least Will is putting Cody to bed, and keeping me from that argument.

"In your bed, Cody. Cody!" Will shouts and runs after his small pattering feet down the hall.

A giggle escapes, me gazing upwards at the second floor, knowing *he's* now dealing with what I go through every night, trying to get Cody to sleep in his own bed.

Eyes front, Mia. You want to get done at midnight? I move my attention back to the task at hand, repositioning my imaginary maid's hat. I focus back on the stained carpet. Back to scrubbing. *Ugh, just what I want to be doing.*

***

Friday morning is like all others with our school morning ritual, except today is our class field trip to Shark Reef. The largest tanks in Las Vegas are right in the Mandalay Bay hotel, displaying many different species of sharks and other fish.

Several random big lizards and birds I hear are there too. Mandalay Bay's one of the most popular hotels in Las Vegas, partly because of Shark Reef. I've been wanting to go for a long time, but haven't thus far. Needless to say, today is thrilling for me and the kids. Of course, the kids are excited, but mostly me.

Ms. Dorsey ends up choosing me as one of the two chaperones to go. Although, I already knew, since Audrey let the cat out of the bag at the party last week. The other chaperone is a mom by the name of Sasha. Cody and her son, Ivan, are friends, and she seems very nice.

Even though we don't hang out outside of school, I see her on campus once in a while, and we exchange small talk. Sasha's always pleasant, and frankly, I'm glad it's her going to Shark Reef, and not Audrey.

Why couldn't I grow several more inches, have long spidery legs, and develop an exotic look? My envious inner goddess thinks whenever I run into her.

She's a tall drink of Russian water with the natural confidence I would expect, but with a soft approach. Sasha has dark-blue eyes, shiny blonde hair, with fair flawless skin. She told me that she's an emergency room nurse, and works constantly, and is exhausted on her days off.

And who can blame her with such an important, high-stress job. We try coordinating play dates for Cody and Ivan, but they don't ever seem to work out with her schedule, so we stopped trying to arrange them. Not that Sasha doesn't want a play date. She likes our son's friendship just as much as I do.

Choosing her as the other chaperone for such a big field trip, I think, is very smart on Ms. Dorsey's part. Sasha will keep the kids behaving and together. Whereas, Audrey is a bit all over the place.

As I finish brushing my teeth, I think back to this Monday.

I only volunteered for a couple of hours in Cody's class, and when I was about to leave, Ms. Dorsey asked to speak to me outside for a minute. I gathered my belongings and followed her out of the classroom and into the hallway. She made sure to be out of earshot of the kids.

My initial reaction sprung up inside me, thinking I was getting in trouble for something. I started feeling flustered. Jitters rose in panic mode. My cheeks felt flushed in a couple shades of red. As I walked out of the room behind Ms. Dorsey, one main thought came to mind—my diversion tactic.

Pushing the papers on the floor to avoid me laughing has been way overdone. She knows what I'm up to by now, and knows that one of the kids did something they shouldn't have. And instead of disciplining, I laugh, and mostly out of context. So, I hide under the table. Now, she's going to call me out on that! *I shuddered.*

Again, I've never been good under laughter pressure, or dealing with humiliation in any way.

"Do you know anything about someone going through my confidential school drawer?" She turned to me in the hallway and whispered.

Relief struck me, knowing I wasn't in trouble as I had thought. I considerably relaxed.

"What do you mean? Did someone break in it?" I asked, confused, but not for long. Audrey!

Audrey didn't come to our last mom get-together. I just thought she had been upset about the chaperone thing after leaving the party. I figured it would eventually blow over. Still, a weird feeling in the pit of my stomach told me Audrey's snide remarks were more than that.

"Yes, the lock was bent, and my papers were not how I always keep them." She looked worried, especially knowing she kept all the student's private information in that drawer.

I stood in front of her, squirming, having an internal struggle with myself. I didn't know if I should do the right thing and tell Ms. Dorsey what Audrey told me last week, and that I think she broke in the drawer.

Do I rat my friend out? I know it was her.

You have to tell her, Mia, *my good conscience spoke up.* If she were a real friend, and an upstanding person, she wouldn't break into a teacher's private drawer.

"Audrey," I finally said. "I think it was her who broke into your drawer."

She shook her head as if remembering an unpleasant memory. "Audrey and Ishani helped me one day last week with organizing my boards in the back of the room. A particularly busy day, and I didn't notice my drawer had been tampered with until right before going home."

I didn't interject, just listened. Piecing together what she revealed with how I'd been seeing Audrey act.

"I reported it to Principal Shea right away, changed the lock, and haven't asked Audrey or Ishani back to volunteer since. I wanted to wait and talk to you first, hearing your thoughts. They both were pleasant enough that day. Audrey a little over pleasant, almost in a snarky way. How do you know it was her?" Ms. Dorsey asked.

"I had a small post-graduation party at my house, and just before Audrey left, she told me you picked me as one of the chaperones for Shark Reef." I paused, gauging Ms. Dorsey's reaction. "And she seemed really upset about it. Briefly, I wondered how she knew, none of us knew, but I thought maybe in conversation, you might have mentioned it to her. I'm putting two and two together now."

She placed her hands down firmly on her hips. "I'm so disappointed!" She exclaimed, glancing over at the walls with all the kids work displayed. "You just never know. Well, she can't be trusted."

"Audrey didn't come to our last mom's group meeting. Now that I'm thinking about it, she's probably distancing herself knowing what she did."

Ms. Dorsey straightened up, and smoothed out her floral-print dress. "That's a shame. Now I know her true colors. This will have to be addressed by Principal Shea."

She smiled, patted my arm, and walked back in the classroom. I repositioned my purse over my shoulder and walked down the hall, shaking my head.

Being a mother has a whole other dynamic than just worrying about raising children—it's dealing with other moms too. Some act as though we're in the Mom Olympic games; competing for a metal. Only about the status with them, *Detective Mia realized.*

I walked out of school solemn, ready to have a nice distraction playing with Caesar.

"Done," I say, tucking my toothbrush and lotions neatly in my bathroom drawer. I dress in blue jean shorts and a plain black tank top with wide shoulder straps. Ready for a fun-filled field trip day.

I know I'll be gone till school is over, so I decide on taking Caesar to my parents for a small field trip of his own. He loves going to their house, like from our Disney World vacation. My dad spoils him with treats, and my mom plays ball with him nonstop in the backyard. For a Dalmatian, a lot of playing is basic requirement 101, and the constant game of fetch does him a world of good.

In single-file, each student lines up, waiting for the buses to come. Most are being good, some wiggle side to side in excitement. I call that having ants in your pants. To be expected for this age group, even I have ants in my shorts, anticipating seeing sharks and the mysteriousness of the ocean.

Taking me completely off guard, one of the girls sprints out of line. In a flash, the student appears to be going AWOL.

"Syiriah, get back here!" I take off running after her without a second thought.

Mrs. Jansen closes in behind me.

"Syiriah, stop!" She yells after her.

Syiriah has nowhere to go, but in circles around the enclosed blacktop. She's running at top speed. A flashback of Cody on his first day of school hits me.

"The sharks will eat me!" Syiriah screams over her shoulder. Her sprint gets faster. Long braids sway side to side in the midst of her rush.

"Stop, right now!" I finally catch up, and reach out to grab her hand, stopping her.

"No, I don't want to go! I don't want to go!" She kicks and screams with me picking her up.

"They won't eat you, honey. The sharks are all kept securely in tanks, confined to an area." I softly pat her back, and add, "It's okay."

She visibly calms down by the time Mrs. Jansen gets to us.

"What's wrong? Syiriah, you can't run off like that!" Mrs. Jansen exclaims out of breath. She drags air into her lungs.

"I know, I'm sorry." Syiriah starts crying, and tears fall down her cheeks. "I don't want the sharks to eat me, that's why."

I sympathetically smile at the teacher. Mrs. Jansen transforms from being angry to empathetic, realizing Syiriah isn't trying to be defiant, she is just plain scared.

"Sweetheart, you're looking at the sharks through very thick glass. They are completely enclosed, and can't survive out of water anyway." Mrs. Jansen takes Syiriah's hand, and I place her standing back on the ground.

"But *Jaws* eats people." She looks up at her teacher. "I just saw the movie."

My eyes widen, staring at Mrs. Jansen, who's in the process of shaking her head in disbelief.

"That's an awful scary movie for you to be watching, in my opinion. *Jaws* is fiction. Remember we talked about fiction verses non-fiction in class?"

Syiriah nods, appearing satisfied with knowing *Jaws* is fiction. We walk back around the building, and just in time. The buses are arriving.

Cody steps out of line to greet his classmate. "What's wrong?" He asks.

"I don't want the sharks to eat me," Syiriah answers, a little sad, even though she appears to feel better from what I and Mrs. Jansen told her.

"Don't worry, I'll protect you." Cody takes her hand, and leads Syiriah back in line.

My heart melts like butter in this very moment. All the running and screaming suddenly vanishes from my nerves.

My boy. I admire with a wide grin.

Chapter 36
Shark Reef

A Shark Reef employee greets us as soon as we get off the buses. There to brief everyone on the mini presentation they've set up for our kindergartners. The man leads us into a room with several large round tables and multiple chairs set up around each one.

Tanks of all sizes lined the room's walls. A small stage takes up the entire length of the room up in front. A few more employees that are dressed in blue jumpers with the Shark Reef logo printed on them stand to the side. The man walking us in must be the one in charge. He's in a beige jumper with multiple badges sewn on, on top of the Shark Reef logo one.

I vaguely notice he can't keep his eyes off Sasha. Who can blame him? She's hot, with this kind of domineering look, making her that much more alluring.

"Hello everybody, I'm Todd. Please take a seat. We have a short activity and presentation planned to give you an overview of Shark Reef. Then I will give you a mini tour explaining all these tanks in the room." Todd pauses to motion around him.

"And I'll explain what creatures are inside each one." He smiles, then goes on to explain proper Shark Reef expected behavior, stopping to smile in Sasha's direction every now and then.

The three teachers, Sasha, and myself, walk around the tables during Todd's speech, scooting in children's seats properly. The students are being really good, listening to him. No outspoken, or odd, behavior *yet*.

I wonder if Sasha's presence has anything to do with the kid's good manners. She even makes me feel like I need to be on my best behavior, too. *That's a stretch in itself, Mia.* I smirk.

I imagine myself crawling under one of the tables if a child, mainly Cody, says something embarrassing. Sasha will march right over to me. Watching her Converse tennis shoes come closer, I crouch down more so on the floor, hoping she won't see me.

"Mia, stop it!" She'll whisper loudly in her stern Russian accent, being we are in a meeting room type venue. "Get up, and get a backbone!"

Of course, her intentions aren't to be mean, but I know her to be blunt, and she'll feel as if she will be giving me sound advice.

She would be, Mia, Teacher Savior me speaks up. *It won't hurt to be less skittish and less afraid of what others think if something should go awry.*

I'm quirky, that's all. I can't imagine changing my ways overnight. Although, a few days with strict Sasha might just be the push I need.

"And that concludes our activity," Todd announces and looks out over the many tables of kindergartners. "Any questions before heading in there?" He asks, and makes a quick glance to each teacher, me, and Sasha. Holding his gaze a bit longer on the Russian Goddess.

We shake our heads and gather the kids by each class. Putting them in single-file formation, we head into our Shark Reef journey.

"Are you sure there's no *Jaws* in here?" Syriah whispers to me, entering the main aquarium room. It's a massive space with 360-degree views of sharks swimming around us; overhead on the other side of the glass ceiling, beneath us under the glass floor, and on all sides, sharks glide through the water.

Hammerheads, Nurse Sharks, Angel Sharks, and others I don't recognize. Cody's sea creature shows teach me about ocean life and everything involved, teaching me natural phenomena's I wouldn't dream about in my wildest dreams.

"Yes, I'm sure." I smile at her, feeling this can be a great teaching moment, so I bring her over to sit beside me on a bench. "Here's a fun fact. *Jaws* is a Great White shark in the movie, right?"

"Right." Syriah looks up at me with big chocolate-brown eyes. She's intent on listening.

"That is a real type of shark, even though the movie is one hundred percent fiction in the story line. However, there is no *Jaws*, he's made up. Also Great White sharks cannot be held in captivity, like here in an aquarium tank. They need to be in the wide-open ocean, free to swim and hunt for their food."

I can tell I have her complete attention. "Great Whites are the best hunters out of all the sharks, but they don't go after humans. They eat other fish, seals, sea turtles, etc. Does that make sense?"

"Yes." Syiriah nods, then adds, "I want to see a Great White now." She covers her mouth, giggling.

Good job, Mia. I cheer, turning frightened Syiriah around to being eager to learn more about these wondrous creatures.

I see Cody walking along the glass walls of the tanks, taking it all in, especially entering the tunnel with sharks swimming right overhead. This is his wheelhouse of knowledge and hobbies, and why he hadn't minded comforting Syiriah back at school.

He's not afraid with knowing everything he does. But, I also don't let him watch *Jaws*. The movie probably won't bother him anyway. Boys think gore and fighting is so cool. While most girls sit back squinting and cringing at the sights. This is the main reason why teenage boys will take a girl they like to watch a horror movie on their date.

As the murders happen, chase scenes ensue, and blood breaks out, girls will move closer to the guy sitting next to them. Prime opportunity for their date to place his arm over her shoulders, and get close.

The Stingray Feed is about to begin, and this seems to excite the kiddos most. The touch pool, as Shark Reef calls it, is gigantic, taking up a huge space. Apparently, we get to pet horseshoe crabs as well as see the stingrays get fed. I have to say I'm a bit curios how this all works.

As much as I feel like a kid with experiencing these new adventures, I need to remember the task at hand—chaperoning. No complaints here. I think that with this extra treat of such an adventurous field trip, the boys and girls are too mesmerized to act out, making my job easier. Even the Russian Goddess is smiling and carefree.

"Mia, have you been here before?" Sasha moves next to me.

I seriously can't get enough of her accent. Makes me want to go to Russia, or take up learning the Russian language, or simply be more confident in myself—do something related to Russia.

"No, I haven't. Have you?" I glance over at her after a horseshoe crab swims underneath my hand. I'm giddy, chuckling at the slick sensation of the water creature.

"No. I try to find the time to do these type of things, but always seem to get pulled back to work." She sighs. "We weren't even able to coordinate that play date for Cody and Ivan, because of my schedule being mostly at nighttime. I sleep during the day." I nod, understanding, as Sasha continues, "But in

Russia, we dedicate our life to work, and doing a good job at it. So, I know no different."

"How long have you lived here?" I ask, idly wondering if the accent ever fades, or if you get to keep it for life.

"Twenty years, but we speak Russian a lot at home. I want to make sure Ivan knows the language, and is able to talk to our family back in Russia. We've been back a few times since Ivan was born. I think it's important for every child to learn where their ancestors are from."

Sasha reaches down into the touch pool to feel a passing horseshoe crab. She laughs as it skims the palm of her hand.

"I think that is important, too. I'm glad to finally be spending this time with you. The boys are such good friends," I say, smiling.

"Yes, I agree," Sasha firmly responds. She holds her index finger up. "We will get the kids together soon. I'll make sure to find the time." She nods, matter of fact.

I'm thinking this might be a perfect moment to mention my mom's group. It seems like that type of support will do her good, being she doesn't have time to go out on play dates and share similar stories with other parents.

"We have this mom's group where we meet once a week to talk about mom-type stuff, and figure out solutions to any mothering challenges. Would you like to join us?" I ask, trying to gauge her reaction.

When she doesn't respond, deep in thought, I add, "You don't have to come to all the meetings, or anything. I know you don't have the time, not all of us do, but when you have a chance, the invitation is open to come along."

"You know, that might be just what I need!" Sasha's face suddenly lights up, giving me the feeling she doesn't have many mom connections at all. "I will try to make it to the next get-together, for sure. Thank you."

"Great! You're welcome. Just let me know. They really help, and we have a great group of moms. Talk to a fellow mom. Join us and you can't go wrong." I giggle from putting my slogan to use that I had come up with for next year's mom's recruiting campaign.

Sasha grins, wide-eyed, and excited.

Conveniently, I left out Audrey and that whole situation. I don't need to get into details, or scare Sasha away. Plus who knows if Audrey will even come back to the group with what she pulled. I haven't told the other moms, and I don't plan to unless it somehow comes out.

Sasha will fit right in, adding a good dynamic for the rest of us. I pat her arm, with my clean hand (the other hand is for the touch pool), and say, "I'm going to walk around and make sure everyone is doing good."

"Me, too," she agrees, and walks one way, while I walk in the opposite direction, to cover all sides.

Recruited another mom, Mia. Great work in supporting the pathway to better motherhood days for all us moms! I put an imaginary check mark next to this small task I constantly work on for our group.

"Whoa!" A child burst out shouting. Then another child shouts. Then another.

I look down my end, nothing, but then spin around on my heel, only to see a domino effect of students teetering over the edge of the touch pool, like performing the wave at a football game. Ms. Dorsey is the first to run over, holding onto one of the children's arms.

She pulls back. I get to them second and start pulling the kids back to standing upright. Sasha and the other two teachers run to the last child on that side to stop the falling domino effect.

Apparently, one of the boys leaned too far over the edge, acting silly. He had to balance on his stomach, trying not to fall completely in, dragging no less than six kids to almost fall in the touch pool with him. One of which is Cody. None of them end up taking a dip in the water, but they come awful close.

The kids all start to giggle, but the teachers don't find anything about almost falling in the sea water funny. Their seriousness, for some reason, makes the kids laugh even harder. I give Cody a *cut it out* stare, but he doesn't stop.

"Okay, we have to move on to the next exhibit." Ms. Dorsey huffs out. "Obviously, we cannot show proper behavior right now. I don't want to have to cut our field trip short, but I will if this continues."

All had been an accident, and I suppose that's why the students are laughing, because everything happening is so out of the blue and absurd, that it is funny. To me, I don't always agree with Ms. Dorsey and the reasons why she gets upset, but she's right in that the kids aren't stopping their giggling to listen.

Like I could argue that category. I can't even stop myself from laughing, even when I know nothing is supposed to be funny. A chuckle escapes my mouth.

From the side, I see Ms. Dorsey look in my direction, straight-faced.

Not so tough now, Mia, without your papers to push on the floor, or table to crawl under for distraction. I suddenly feel in trouble with the teacher and turn beet-red in embarrassment.

"I'm sorry." More chuckles burst out, cutting off my sentence.

Play it cool, Mia. Play it cool. I straighten up, put my serious face on, and walk ahead with the students. It isn't until I see Cody and his wet sleeves that I lose it, and start laughing. Out loud.

I find myself in a fit of giggles. All eyes on me, and wondering what's so funny at that moment, since the touch-pool-incident happened a whole five minutes ago. I shake my head to try and get rid of the images of children teetering away on the ledge, but that doesn't work.

The opposite effect takes hold. An odd sound breaks through my tightened lips, like a balloon bursting or a fart combustion trill. I turn toward the wall to attempt to calm down.

You're making a fool of yourself, Mia. Continue on being a good example now, laugh later.

I straighten back up, tug at the hem of my tank top, and spin around as Mia the Stern Chaperone. We start to move on to the next exhibit. Ms. Dorsey looks back at me, and so does Sasha. They both look confused.

But then I hear a familiar and welcome sound come from behind me that makes my insanity make sense. *Laughter!* I turn to see if I'm hearing correctly. The two other kindergarten teachers are laughing. Ms. Dorsey and Sasha follow suit. They can't help themselves. Soon, we all laugh to where our eyes begin watering. Other patrons of Shark Reef walk by, trying to make out what's going on.

"You're right, Mia. This was all so absurd." Ms. Dorsey tries to subside her uncontrollable giggles, but they just keep coming in spurts. She ends up wiping her eyes with a tissue from her pants pocket.

For once, the kids don't make a peep. They're standing single-file, stunned, not understanding what's going on with all the teachers and chaperones. To them, we aren't supposed to laugh this hard. We're adults, for goodness sake. This never happens. Especially Ms. Dorsey not being able to control herself, to even speak.

She's usually on the more serious side when it comes to keeping children properly behaving. But not today. Not now. And certainly not watching tears trickling down my cheeks, laughing so hard in return. Yawning isn't the only contagious act, so is smiling and a good laugh.

Today, I do not feel alone with my out of the blue behavior. I have company, and it feels off the charts amazing.

"Okay, kids, let's continue on. We still have more to see." Ms. Dorsey waves the students to walk forward. She gathers herself together and clears her throat. Only this time, she's more lighthearted in her actions.

I think she needs this letting-go moment more than anything. Being a teacher is such a stressful job as it is, and lately, with knowing Audrey most likely broke into her confidential drawer, all weighs on her. Possibly making Shark Reef more of a chore than fun.

You turned it around, you awesome mom, you! Internally, I'm jumping for joy.

"I'm definitely joining your group, Mia. I need more of this in my life." Sasha nudges me, chuckling as she heads up to cover the front of the line.

A mother seeing others handling the stresses of motherhood, sometimes by just laughing, because what else can we do, gives us all comfort in knowing we aren't alone.

With a grin that doesn't go away, I proceed with the children up to the long aquarium tunnel ahead. The same types of sharks from the 360-degree area swim overhead, and on the sides throughout the tunnel. A gorgeous blue serene sight. These scary looking creatures feel almost docile in a way gliding through the water. I feel at ease.

Glancing at Syiriah, she's not scared at all. In fact, she has a smile in awe of everything. Cody stands by her, smiling too. Maybe the comfort of a friend who isn't scared puts her at ease, enough to enjoy the sharks.

Lesson of the day to parents—do not show a child the movie Jaws before going to Shark Reef. The damage control that had to be done today was unnecessary.

What a trip of learning, bonding, and adventure.

When we arrive back at school, I gather Cody's and my things in the classroom. Sasha got Ivan's and her belongings also. Having been chaperones, we're able to leave right after the field trip with our sons. Only thirty minutes early, but that's a gift for moms who always have a plethora of things to do.

"We'll walk out with you," I let her know while waiting with Cody for her and Ivan to finish looking through the classroom's lunch bin for Ivan's lunchbox.

"Mia." Ms. Dorsey walks over. "My classroom is open for you to volunteer any day. Remember that for future years. Would love to have you back." She gives me a giant teddy bear hug. I return the hug, just as tight.

This time, my eyes begin to water for a different reason than at Shark Reef. A combination of Ms. Dorsey's invitation to come back, the final marking of the end of kindergarten, and possibly knowing I face a bit of a scrub down with Cody at home. I'll have to wash off the seawater from the touch pool.

Round and round mothering emotions go, where they'll stop, no one knows.

Epilogue
Discipline

Since school ended, marking the start to summer break, Cody is starting to write a book, entitled *Never Leave Your Mom Home Alone*. The title is catchy, leaving the anticipation of, *why not leave her home alone?*

With no school daily, he now has the time to write about what has been going on the entire school year. Well, until we schedule summertime play dates, that is. (I'll be also scheduling drinks with Ella, frequently.)

Delving deeper into the reason behind his work in progress will explain so much. I clean up toys, and also put certain belongings high up that he's been suspended from for bad behavior. All while he's at school. Certain toys have been away for a while now, because I have not let him off on good behavior, yet, to get those special things back.

Cody feels he needs to write about the horrors of what happens when he comes home from school to find a neat house, and his temporarily suspended belongings are nowhere in sight. Primarily, he is letting other kids know that this can happen to them too, so never leave your mom home alone.

This is obviously *Cody's* view on my mothering. And he thinks he should get away with everything. Well, you know what I have to say about that; wait till he becomes a father himself. He will see how his way of thinking changes.

I've heard so many moms and dads express these exact same feelings to their little ones. "Wait till you become a parent, then we'll talk." I sure know I say this about a thousand times.

But alas, it goes in one ear and out the other.

Big sigh.

My discipline hat is frequented, almost as much as the chef, maid, life coach, homework advisor, and chauffeur hats we parents wear. But maybe it's not worn as much as my own personal hat, my favorite one—the Detective Mia hat.

Again, here is an opportunity to take a moment to say I'm sorry to my mom and dad. I had a different perspective on raising kids when I was Cody's age, which I now see as definitely unrealistic.

Honestly, I think it's cute he is writing a book, because he's mad about me putting toys away. To him, this is serious business. And boy, do children take things seriously when it comes to toys.

If Cody's book ever makes it to print, you will understand what he's writing about. Kids just have a different perspective about how life should run.

In conclusion to many of my experiences, discipline must follow certain actions, like temporarily taking belongings away. I've done this on multiple occasions. The best part, or should I say the most challenging part, about having to discipline Cody is that he really doesn't take it well. Really not well. Point in case, he is writing *Never Leave Your Mom Home Alone*.

He will say things I've never heard from anyone, or anywhere, before becoming a mother. I end up standing in front of him in utter shock.

"I'm going to tell everyone you are a very bad mom."

"The garbage man should take you away on garbage day."

"I want to live in another house."

"I am going to pack my things and leave."

Well, he can try that, so I'll help him pack, knowing full well that his motorized Jeep won't make it to the end of the block before the battery runs out.

He'll be back.

Off he goes when Saturday morning rolls around. We are only about two weeks into summer break. Cody is writing his book in the kitchen while arguing a point with me about discipline. I don't agree with what he's saying, and he gets upset. Beet-red upset.

Cody jumps in the driver's seat of his Jeep and sets his backpack down on the passenger seat. The battery revved up as he puts pedal to the metal to head down the sidewalk. No clue where he's going, but I wave bye anyway and smile, watching him drive off. He looks as angry as a hornet, but I keep on smiling and waving.

About halfway down the sidewalk, his Jeep starts to stall and lurch forward in sharp movements. As machines do when the battery is going out. As I suspect, he doesn't quite make it to the end of the block. If the Jeep's battery is fully charged, it may have gotten close to the corner.

Cody pounds the steering wheel. His foot stomps on the gas pedal over and over. Replicating how an adult acts if their car conks out. He gets out, slinging his backpack over one shoulder, and strides back toward me.

I hold my arms open. "Come on, let's talk, and I'll make you a cup of hot chocolate."

"With marshmallows?" he asks with a sharp tone.

"Sure, with *lots* of marshmallows." I look down, smiling wide to try and soften his bad mood.

He gives me a quick hug and goes into the house. I walk down the sidewalk to grab his Jeep, and shake my head all the way back to the driveway. *Discipline.* I sigh.

On second thought, the garbage man taking me away might not be so bad. It means a break from the house, and the chaos. And how awful would the dumpsite really be to spend a little time in. My house is already a mess—I'm used to it.

There are smells coming from Cody's shoes that I've learned to tolerate over time. And the garbage dump is like its own private oasis in the middle of nowhere, *almost* like a personal vacation. The one thought about daily.

A tropical island is the vision, but the waste-yard retreat will work in a pinch. I stand in front of my still errant child stirring his hot chocolate, shoulders shrug up, thinking that trash day isn't coming soon enough.

There are moments I find myself saying out loud, "Whoa, hold on. Wait just a minute. What did Cody just say to me?" Or, "If he thinks he's going to talk to me like that, he has another thing coming." I am in disbelief at what comes out of his tiny mouth.

And any preposterous foreign statements are said all because I'm taking something of his away or grounding him for an action *he* does wrong. It's called discipline, and he really does not take it very well.

I'm right back to my escape room. Sitting, ruminating about this challenge late at night. Quiet. Stillness. Nobody asking me for anything. Husband and son are fast asleep. Caesar's snores can be heard momentarily in the distance, but for the most part, it's just me and my mental wellness, enjoying the peace of silence.

A deep breath is taken; knowing garbage day comes once a week, and the possibilities behind that day. Hey, all parents need a respite. The whole discipline challenge reminds me why we need breathers.

The use of the discipline hat is the craziest issue Detective Mia has on her plate. Always on the hunt, prowling from within my mom's group, internet, and streets, for answers. Only to come up with, we have to wing it. Every child is different with no sure-fire way of discipline relief.

Taking favorite things away is as close to a solution as any in our household. That certainly helps me in my constant goal in developing a better motherhood routine. Cody, among the other children from my mom's group, is immune to any other form of discipline, so taking away favorites is what does the job, mostly.

I seem to be winging it all the time, and continuously learning from my mistakes, as in all areas of being a mom, and in life. I also repeatedly change my thoughts, too.

Honestly, the ultimate secret to a better motherhood routine is right under my nose—it's okay to change with the times, and take comfort in learning what works through Cody's ever-growing actions. Not only in discipline, but with raising him in general.

A lot happens as part of my mom's life, making me do off the wall things. Laughing when I'm not supposed to. Commenting off subject. Exiting stage right to avoid embarrassment. Looking forward to trash day with maybe riding off into the sunset on the garbage truck. Discipline is only the tip of the iceberg.

Whether there is screaming, running amuck, being defiant, being brutally honest, or just plain being a natural-born comedian, I do my best to find humor. Laughter really is the best medicine.

I wouldn't trade any of my mothering experiences for the world.

Over anything, Cody is my heart. He teaches me new things all the time, and I'm always in awe with how smart he is. His playful nature makes me laugh every day. And his smile makes tough days seem brighter. Most importantly, he has a heart that wants to heal all, having kindness that will truly lift up humanity as a whole one day.

I love my son to the ends of this earth with always wanting the best for him, even when it means sacrificing my own needs. Above all, he will always be my baby, no matter how old he is.

In ending to my ongoing crazy mom-life, humor finds a way to be the icing on my motherhood cake—my true savior. I want to thank you for letting my experiences provide you with the humorous break in your busy day.

I hope much of my life has resonated within you. Essentially encouraging you to realize you are not alone out in the parenthood ocean. We are sailing in a yacht together.

May the force be with you on the high seas of parenthood.

Best of Luck!

Mia.

www.ingramcontent.com/pod-product-compliance
Lightning Source LLC
Chambersburg PA
CBHW051524150726
47997CB00001B/379